HEAVENWARD

Book One of the
"Celestial Creatures" Series.

Olga Gibbs

RAGING BEAR
PUBLISHING

Heavenward

Published in 2018 by Raging Bear Publishing.

A CIP catalogue record for this title is available from the British Library.

Paperback ISBN 978-1-9164710-0-9

Cover design by Perie Wolford.

For upcoming publications visit www.OlgaGibbs.com

This book is for my family. For all I put them through.

And for all survivors out there.

He shall give his angels charge over thee,
to keep thee in all thy ways.
Psalm 91:11

And I saw an angel come down from
heaven, holding in his hand the key to the
bottomless pit and a great chain.
Revelation 20:1

CHAPTER 1

I can't breathe.

My lungs are shrivelled inside my constricted chest, unable to draw a single breath. It's as if I'm buried alive under tonnes of heavy wet soil and the weight of it is pressing on my chest, breaking my ribs, filling my lungs with its black wetness, leaving no space for air.

I want to scream, but I can't even do that. Not a sound escapes me.

I sit up in my sweat-drenched bed, my pyjamas sticking to my back, as I stare with my unseeing eyes into the charcoal darkness of the night. My heart is pounding somewhere in my throat. Its echo is booming in my ears, blocking out the sleepy world around me.

With a shaky hand, I reach out to my nightstand and the nightlight wakes up with a dry click next to me. Its small orange circle is flaccid and weak and doesn't illuminate the room but it is strong enough to disperse my nightmare and remind me how to breathe.

I exhale and fall back.

I know I won't get back to sleep again tonight, so I lay here, watching the ceiling above me awakening with the weak light of an English morning in the North.

A loud knock on the door startles me.

"Ariel! School time! Come on, time to get up!" Fat Paula's voice booms through the door. She doesn't wait for my answer, proceeding down the hall, knocking on all the other doors, calling the rest of the girls up for school.

I push myself to get up and get ready.

The glum, feeble sunlight trickles slowly through the net curtains, throwing a dim light over my messy room and my school uniform, folded over the back of a chair.

I never have the energy for make-up, so I just get dressed and brush my hair and teeth, but even that's an uphill struggle every morning, with so little sleep the night before.

And, again, I'm running late.

The school bus's horn blares sharply like a wounded goat as I grab my backpack and run down the stairs, hitting my knee on the heavy wooden banister as I turn the last step.

"Ariel, breakfast!" But I'm out of the door before Paula has the chance to remind me that I haven't had my meds this morning either. I hate taking them – they make me feel drowsy and powerless. I can't stand the feeling of being drugged up. Not again. Not after everything that's happened. But nobody listens to me. The staff keep feeding me them as if they're working towards a volume distribution bonus for a pharmaceutical company or something.

The cold English morning greets me with the usual fog and drizzle. I stop to take in the cold salty air, craning my head up to the sky. I love looking at the sky. It always gives me a feeling of peace and belonging somehow, although, most of the time, all I see is thick and grey clouds above me.

The old school bus, with its nauseating diesel stench, is still empty, with only a few younger children, like scared small birds perched on a branch, sitting at the front. I head towards my usual seat at the back, stretching my legs across the worn, once blue seats, nearby.

With a heavy sigh, the bus closes its door and chugs along its usual route, collecting pupils and providing me with a daily detour of the depressing place I now call home.

The town is an alternative apocalyptic vision of poverty and despair. I haven't been here long, but I already feel ready to crawl into a grave and wait for death to come.

Most of the dilapidated buildings around the town centre are boarded-up, no longer occupied by people or businesses, and it feels as if propping each other up is the only reason the buildings are still standing. The single short shopping street runs through the heart of this once busy, but now godforsaken seaside town, desperately flaunting its small and pathetic stores, which only sell the crap no one wants or needs.

The desolate streets are ghostly quiet this morning. Only an old man shuffles down the road with his back bent as if burdened by the sins of the world.

The crumbling old parish church with its caved-in roof hides behind a broken church fence and a neglected graveyard, now overrun by weeds and invading ivy.

After a compulsory thirty minute excursion through the fourth circle of Hell, the bus slowly pulls to a stop outside my school.

The grey, washed-out three-storey building is surrounded by a tall metal fence. I swear this building was an HM prison before someone gave it to the council to be used as a school as surely no one would build this atrocity as a school on purpose.

Heavy off-road vehicles and even a few tractors are parked outside the school, bringing in the local farmers' children. The boys jump out of their Rovers and Defenders with exaggerated athleticism and swagger, and walk towards the building where the different cliques are already calling to their members and followers.

The girls slip out of their cars slower as if to give everyone time to appreciate the effort they put into getting ready for school this morning. Mind you, with skirts that short, you have to take care while climbing out of a car.

Everyone's face is familiar. Everyone knows everyone in a school that small. Friendship groups form and dissolve but, ultimately, there are no secrets and gossip is booming. The only way for me to survive in here is to keep clear of them all.

Once out of the bus, I suck in all my "lady lumps and bumps" as I try to slide between the bodies of the popular kids littering the lawn in front of the school but my attempts fail, as I get dirty glares from a few princesses when my pauper clothes brush over their Topshop bags.

It's a good thing I'm holding my breath, as I might've passed out from the heavy cloud of perfumes and aftershaves lingering amongst the bodies. I pick up the pace, desperate to get out of this stew of drama before I draw any more attention to myself.

Carefully keeping my eyes down, I ram full speed into something solid and warm. With the momentum still pulling my feet forward, I trip and am about to land backwards on my arse when two big hands shoot out, grabbing me by my shoulders. With my arms behind me and my feet ahead of my body, I look like a water-skier, pulled forward by an invisible cord.

Once I finish fumbling with my legs and finally manage to find the ground, I crane my neck upwards to see who's there, still holding me.

A boy. He is muscled and tall. I only come up to his armpit. His school blazer is too tight on his big frame, looking like it might burst at the seams on his large shoulders. His luscious, tousled, dark hair is cut short on the sides, falling onto his forehead, over his left eye. Vivid, light blue eyes shine under his wavy fringe, prominent on the backdrop of his dark hair and tanned skin. With a perfect, straight Roman nose, high cheekbones and defined jaw, this boy could easily look the part in Hollywood or at least earn a decent living as a model.

"Hi." His voice is velvety soft as he smiles down at me.

His gorgeous, all-Hollywood, charming smile shows off his perfect white teeth and an adorable dimple on his cheek. The warmth from his hands seeps into my arms, spreading along my body like a fire, and suddenly I feel hot. My nose is tickled with the delicious smell of green moss and undergrowth, like the smell of the muddy earth floor after a long rain, when it's surrounded by the wet bark of pine trees with a sharp bursts of pine needles, and without thinking I take another deep breath, inhaling the glorious scent.

At the back of my mind, I sluggishly wonder how pathetic I must look to him. Clumsy, spread like a beach-stranded starfish who all but melts in his hands, so with the last ounce of sense left in my head, I stop myself from closing my eyes when I inhale and stop a contented sigh from escaping my lips as I exhale.

"Hi", my voice is coarse and unsure, even for my ears.

Get a grip! I reprimand myself and shake my shoulders back out of his grasp. I know better than to get involved with a boy. I know only too well how bad that can end.

"Sorry, I didn't see you there. Thanks for catching me though", I cut off abruptly, all business like.

"No problem, always a pleasure. I'm Sam", he offers, keeping his polite smile.

"Ariel", I answer, outstretching my hand for a shake.

"Like The Little Mermaid?"

He grins at me and suppressed laughter rumbles in his chest.

I open my mouth in disbelief and slam it shut again, withdrawing my hand and with it the offer of a handshake and friendship. Instead, I fold my arms over my chest, glaring at him.

"Yes, like the freaking mermaid. Do you have a problem with that?" I narrow my eyes at him.

"No, no. No problem", he blinks at me with feigned innocence, raising his hands, although his bright mischievous smile betrays his sincerity.

"I need to get to my class", I snap, "so if you don't mind..." I trail off as I take a step around him, but the boy steps sideways as well, blocking me in.

"Sorry, I didn't mean to upset you. I was just joking", he tries for sincere, overacting with his 'puppy eyes'.

"As I'm new here and haven't met anyone else yet, I thought maybe we could be friends?"

What a cheek!

"Welcome to our school, Sam", I cut him off, taking another step around him and this time he allows me to walk around him.

"I'll see you later", he calls after me, way too loud, and everyone turns their heads towards us, watching the closing moments of the scene as I stumble away, keeping my eyes to the ground under the gaze of speculative glances.

The warmth from his hands still tingles on my skin and contradicting my annoyance, a smile forms and spills over my face. Suddenly I want to giggle.

"For Godsake! Get a grip!" I repeat as I push my slipping glasses up my nose, and go marching down the hall.

My English class is empty and silent when I get in. Only a lonely, trapped fly is buzzing and beating on the window, desperate to be free.

Over the next fifteen minutes, the room slowly fills with pupils.

But when the door creaks open once again, the morning chatter of the room subsidies to a hushed murmur, and as I raise my eyes from my notebook to see what had that effect on the class, I see *him*.

Sam.

He stands by the door. An arrogant half smile plays on his full, perfectly curved lips, flaunting an irresistible dimple on his right cheek as he inspects the room. With a barely audible sigh, a few girls melt in their chairs, stupid smiles pulling at their lips as they eagerly eye Sam.

His eyes meet mine and he gives me a wink, and a brighter smile blossoms on his face as he makes his way towards the end the room, past me, choosing the seat right behind me.

Shit!

"Hi Mermaid", he whispers behind me, but I ignore him as I slide down in my chair, burying my face behind my notebook, away from the speculative glances directed behind me.

"Hi, you must be new". Daisy, the popular girl, isn't wasting any time on pretences or foreplays. She plonks her arse on his desk, engulfing me in a sickly sweet cloud of her perfume.

"I know everybody here and I've never seen you before. And I would've remembered *you*", she murmurs behind me.

I make sure I don't react to the conversation as I keep my back bent over my book and my eyes firmly on the page. At the end of the day, I really don't care how successful her hunting will be, just as long as I'm left out of it.

"Hi. Yes, we just moved in. I'm Sam and you are?"

I can hear a smile in Sam's velvety voice, and I want to turn to see his face when he looks at her, but instead I clasp my hands, squeezing them tight between my thighs.

"Daisy", she purrs in her sugar sweet voice.

"Nice to meet you Daisy", he replies.

It feels like this friendly exchange behind me should result in a handshake but I know better than to expect Daisy to shake hands with a boy.

The last few pupils walk in, freezing on the spot at the sight of the new boy with Daisy on his desk, and then they push through the shock and shuffle to their seats, warily glancing back in Sam's direction.

With the bell, bringing up the rear, in walks Mrs Power and that's the cue for Daisy to get back to her seat for the lesson.

"Ok, Sam. I'll see you later", Daisy murmurs. That sounded ominous and mildly like a threat. So the hunt has begun.

"Morning everyone. Let's start from where we left yesterday. Who can tell me the purpose and the role of Banquo's character in Macbeth?" Mrs Power's perky, theatrical voice travels to the end of the classroom. Soft sounds of dismay stir through the room – I guess it's not only me thinking that a perky quiz is too much for first thing on a Monday morning.

As the day sets off on its usual path, I try to concentrate on the teacher in front of me and ignore the glances the entire class steal to the seat behind me.

The school bell rings and I'm out of my seat, gathering my books and shoving them into my bag as fast as I can before making a beeline for the door in a bid to avoid the "wannabes" attack on the new pretty boy, which, undoubtedly, would block me in.

I exhale once I'm in the wide hall.

I head to my next class when a familiar tall and lanky frame rushes towards me, pushing through the crowd with her elbows. A scrawny tornado of activity breaks off in front of me.

"Have you heard? We have a new girl in our school and she's in my science class!" Annie, a geeky girl from science club, gushes out, like she's afraid to run out of oxygen. "Apparently she's just moved here with her parents from London. Whatever possessed them? The teacher's already suggested she should join our science club as her grades from her previous school were apparently astounding". Annie rolls her eyes while making air quotes with her fingers. Annie doesn't like competition, especially ones who might take away her spot in the countywide science championship.

"And we have a new guy as well. He just had PE with Rachel", Annie whispers, her eyes bulging. "Apparently he's quite fit for a nerd. Rachel says that he must be a nerd if he wears glasses", Annie huffs.

"I wonder if he'll join our science club", Annie exhales the last sentence with such a stupid smile on her lips that someone might think that this mystery boy has already declared his undying love for her.

"Anyways, I better go. Mr Putt has been in a shitty mood lately and has been giving out late-arrival detentions left, right and centre. See you tomorrow", and with that, she returns to her previous course, ramming like a torpedo into the crowd, colliding with unfortunate students, barking at them to watch out.

Three new students in one day? Very unlikely in a town so small, but who knows, maybe they are related?

The school is buzzing. The gossip machine is working hard but I happily manage to avoid gossip and drama for the rest of the day, and I'm only reminded about the new students when I walk into the school lunch hall, which doubles as a gym in our small school.

The lunch hall greets me with the deafening buzz of hundreds of voices, hundreds of cutlery pieces scraping on hundreds of plates and sudden outbursts of uproarious laughter.

The mist of frying oil hangs thick in the air, clinging to hair, skin, clothes and walls. The hall's nauseating smell of a fish and chip shop is a clear warning to every student.

I pause for a moment by the door, adjusting my backpack on my shoulder and scanning the crowd, before immersing myself in another episode of the survival show, called *Lunch Hall*.

Sam's large, muscular frame stands out against the other students at his table. Daisy is next to him, smiling way too sweet, leaning in too close and purring while rubbing his biceps. She profusely flirts with him and he is more than happy to encourage her. All the chairs at the table are filled with the popular kids.

A few tables away from them, the new girl is surrounded by a tightly bound circle of teenage boys. There must be at least a quarter of the school's boys around her. They are eager to get her attention, as they climb over each other, charming her with their wittiest jokes and dazzling smiles while giving each other death stares the moment her gaze leaves their faces.

But I have to admit, I can see why boys would be attracted to her. She is the prettiest girl I've ever seen. She has a delicate, angelic face with bright, sapphire-blue eyes, red, luscious lips, and luminescent, peachy skin, framed by sun-kissed, glossy blonde curls.

It's comical to watch boys tripping over each over for her attention. I can't believe that none of these newly recruited adoring fans can really see how pathetic they look and I wonder, if I was to line them up on one side of the table and put her in the middle, would they all look like the scene from the '*Last Supper*', where Jesus Christ is in the middle with his disciples hanging in on his every word?

My mood instantly sours as my thought jumps to my mother. She would probably make me stand in the corner of the room, with my knees on salt, in front of the cross, begging for forgiveness from the Lord for such blasphemous thoughts, comparing some random girl to the mighty Lord himself.

To distract myself and to stop my mind venturing further, I scan the hall, trying to locate the third student Annie was talking about among the buzz and commotion of the rush hour lunch hall.

I swear under my breath, cursing him and his choice of seating arrangement, as I spot him sitting at my table at the back of the hall.

The boy is slim and not buff at all. His lean shoulders are hunched over his empty tray as he absentmindedly traces the pattern on the tray with his finger. His brown hair falls over his face, hiding his features. Solid muscles flex on his arms under his rolled-up school shirt sleeves. Today is not the day I'm willing to compromise on my solitude, so I stop and scan the hall for another free table. Just my sodding luck, everywhere is busy.

To centre myself, I inhale the oil laced air and march to my usual seat, trying to ignore him, thinking that if I ignore him, there'll be no need for him to talk to me either.

As I take the seat, the boy lifts his gaze from his tray.

"Hi", he calls to me in a soft voice over the rumble of the lunch hall and I feel as if I've been punched in the gut as the hall tilts, emptied of all the air at the sound of his voice.

Something familiar, content and secure rings in his voice, pulling at me, and I want to run to him, to wrap myself in his arms, knowing that everything will be okay. The pull is

13

so strong and unexpected that I sit there, stunned, grabbing hold of the sides of my chair, afraid to fall over, afraid of the incomprehensible, insane reaction of my body to his voice.

What's going on? Who is he? What is going on with me today?

"Hi", I croak, overwhelmed, lifting my shocked eyes at him, unable to explain such a creepy reaction to a complete stranger. My clammy hands are shaking.

"I'm Rafe. Is it okay if I sit here?" he asks with a kind and beautiful smile.

The boy is not unfortunate looking. His full and luscious light brown hair falls like a cascade of shining silk down to his shoulders. His beautiful, hazelnut-brown eyes twinkle when he looks at me and, like me, he wears glasses, only his are not cheap like mine, but elegant and refined, suiting him rather well, making his eyes look bigger and brighter.

His perfectly smooth skin with not a teenage pimple in sight is stretched over his high cheekbones and slim straight nose, but I spot a small white scar on his left cheekbone, which adds to the mystery, making him look even more handsome and irresistible. His full lips and black endless eyelashes would be the pride of any girl.

"Hello? Can you hear me?" His voice pushes through my fogged mind and it takes me a few more seconds to realise he's been talking to me.

"What?" I croak through the shock.

"Is it okay to sit here? It seems to be the only quiet table in this place", he asks, giving me another soft smile.

"Yes, I know..." I start in a weak voice. I stop and clear my throat. "And that's why this is my table. Just for your future reference", I snap and suddenly I feel angry with him, but mostly at myself for my reaction to him.

"Sorry, I didn't know", he flashes his perfectly white, straight teeth at me, gazing into my eyes. "I didn't see your name on it, although I looked really hard".

Is he making fun of me? Probably all the attention that he got today exploded inside his head like an aneurysm, turning his stupid brain into mush. Or maybe he is Sam's brother after all, one as arrogant as the other.

"How could you have possibly looked for it? You don't even know my name", I bristle, cheesed off that I'm drawn into the conversation after all.

He gets up, gathers his tray in his hands and walks around the table, taking a seat next to me. I push my chair away from him, scraping its metal legs across the old vinyl floor with a teeth wringing noise, giving myself some space, and hinting to him that we are not mates.

But before I move away, his warm scent of crisp, salty ocean waves, ripe fruits and sun hits me, and for a second I'm wrapped in that smell of holidays... or happiness.

Rafe's unfazed smile plays on his lips while his calm eyes lock on me, watching my passive aggressive dramatic moves.

"That's a very good point", he continues, ignoring my hostile scowl. "Why don't you tell me your name then?" And although his posture is relaxed and his smile is wide, I can see a strange twinkle in his eyes, too intense and studious for my liking. I wonder if that's how he looks at a frog before he dissects it in biology class.

"Okay, listen. Let's stop right there", I snap, raising my hand to stop him. "I'm not interested. I'm here to eat and to be left alone. That's it. So if you want to chat, maybe you should find yourself another spot", I purse my lips, folding my arms over my chest. My ultimatum is clear and final.

"Okay, okay." He raises his hands up and laughs, a soft musical sound, which weirdly gives me the chills, raising the hair on my skin. "Next time I'll keep in mind that I'm only allowed at this table if I keep my mouth shut. I'd better go. I need to find my next class. See you later".

And before I can object to the 'next time' or come back with something witty, he is gone, and I stare at my lunch, gathering my equilibrium and trying to relax a bit.

Just before the bell rings, I throw my rubbish in the bin and head to my next class, when I feel someone lightly tug at my sleeve and I grind to a halt.

I turn to find the new girl, looking at me with her mesmerising sapphire blue eyes, framed by her black endless lashes, giving me her open, charming smile. She is even prettier up close.

"Excuse me. Hi", she chimes in a soft musical voice. Her words come out in a rush. "You're in the science club, right? Annie told me. My name is Mia. I started today. I don't know many people here and although the boys are very friendly, the girls aren't so much. I was wondering if maybe we can sit together at lunch tomorrow?"

She babbles with such speed and force that I feel like I've been pushed down the tracks by a train and, before I can stop for a minute and think and remind myself that I'm not the sociable type, and most definitely don't want her crazy baggage of hormonal admirers, I hear myself mumbling something in agreement and offer to help her get around the school.

"Thanks!" she beams at me with a beautiful, open smile and suddenly jumps up and hugs me while I stand there, totally dumbfounded. And before I can think of what to do with myself or my arms, she is gone, followed away by her most stoic groupies, the ones with stronger stamina.

Wishing for this weird day to finish as soon as possible, I spend the rest of the day snaking from class to class, spending more time in the bathrooms during the breaks than necessary for any bladder.

But every misery comes to an end, and this day is no exception. Once the final bell of the day rings, I exhale with relief, gather my books and rush to the bus stop.

* * *

"Hey, look, the geek is in the house", Molly's nasal bitchy voice greets me as I step through the door. "How was the school for geeks and nerds?"

I roll my eyes.

God give me strength.

Ignoring her, I head for the kitchen to make myself some tea. The staff's shift change happened while I was in school and now I'm greeted by Martha, a small, always laughing lady with a broad Scottish accent.

"How was your day, darling?" Martha asks, busy stirring something for dinner in a big pot.

"Yeah, okay". I'm not in the mood to chat and plan to escape into my room as soon as my tea is made.

"No, please. Give it back", a young tearful voice cries out from the lounge.

I leave the boiling kettle and my unfinished tea in the kitchen and stride into the lounge. The closer I get, the clearer I hear Molly's hyena chuckles, providing the accompaniment to the soft pleas and cries. Martha follows me, quick in her pursuit.

The lounge is brightly lit with the five bulb plastic chandelier under the ceiling. The TV blurs evening nonsense in the background. Molly's tall and fat frame stands in the middle of the lounge, towering above the youngest girl in our home, twelve year old Evie. Evie is young and small and it's not the first time she's been picked on by Molly.

A piece of paper is clutched in Molly's fat hand, raised high above her head, while Evie desperately jumps around her like a young goat, trying to snatch it out of Molly's grip.

"Molly, what's going on in here?" Martha's voice demands behind me but Molly ignores her completely, as if she'd never spoke.

"Please", Evie cries out.

Her futile jumping attempts entertain Molly immensely as another rumble of chuckles pours out when she lowers the piece of paper just a bit, to encourage the next set of jumps, and at that instance, my decision is made.

I march to Molly and, with gathered momentum, jump up in front of her, snatching that piece of paper out of her grip. The paper rips with a sharp sound, coming away in my hand, leaving behind a tiny corner in Molly's sweaty palm.

"Oi!" Molly's face turns purple. Angry red spots are dotting it, making her resemble a cheetah. "What do you think you're doing?"

Her chavvy nasal voice stretches the vowels above my head. She is only slightly taller than me but twice my size and, from my previous confrontations with her, I know that she is twice as strong.

"I don't think that was yours!" I bark. My eyes are fixed on her, as I hand the paper to Evie, who is crying softly somewhere behind me. The paper is pulled out of my hand and I can hear the hurried rush of Evie's footsteps up the stairs.

Molly's loathing glare rakes my face, and I think she is about to hit, when Martha's small body squeezes between us. She looks up at Molly, pushing me away with her back as she tries to put some space between us.

"That's enough, girls." She backs up two more steps, pushing me away with her. "We'll talk about the consequences tomorrow. Now I would like both of you to get to your rooms." Her voice is like rigid steel and I know that now she means business. Her gaze darts between me and Molly as she adjusts to stand between us.

"I mean it", she snaps.

"Fine by me", I snap back and with a last warning glare at Molly, I walk up the squeaking stairs and into my room, slamming the door behind me.

What an awful day!

CHAPTER 2

I'm running down brightly lit, empty corridors. My panting and rushed footsteps are echoing along the walls. I'm desperate as I scan the white stone walls and cobblestone floor, looking for some route to divert to, a niche to hide in. I know they are after me and I'm being hunted like an animal.

A brighter light is spilling through the wall on the right and a memory of the room down there sends me into a sprinting rush, but as soon as I turn the corner, I halt, as if hitting an invisible wall, losing my footing on the corner of a stone, and trip.

I scramble to my feet, but it's too late. I've been spotted. I've landed smack in the middle of the vipers' nest.

A group of beautiful angels in red clothes under their sparkling armour are just as surprised as I am, but as I take a step back, the heavy doors boom shut behind my back with the finality of a coffin lid.

The shock wears off their faces as the menacing light ignites behind their eyes and creepy smiles spread over their lips. This bunch can't believe their luck.

The white walls of the grand cathedral hall shoot high and disappear in the piercing depth of a crisp blue sky. There's no ceiling in this room – only the open dazzling blue sky above. The monumental hall is filled with warm, incandescent sunlight and the breezy summer smells of the ocean, ripe fruits and the sun. This room usually feels and smells like happiness.

But not today.

An overwhelming sense of dread and fear pushes adrenaline around my body. One by one, they draw their weapons, surrounding me, ready to pounce – I'm the obstacle for them, the risk they are no longer willing to take, and now they just need me dead.

Only a few in this lethal crowd have swords while the rest of them are wielding medieval weapons. Some women are holding or flexing long-tailed whips, which are glowing with a bright white light with tails of fiery flames, while men are balancing in their hands long poles with spiky, heavy metal balls attached to both ends, or poles with curved blades and sharp tips at each end.

The sharp crack of a whip slaps behind me, and with the next one an agonising pain rips at the back of my legs, sending me down on my knees.

The next crack of a whip brings burning, scream wrenching pain to the side of my body. Like the predators they are, my enemies stalk closer, closing the circle tighter around me. Defiance and anger have replaced the weakening fear in my veins, brought by a sickening sense of betrayal.

My pure-white armour is a sparkling heap a few yards away from me, with my sword resting on top of it. My sword is liquid fire, moulded into the shape of a wide and long blade, with the blue of the flame next to the sparkling white hilt, radiating orange and reds into the tip.

The fire in my sword is alive. Its colours ripple along the blade and the shape of the blade shifts, changing ever so slightly, as if it's breathing. My sword is alive and it's calling to me, it wants me, but I'm afraid it's too far out of my reach.

But as I try to get up, another flex of the whip sends me back to my knees, with the pain erupting wide across my back. The group isn't laughing with every strike, not taunting me, not even talking to each other. The complete silence of the assault feels like an execution.

A sudden hush rises like a tide. It stirs amongst them, moving from the outskirts to the centre where I kneel, like a ripple in the water in reverse, and slowly the crowd parts, giving way to a large man with piercing blue eyes who strides through the mob towards me. His pearly white blonde hair is long, braided and pinned on top of his head, like a crown. It's hard to tell how old he is, he looks ageless.

His sword of liquid fire is drawn at the ready as he slowly, without a rush, without a word, without even acknowledging me, walks around me, and with one swift move, he plunges his sword of fire into my back.

And again I scream. I scream until my lungs are sore, until they burn inside and I want to crack my chest in two, just to let them out, to ease the pain and let them have some air.

I gulp down the water from the glass on my night stand in a vain hope to wash away all my craziness and to forget all that just had happened to me.

But I know better than to hope for miracles or anything good. Nothing good ever happens to me. I know that by now.

I force myself back into bed, hoping for a dreamless sleep, but my mind is busy, churning away at the new details of my dream.

With a heavy boom, the door shuts behind me, cutting the last chance of escape, trapping me in that bright, open-sky room. I know that pleading with them will not achieve anything. I know that I'll not change anyone's mind and this is the end.

Their faces are more defined, and somehow clearer today.

I have the time to look at each one of them in turn. I slowly scan their gorgeous faces. Faces of the executors, the murderers, one by one.

I jump upright in my bed with the shock of realisation. I know those sapphire blue eyes, framed by those black and long lashes and those blonde, glossy curls.

I must be going insane. I must be.

No. Let's think rationally for a moment. It was a busy day today. Let's face it, three new faces in our school is extraordinary. As extraordinary as the school itself winning the UK Establishment of the Year award, bloody unheard of. So naturally my mind took that shit to heart and decided to cook up something exciting (like I need any more of it!), and hey presto, one of the people, who hunts me down and then executes me in my nightly dreams is the new girl.

And like a mantra I start to repeat to myself the words, which the therapist feeds me every session: *"It's time for us to recognise where the dream stops and reality begins"*.

I'm already exhausted and scared and no matter how hard I repeat these words, I struggle to distract myself from the possibility of encroaching schizophrenia, so I reach with a shaking hand for the book on my night stand, afraid to go back to sleep.

* * *

The morning bus ride is a carbon copy of yesterday.

I spend most of the ride rummaging through my backpack, praying I have everything I need for today. I feel tired and exhausted.

On laden legs, I plod through the school and down the always busy and bustling corridors, unwillingly colliding with misfortunate students. My mind is foggy and disjointed.

I yank the music studio door open with only a minute to spare and I almost trip over my own feet again when I see Rafe, reclined casually behind the desk at the end of the room.

Dropping my gaze to the floor, I scurry to my own desk, carefully avoiding eye contact with him, cursing the sudden influx of new students in our school and their gravitation towards drama, nicknames and lunch table choices.

"Afternoon everyone", Mrs Farley hurries in with a stack of books in her arms, accompanied by the rustle of her long gypsy skirt. "Today we'll continue our compositions. Remember that most of the techniques we are using here should be in your exam pieces. The more expression and dynamics shown, the higher the mark".

With a thud which sends a mild shock wave through the floor, she drops the books on her desk and turns towards our group.

"Mel, Emma, Olivia, Ariel. I would like you to include Rafe in your group. Although you've progressed further than others in your composition, I think you will be able to assist him on his quest to find his musical path", she says in a sing-a-song voice, clasping her hands over her chest. Mrs Farley is a good teacher, nice and calm, but she does like flowery phrases.

On cue, Rafe gets up, slings his bag strap over his shoulder and strides towards our long table. The oxygen count drops in the room, as my female only music class inhales as one, watching Rafe's fluid, confident strides, the swing of his hair, and the flexing of his muscles as he makes his way to our desk.

Rafe stops at the end of our long desk, expectantly looking at the four of us with a bright, mesmerising smile. I feel, rather than see, the stupid smiles spread over my teammates' faces as they exhale with little whimpers around me, almost sliding off their chairs.

I roll my eyes.

Oh, for god's sake!

And when my eyes return to their natural position, I notice him looking directly at me with a mocking grin, stretching his lips even further. Of course he saw my eyes rolling, but quite frankly, I don't care, and the girls need to get a grip.

I lift my butt slightly, grabbing the sides of my chair with my clammy hands and with a noise, I drag my chair along the discoloured, vinyl floor, making space at the end of the table for our new study partner.

"Thank you, girls", says 'Prince Charming' with a smile. "I hope I'll be able to contribute to your team and not keep you behind." His charming smile is off the charts.

"Oh, no, don't worry".

"You'll be fine".

"We didn't get that far".

My teammates gush at once, chirping like spring birds on a sunny morning.

I hold a steady gaze ahead of me, pinned to the whiteboard on the wall, ignoring all the commotion of mating and the effect his voice has on me.

"I hope it's ok with you, Ariel".

I jerk my head as I hear my name spoken in Rafe's melodic voice, which sends a zap of electric tingles through my body.

"Yeah, that's fine", I try to sound as casual as possible, attempting to disperse the glowing heat enveloping me, to stomp on the goose bumps raising the hair on my arms from hearing him say my name.

Pink heat swaddles my cheeks as Rafe takes a seat next to me and the crisp smell of ocean with its ozone and salt fills my head.

I can practically hear the waves crashing around me and I can smell the succulent fruits in the air, and at that piercing moment, I feel like I know this smell. There's something familiar, comfortable and reassuring about it. I hold it in my lungs while marvelling in this new feeling of safety. For the first time in my life, I feel balanced and grounded. I feel like there's a power within me, stirring, trying to unfurl, to show me what I can do, and I desperately ransack through my brain, trying to place it, but my mind's coming up blank.

The pull of his scent and his voice is so strong that I can't help myself, as my head snaps up and our eyes meet. His warm, hazelnut brown eyes gaze at me with earnest, not a gleam of a smile left in those soft eyes.

The draw is so intense and mesmerising that I feel like I'm being dragged into a vortex.

I'm hooked, like a fish at the end of a fisherman's line, like a butterfly in a child's net, and I cannot find the strength in me to pull my gaze away from his, or even blink.

This vortex is speaking to me. It whispers stories of trust and honour, of harmony and love, of the universe and God. It vibrates in my head with a kaleidoscope of images, none that I've seen before yet all strangely familiar. I hear Mrs Farley's voice in the distance, rumbling like the sound of a faraway motorway.

"Ariel! Ariel!"

And like that I'm released from the vortex. I slowly turn my head to the teacher, only to find every pair of eyes on me.

Shit. How long has she been calling for?

"Ariel. Can you please play to the class a piano solo that you've included in your composition?" Mrs Farley asks.

I fumble with my fingers on the keyboard and eventually my piece flows through the room, but I my fingers slip as I feel unsettled, lost, confused and too exposed. I need some air.

"Mrs Farley, I need to go to the bathroom please", I raise my hand as the last chords of my piece subside into silence.

"Yes, of course. But please don't be too long". I'm dismissed.

I fight out of my chair and through the narrow space behind Rafe's seat, away from my desk as fast as possible, avoiding eye contact with him at all costs.

I practically run into the bathroom. Once inside, I stop in the middle of the room, unsure what to do now. I stand there, commanding my flimsy, overreacting heart to resume its normal pace, but it's all futile.

I'm hyperventilating, struggling for each breath as the metallic taste of panic scratches on my tongue, filling my mouth, spreading numbness to my limbs.

I'm afraid to move, to spill my panic for everyone to see. I plead with myself to get a grip, desperately trying to gather my thoughts, which have scattered like frightened rabbits.

I double over, trembling, covering my head with my arms, trying to breathe. My legs give way and I collapse in a pile on the sticky bathroom floor.

My dreams have spilled into my waking life. I'm having psychotic episodes now. No! Oh god, no!

I cry. I sit there and cry, rocking myself, mourning my short and broken life which insanity has taken away from me. I sit on the grubby bathroom floor for a while, but I don't know for how long, and eventually my tears dry out.

I rise unsteadily as the end of lesson bell screeches in the bathroom. I get myself up, rinsing my hands and face before plodding back to music class. I hope everyone will be gone by then.

But Rafe is still there, sitting at our desk, gazing into space. He turns his head to me as I step into the room. I plod to the desk and grab my bag, laying my hand on the books.

"Ariel, can we please talk?" he asks, sounding serious, even grave, with no sign of 'Prince Charming' left as he places his warm hand over mine.

I wish he would stop saying my name and standing so close.

Anger rises inside me with pulsing tides, replacing the vulnerability of my fear. With each heart beat anger releases a flock of vultures inside me, clouding the world, demanding blood.

I spin to face him. Anger contorts my features and I can only imagine how I must look.

"Listen, mate. Enough is enough. I told you before to leave me alone. I'm telling you again and it's the last time. Stay away", I hiss at him.

I slam my fist on his wrist and he releases me with a shocked and surprised look. Not losing a second, I'm out of the door.

CHAPTER 3

The lunch time hall is as busy as usual.

The buzz of hundreds of voices with occasional bursts of female shrieks and thunderous roars of boys' guffaws vibrates the walls and floor in the hall. An occasional argument will ignite without a warning but will be extinguished just as promptly by a PE teacher, who tells boys to take it outside or to the headmaster's office.

I'm relieved when I see my table remains empty in the corner of the hall. I sprint to it, hoping that my presence will discourage anyone else from joining me and the nearby rubbish bins will finish the job for me.

Basking in a brief feeling of relief and freedom, I slowly peel my orange while looking around the hall, watching free shows of macho competitions and Miss Popularity contests, when a new group walks through the doors.

Sam, with Daisy by his side, and her girlfriends with an array of school athletes as their boyfriends. The group stops by the doors for a few seconds, long enough to scan the hall for the best table and to give everyone a chance to appreciate the beauty of Sam and Daisy together.

I'm about to roll my eyes and get back to my orange when Sam's eyes meet mine and a wide gorgeous smile takes over his lips, highlighting that irresistible dimple on his cheek. My hand with the orange freezes midway to my mouth and I gape, mouth open, as he turns on the spot and decisively makes his way towards me.

It takes Daisy a few steps in the opposite direction before she realises that her trophy is no longer following her, and as Sam approaches my table, more heads turn in our direction and slowly the chatter in the hall dies to a murmur.

Everybody's stunned. Daisy, me, every student in the hall. Everyone but Sam. Relaxed and graceful, he pulls out the chair next to me and reclines his big frame in the most elegant and confident manner, stretching out his long legs.

Still with my mouth open and my orange segment suspended in mid-air, I stare at him, scrambling in my brain for something smart or sassy to say.

Keeping his tranquil smile, Sam reaches for my orange and, with the refined elegance of a king, separates a segment and sends it into his mouth. I'm transfixed by the motion of his beautiful and long fingers touching his full lips. Mind blank, I follow his motions with my eyes like a mouse caught in the gaze of a cobra.

"How you doing, babe?" His velvety voice pulls my eyes finally from his lips. Snapping my eyes to his, I plead with myself to muster the cool, although I fear that that miserable train left the station long ago.

"Hum..." The sound coming out of my mouth is mousy and scratchy. I clear my throat and try again.

"Fine. You?" My voice is more audible but still sounds pathetic.

"Oh, thank you for asking. I'm perfect. Your orange is really sweet and juicy by the way. I like it".

He gives me his charming half smile and a conspiratorial wink, and a feeling of an unspoken innuendo floats above the table.

I clear my throat again.

"Why are you here? Daisy is waiting for you", I say, waving my hand to where Daisy still stands, frozen to the spot.

"Well, maybe I don't want to eat lunch with Daisy today. Had you thought of that?" A twinkle of mischief bounces in his eyes.

"Sam, everyone is looking. Why don't you go and make up with Daisy? Whatever spat you two had, I really don't want to get in the middle of it", I say, glaring at him.

"There's no spat, Mermaid. I never said that we are in a relationship or even worse, exclusive. She follows me around like a puppy and I let her. I'm just a friendly kind of guy". He idly reaches out to my orange and takes another segment.

"You are a player kinda guy", I say sternly, sounding too much like a teacher, even for my ears.

"That I am", he says as a wide grin spills across his face, blinding me for a second.

"I hope you are not here to practise your 'player' skills. I'm not interested. In any of it", I do another sweeping motion with my hand to include the entire lunch hall, slowly gathering its previous mojo.

"You are not interested in lunch?" he raises his eyebrows, mocking me.

"You know what I mean. Drama, boyfriends, cliques. I'm not interested in any of it. I'm here to study and get out as soon as I can", I remark.

"I'm here to study too", he pouts his beautiful lips like a toddler, looking at me from under his thick, black lashes.

I can't help but laugh and he gifts me with another one of his dazzling smiles.

This must be the last straw for Daisy's humiliation, as with a furious scowl, she stamps her foot, spins on the spot, and almost runs out of the hall. Suddenly awakened, her girlfriends follow her in hot pursuit, leaving their forgotten boyfriends to meander and find places to sit.

"You know I'm going to pay for that, right?" I sober, already imagining the crap I'll get tomorrow.

"Eh, don't worry about it", he dismisses my worries with a wave of his hand and then reaches for another orange slice.

"Would you mind?" I lightly slap his hand before he has a chance to grab the rest of my fruit. "Get your own lunch".

Slowly the lunch hall returns to its busy, loud self and nobody pays attention to us anymore.

"Ariel, we need to talk", Rafe's familiar voice says above me, bringing the smell of the ocean with him.

Resigned, I lift my eyes to find Rafe, standing expectantly next to our table. He is wearing a cheesed off scowl on his face. I don't know what his problem is, but I'm definitely not going to let him take it out on me.

"I thought we agreed to stay away from each other", I sigh, dropping my eyes fast, as the memory of the vortex still disturbs me.

I shoot a careful glance at Sam, who's closely watching the furthest side of the hall and doesn't make a move to participate in the conversation. Only the tension in his posture tells me that he is aware of the company.

"Ariel." A calmer plea of my name sends shivers down my spine and raises the hair at the nape of my neck.

Why do I react to him like that? This sensitivity to him angers me.

"Rafe. Please. Enough", I say, desperately trying not to yell and not to run. I've given enough entertainment to the lunch hall for one day. "You'll force me to stop coming to school".

Carefully Sam unfolds his long legs, turning in his chair to look at Rafe.

The air freezes a couple degrees as they stare each other down. The fierce scowl on Sam's face changes his perfect features into something animalistic, while Rafe meets Sam's glare with the stoic expression of an ancient marble statue.

Neither of them is backing down and the speed, with which the situation has escalated, feels like these two have been in this position before and they've simply picked up from where they left off.

The silent intensity of this standoff radiates its heady energy in wide circles, like ripples from a stone thrown into a lake. A few closer tables sense an upcoming fight and blood lust lightens the boys' eyes, while girls squirm in their seats with excitement, murmuring something in hushed voices to their girlfriends.

"Rafe", I call.

I'm doing my best at a stern voice, but the sound escaping me is more of a plea. When his eyes finally meet mine, he somewhat relaxes, settles, and after a few long seconds, exhales. I didn't realise he was holding his breath.

"I'll try to speak to you later. Trust me, you need to hear me out."

And with that, he leaves the hall, dumping his entire tray into the bin on the way out.

Now it's my turn to breathe out, only mine comes out with the high pitched farting noise of a rapidly deflating balloon.

"That was intense", I mumble, eager to fill the quiet and as a way of apology.

"What was his problem?" Sam asks, returning to his cool and elegant self.

"I don't know. He keeps saying he wants to talk, but the problem is I don't want to talk to him", I say.

"Some guys, huh? Don't know how to treat a girl", Sam winks at me.

"Well, thanks for all that excitement. I'd better go now, before lunch hall gets any more drama performances starring me", I say as I get up, gather my bag and am about to pick up my tray when Sam scoops it in his big hands, dumping it for me on the way out.

"Thanks", I say.

"Always a pleasure, Mermaid", he smiles at me.

"Okay, let me walk you to your next class", he says, once we are in the corridor, scanning it in every direction with exaggerated vigour like a professional bodyguard.

"Why?" incredulous, I look at him.

"So nobody else tries to talk to you while you are avoiding them", he chuckles.

On the way to class, more curious glances inspect this unlikely duo, following us with a train of whispers and a fresh dose of gossip.

We stop outside my math class.

"Okay, Mermaid. I'll see you after school, probably on the bus. Dad can't give me a lift today so you'll have the pleasure of my company on your ride home."

Before I can interject with an excuse, Sam is off to his classes for the afternoon.

CHAPTER 4

With the last bell of the day, I make my way to the bus stop, only to be stopped in my tracks by the sight of Daisy and her crew gathering there. Before I have a chance to turn around and head in the opposite direction, she spots me.

"Look who's here. If it's not Miss Universe herself", Daisy yells at me across the small lawn, separating us. Like vultures sensing their prey, the students around slow down to a stop in an anticipation of a bitch fight.

Once spotted, I don't see how I can turn around and walk away. The humiliation of the retreat would be just as bad and right now, I won't chance having my back unprotected to her.

I walk, ignoring her, hoping she might let it go but, as every pair of eyes in the yard are locked on me, I know it isn't a situation which can be solved with denial.

"Oi, nutjob! I'm talking to you!" she yells at the top of her lungs.

Rage unfurls slowly inside me, stretching, yearning, waking up.

I swear to myself. Daisy won't let me leave this patch of grass. And I need my bus.

I slow down to a stop, bracing for what's about to come. I take mental stock of my options, wondering how far Daisy will be willing to push it. I don't think Daisy has the balls to take it to a fight, she's too much of a wimp for that. Public humiliation is what she's after. But in saying that, no one's ever stolen her boyfriend from her, so right now I'm in uncharted territory.

She comes at me swagger and all, crossing the yellow, balding patch of grass, flanked by her five girlfriends. She stops just a few feet away from me, blocking my way.

Her girlfriends snigger behind her, excited to be a part of a public put down. In their minds, they are already counting the popularity perks coming their way out of this.

"Nutjob? Or should I say Miss Nutso of the schizo house?" Daisy announces loudly in a sing a song voice. "I bet you run around naked every night while barking like a dog!"

Daisy scans the gathering crowd with a smile, like a showman warming up the audience, checking for impact. Encouraged by her girlfriends' giggles and gawking of the crowd, she is pleased with herself.

"You would know, running like a dog after the guys yourself", I rebuff, willing my voice to sound strong and clear.

A few students snigger behind my back and Daisy's face turns punchy pink in an instant. Anger morphs her face into a grotesque mask of hate.

"At least I'm not as ugly as some. Look at yourself, an ugly, useless waste of space. Who'd ever want that bag of crappy nuts?" She seethes, taking a few steps towards me, her face now just a few inches away from mine. "You'd better remember your place, rat, and I'd better not see you near Sam again. Got it?" she hisses, hate contorting her features and, like birds in the forewarning of a storm, Daisy's girlfriends fall quiet behind her.

Who does she think she is? I think *I* might punch her.

My abandoned friend Rage is awake inside me. She helped me through my darkest times and never failed me once. She's the one I can rely on to be there for me and she's not about to fail me now.

"Get out of my face, Daisy", I say. My voice is calm and now I can clearly see that as long as I'm here, Daisy will never forgive me for Sam's attention.

"Or what?" She takes another step forward, closing the last inch between us. Her eyes are vicious slits. The side of her lip is drawn up like that of a rabid dog's. She's so worked up that only now do I see that a fight is exactly what she is after.

I take a small step back. If she tries to hit, I'll need room to move, either for ducking or for swinging my arm. Either way, I need space.

"You really don't want to go down there, Daisy", I snap, keeping my gaze steady on her. "You really shouldn't pick a fight with a crazy person, you never know what they might do", I tut at her, slowly shaking my head, a little smile playing on my lips. She thinks I'm crazy? I'd better prove her right.

"Have you ever thought that if you would've been just a little nicer and chased boys a little less, more boys would actually be interested in you? Can't you see how you're embarrassing yourself all over a boy?" I shake my head. "Trust me, no boy is worth it".

"What would a psycho like you know?" she fumes. Her hands ball into fists by her sides, slowly rising. I'm sure she is about to hit. I really don't want to hit her, but I know that I'll only ever allow her to hit me once. I release the backpack's handle from my hand. It drops to the ground with a soft thud.

"Daisy, no need to be such a bitch, darling", Sam's calm voice interjects unexpectedly. All heads turn in his direction as if commanded by a puppet master.

He stands just outside the immediate spectators circle, observing the show, his arms folded over his chest. I don't know how long he has been there. His crossed arms and relaxed posture don't match his scowl, stone cut features and tightly pressed lips. He is pissed.

With a relaxed stride, he approaches the nucleus of the fight, strolling through the crowd of bystanders which parts for him like the waters of the Red Sea for Moses. He is in front of Daisy now and I can feel the excitement of the crowd spike up.

I take another step back and he takes my spot, facing her, while Daisy regards him with frightened eyes, confused about his plans, but still hopeful as she goes for her charming smile, which dies the moment Sam speaks.

"Listen, darling. You need to find pride in yourself somewhere", he reprimands her as his clear voice cuts through the silence. "You can't keep running after me like that. I told you before that I'm not interested but you are still here. Making a fool of yourself. Not cool". He shakes his head, emphasising how disappointed he is.

Daisy's jaw slacks. An incredulous look of disbelief spreads across her face. It's for everyone to see that it's not what she expected and hoped for from him, not at all.

"What are you talking about, Sam?" Daisy finds her voice, pleading with Sam with her words and her eyes. It's embarrassing to watch someone's public humiliation, and I never found any enjoyment in it. I find the old, cracked asphalt under my shoes more interesting at the moment.

"You said you liked me! We went out", she cries out. "How could you possibly find anything interesting about *her*? Have you seen her?" Her voice raises an octave with every word spoken and she screeches the last words. I practically feel her finger pointing at me and every set of eyes turning my way, determining whether I am suitable for a job I hadn't applied for.

I don't want to listen to any of it anymore. It's none of my business and I have participated more than enough in this freak show.

Without a word, I bend over, pick up my backpack and start for the bus stop. Around Sam, past Daisy, through the crowd, stepping carefully over bags and around rain puddles.

"How could you do this to me? Do you know how embarrassing this is?" Daisy's high pitched screams ring behind me and I plead in my head for the bus to come so I can distance myself from all this drama.

"You are embarrassing yourself right now", Sam's calm voice chastises behind my back. "I told you before…" The rest of the sentence drifts away into the wind, as the distance grows between us.

I sneak a look over my shoulder, watching Sam approach Daisy, murmuring something in her ear, standing very close. His face is soft and kind and Daisy's longing eyes are trapped on him.

He reaches to her face, holding it in his hands while cooing something to her. Eventually she nods. He bends down and places a light kiss on her cheek and starts towards the bus stop and before I turn away, her hurt and hateful eyes meet mine.

Oh boy. And now it has begun…

"Are you all right?" His voice is behind me, very close. His lips hover above the top of my head and I feel the heat of his body next to mine. His presence comforts and disturbs me at the same time, it sets me off balance. I want to push him away and curl up in the warmth of his embrace.

Taking a side step, I turn to glare at him. I'm annoyed at him, at Daisy and at everything that just happened, and at myself, for feeling so vulnerable and needy.

"Remember, how I told you I don't want any drama?" I hiss. "How I don't want any cliques, stolen boyfriend' fights and other crap? And sure as hell, I don't want a boyfriend, especially Daisy's", furiously, I spit out my last words, turning back to watch the road.

"Sorry, I didn't mean for any of it. I didn't think Daisy would take it out on you", he says, his voice warm and sincere. "I tried to explain to her that you and I are just friends. Hearing it at the same time as I was telling her that she and I were only friends didn't go as well as I'd hoped".

Finally, the metal tin of a school bus arrives in a cloud of black diesel fumes. With the wheezing sound of an old man, the pneumatic doors open and I'm in, heading for my peaceful island at the back. But as I plant my butt on my usual spot, stretching my legs to block out the seats next to me, Sam struts down the aisle, heading towards me.

"What are you doing here?"

It's not a pleasant surprise and I'm not even trying to hide it.

"I need to take the bus today. It's a school bus, right? So move over. There aren't that many seats left", he lightly nudges my feet on the seat.

Reluctantly, I take my legs off the seats, aware of the heads turning in our direction with raised eyebrows and curious glances.

"Do me a favour. Don't speak to me", I snap. "I'm sick of this shit more than you can imagine". I stick my ear buds in before he has a chance to respond and turn to the window to watch the floating landscape, unchanged since this morning or months before that. The bus takes its usual route, stopping now and again to eject rowdy pupils out of its rusty core.

Suddenly my ear bud leaves my ear and a warm breath caresses my earlobe, sending chills down my spine. "I'll see you tomorrow, Mermaid, and I'll try to behave", Sam whispers.

His lips are all but kissing my ear and I'm frozen to the spot with all my senses doing somersaults and vault jumps and, before I can think of anything to say, he strolls to the front of the bus and asks the driver to stop.

CHAPTER 5

The house is loud this evening and filled with the usual arguments over stolen make-up, overrun bathroom times and imaginary boyfriends.

These 'boyfriends' are the hot topic in the house. Of course, none of the girls have a boyfriend, but they like the sound of it so much, the normality of it and they so desperately want to be wanted, that pictures of random guys who are so obviously models from a catalogue, appear on their phones with stories of 'till death do us part' kinda love.

These stories always amuse me and sometimes, if I'm in the mood, I would sit with the girls in the lounge or at the dinner table and listen to those stories, questioning the ever-changing details.

I sit at my desk in my pyjamas, finishing off my English homework. My favourite radio station plays in the background and I tap my foot in time with the song, humming the lyrics under my nose.

A light knock on the door pulls me from my homework.

"Yeah?" I shout. It's an invitation, and the door opens to let Paula in. She looks serious and composed.

"Ariel, your social worker is on the phone. She needs to speak to you about your sister", she utters, scanning my face with her gaze.

Dread envelopes me in its cold blanket as I run downstairs, jumping over the last two steps.

"Hello?" My voice is coarse, giving away my dread.

"Hi, Ariel, it's Jo. There's been a... development with your sister and I wanted you to hear this news from me". My social worker sounds distant and professional.

I don't say a word. My knees suddenly feel weak and I want to sit down but there's no chair in this small room.

"Ariel, your sister's been taken to hospital today", Jo continues into the silence. "There has been an accident. She has sustained broken bones, fractures and a concussion. Doctors are saying that she is in a critical but stable condition, so they are hopeful".

My mind reels, unexpectedly tilting on its axis and I think I might throw up. Fear numbs my head, filling my ears with cotton wool and I hear Jo still speaking, somewhere in the distance, but I can't make out a word.

"Was it him?" I croak down the line.

An answering silence stretches over the phone.

"Was it him?!"

My heart picks up the pace as her silence says more than she ever will.

"We are in the process of carrying out our investigation", she says carefully, "but in the meanwhile, your sister has been placed under our care. She'll remain in our care at least until the investigation is completed. I'll come and get you to see your sister when the doctors say it's okay for visitors." Her composed voice echoes in my spinning head.

She pauses once more.

"I'm sorry, Ariel".

I pull the phone away from my ear, fighting to pry it out of my frozen fingers, before handing it to Paula. My hand and knuckles are sore from gripping the phone so tight.

I turn on the spot and walk upstairs, to my room, as I hear Paula say something into the phone in a hushed voice behind me.

I step into my room and slam the door behind myself.

I'm worked up, angry, furious. Choppy, shallow breaths come out of me and my lungs feel restricted and small. I can't sit down and can't stop myself from pacing. My hands ball into fists by my sides. My head pounds. Anger and hate swell, surging high, spreading its searing heat to every part of my body and clouding my mind with a blinding red blanket. Pressure builds inside me, somewhere in my gut, pushing at me from the inside, at my internal organs. I think I'm ripping apart from within and then it starts pounding, like an iron mallet colliding with my insides, crashing at my walls, again and again.

Blinding fury comes next like an avalanche. I want to hit him, want to hurt him, badly.

Pulsating hatred electrifies me. With my every step, with my every thought. of my sister, of me. With my every memory. Of him. Of me. Every hit I took, every hit he dished out. Every depravity he subjected me to. Scared, lonely, lost, silent, pushed, beaten. His touch, his smell. The exploding pain of his gold ring, driven into my face by his fist. His drunken, hungry eyes lingering over my body...

He came into our life with the sleazy, self-righteous facade of a preacher, hiding underneath a vulture who found an easy prey in a weak 'God found' single mother and her two daughters. Low lives like him can smell the naivety and desperation of an ageing woman from a mile away.

I protected my sister for as long as I could. I covered her, taking more of his hits. At the end of the day, I was already the broken one, with demons talking to me in my dreams. I kept my sister away from him.

My mum promised me that she had left him. She promised me she would keep my sister safe. I trusted her. I was told that services kept him away, but she must have gone back to him. I only ran away because I couldn't take it anymore. I ran away from him to stop the abuse, only to find something worse.

I spin in the room, looking for something, anything, to do to release the pressure inside, to stop it from tearing my guts. I throw my arms, sweeping everything off my desk and with it the first release comes.

A bellow comes from my throat like a wounded animal wail. But I don't care about it as my fist flies into the mirror and a million rainbow shards sprinkle over the floor. Blood drops sprout on the carpet like red poppies with my every step. More blood poppies blossom on the carpet around me. They follow me as I look for another kill.

I spy my childhood keepsakes, arranged on the shelf, along with some childhood pictures of me, my mum and my sister, in beautiful silver frames. We look happy in them, like a family should be. My mother is smiling, still happy, tightly hugging her children. Still caring, still protecting.

I pick them up one by one and with an agonising roar hurl each across the room.

They break, shattering against the wall, leaving small piles of ruined childhood on the carpet and I scream more, like a broken beast in agony.

My vision is blurry. I raise my hands to rub at my eyes, shocked to find tears there. I don't remember the last time I cried, I didn't know I still could.

I wipe at my face, leaving bloody streaks in its wake. My legs give way and I collapse on my knees as I raise my face up to the sky and wail.

The room rings as a piercing shriek bounces off the walls, deafening me and it takes me a few seconds to realise, that it's coming from me. I scream, from the top of my lungs with the fury of a broken childhood, with all the hurt, anger and fear of a damaged body and a crippled mind and a young, broken soul.

The pounding starts in my head. It spreads, picking up the tempo, gathering strength. Slowly, it rises to a buzz of a hive full of angry bees. The noise climbs higher and higher, ascending to a loud, piercing screech of a wrongly tuned radio. It completely blankets my thoughts, eliminates everything but that pain, pounding its searing iron mallet into me.

It reaps inside my skull, tearing my eardrums. I cover my ears with my hands, collapsing sideways on the floor, wanting to make myself smaller, willing for the torture to stop, and when I think I can no longer take it, the ear splitting sound of broken glass rings in the room, followed by explosive arcs of icy shards raining over me.

And I scream, covering my head.

Glass shards fly, stinging my skin, sprinkling my hair and, in the next instant, the pounding in my head dies. The deadly rain of broken glass stops.

In shocked silence I lay, curled up in a ball on the floor. The cold October wind rushes into the room, rustling papers, scattered on the floor and moving my hair. I raise my head and survey the sea of shards around me and the black gaping holes of the windows.

The room is quiet and pitch black with only a pearly white luminescent glow dissolving the darkness around me but it's too faint and does not reach too far into the room.

I scan the room, searching for the source of a glow and when my gaze falls to my body, I freeze. This pearly luminescent glow is coming off *me*. My skin is *aglow*, over all that I can see.

Shocked, I stare at my glowing arms. They are like a weak version of luminescent lights in a hospital's corridors. New scratches and old cuts cover my arms, but I can't see any of it, as my mind is transfixed on the white glow. I stretch my arms in front of me, turning them side to side, bending them, flexing my fingers.

But the glow doesn't disappear under my stare.

What is this? What is happening to me?

I tentatively touch my left arm with my finger. I'm not in pain, I'm not hurting.

But as I look at it, the fear that I might have finally lost my mind takes over and in a sudden surge of panic, I rub at my arms and legs, scratched by the glass, in a vain attempt to remove the glow, but it's still there.

"Please, no. God, please, no", I chant like a prayer.

I have finally lost my mind.

I feel light headed and I think I'm about to pass out. The room spins, so I grip the carpet in a desperate need to ground myself, to stop the Earth from tilting. Blackness encroaches from the corners of my vision, bleeding into my eyes and mind.

CHAPTER 6

Exhausted and tired, I drag my feet over the science room threshold, cursing the bright light of the day.

I was relieved to wake up in my own bed this morning.

My room was cold but tidy, clear of any broken glass. Sheets of thick and milky plastic stretch over the gaping holes in my window. A few plasters over my hands and the plastic on the windows are the only reminders of yesterday.

The staff pleaded with me to stay home today, but I'm too afraid to be on my own.

The rest of last night is like an old, faded and then badly assembled video montage of darkness and occasional lucid moments.

I remember the cool hands and the soft voice of a kind doctor and the word 'hospital', which set off panic in me, which only a child subjected to so many hospitals would understand. I remember crying and kicking, the hushed voices of the staff and the doctor, followed by the cold sting of an injection in the arm, and peaceful darkness afterwards.

"Hi."

The innocent scent of lily of the valley hits my nose as Mia's light musical voice chirps next to me.

"Hi." I try to be polite and friendly, giving her a half-smile.

"Are you alright?" Mia asks, examining my broody features for a few seconds.

"Yeah, fine. Don't worry. Just didn't sleep that great last night, that's all." Giving her a small smile I change the subject, "ready for the test today?"

"I think we should be okay", with a wink, she nudges me with her elbow. She is a nice girl so I make an effort with a warmer and wider smile.

In perfect time with the bell, Mr Shaw strides in with the announcement of today's test. Thirty odd voices groan in response to the inevitable and some plead with him for mercy, but that doesn't stop the exam papers moving from the front, reaching the back like rising water on a sinking ship.

Paper in hand, Mia gives me another reassuring wink and sets to task.

"Please remember that you need to use a burner for question eight. You need to conduct a test and record your findings", Mr Shaw calls into the gloomy silence.

Mia is on question eight before me and I can hear the hiss of the gas pushed through the tube as she switches on the burner.

Lifting my eyes from the paper, I half expect to see the usual small flicker of yellow and red flame but the red and orange are replaced by pure bright white with a grey metallic sheen at the base, silver and blue at the top. And with the colour change, the fire's motion has changed – it moves like an intelligent organism with a purpose and not the child of chaos we all see it for.

As I watch stunned, the flame gears up, expanding, spilling onto the table in flowing cascades like when baking soda and vinegar was spilling from my volcano project in Year Four. The flame stretches on the table top in both directions, spilling on the floor in trickles of silver liquid fire.

As if fed by an invisible fuel, it flows, advancing around me in a fiery circle, cutting me off, and the next instant as the flame closes its ring, it shoots up high to the ceiling, trapping me inside its fiery walls, and I scream.

A single terrified shriek pierces the quiet, followed by the screams of a dozen more voices.

Erupted chaos of human panic fills the room: fallen chairs, table legs scraping on the floor, the thud of a fallen body, followed by a scream of pain and a splintering smash of the door, as it flies off its hinges under the weight of desperate bodies.

The high-pitched wail of the fire alarm deafens me. Sprinklers come to life above my head, soaking my hair and clothes. Now I'm both hot and wet, trapped within blistering hot white fire walls and Mia is trapped with me.

"Mia, we have to go! We need to find a way out", I yell above the fire alarm, grabbing her arm and tugging hard.

Searing pain scorches my palm. I pull it back, crying out in shock and pain.

The skin on my hand bubbles up with angry red blisters and, as I watch in horror, they multiply, spreading higher up my arm, and then begin to burst with wet smacking sounds, leaving behind each blister a little pool of blood.

Under my gaze, little pools turn into dozens and dozens of small streams, guided on their course by gravity.

Horror-stricken and unable to move, I bawl with all my lungs can give as Mia slowly turns to face me.

But it's no longer the Mia I know.

Steely features have washed away the familiar softness off her face. Decisive lines cross her forehead as her eyes narrow into the cold, calculating slits. All emotion is drained from them, leaving behind the purposefulness of the executor I once saw in my dream.

My scream dies in my throat, turning to a wheezy croak. I gape as my mind reels, petrified by the possibility of the existence of Mia the Executor and the reality of all the creepy craziness of my dreams.

The heat of the blaze becomes unbearable. It surrounds me tightly, pressing its advantage. Mia is now on her feet, watching unfazed as the fire rages around us and I collapse on my knees in front of her, gasping for breath and nursing my bleeding arm.

Mia looms above me as I raise my eye to her.

"Mia, please", I croak in a choked whisper, but Mia just looks down at me, her head slightly bent to the side, watching like a cruel child who just pulled the wings off a fly and is now watching it crawl. She doesn't cheer, she is not sad – she is a detached surgeon in a sterile environment. Or a cold killer.

The wall of fire accelerates higher curling under the ceiling like a giant wave, eager to swallow and crush me under its weight.

The blare of the fire alarm, the cold shower of water from sprinkles, the heat of the flames, and the smell of burning plastic and wood, all are mixed with a faint hint of lily of the valley and the agonising pain in my arm to create a gruesome medley to accompany my death.

I resign, closing my eyes.

CHAPTER 7

A female shriek and the sound of shattering glass burst into the cacophony of sounds.

A sudden cool wind gusts over my body, dispersing the heat and the smell of burning plastic. The final strike still hasn't come so I tentatively open my eyes and raise my head.

Everything stops around me as my mind goes into overdrive, trying to understand what I see.

Sam towers above me inside the circle of fire. His beautiful face is serious and stern, with none of the usual smugness in sight, and he doesn't seem to be at all perturbed by the weird-looking fire raging around us.

But that's not what sends my mind into overdrive.

Sam's usual appearance of a runway model is weirdly offset by pure, snow-white, extra-large angel wings spread wide behind him, shooting up to the ceiling and taking up a quarter of the room. His wings are glorious with glossy and soft feathers, looking exactly like so many angel pictures I've seen.

They flap lazily behind his back, providing a cool breeze to my body and protecting me from the fire's heat, and although the fire is right behind his back, it doesn't seem to hurt his wings and it feels like he uses them to shield me from the blaze. They are much larger than him and, somewhere in the back of my mind, I wonder how he can fold them without dragging them over the floor or tripping over them.

He looks glorious and powerful – the commander of his universe.

My sluggish brain churns the vision, like a large wheel stuck in the mud spinning, but not covering any ground. I must have finally lost my mind and now there will be a compulsory white suit with decorative straps for me.

The crisp sound of a whip cuts through the other noises and a red, fiery, glowing whip's tail wraps tightly around Sam's legs, binding them together.

Surprise registers on his face. His eyes lock on mine and his lips move, telling me something, but I can't hear him over the roar of the fire and skull-splitting sound of the fire alarm. I don't know what he wants me to do. I don't know what I can do.

Losing his balance, he falls face down with a heavy thud of a chopped down tree, and the next second he is pulled out of the fire ring with incredible force and speed.

Smoke and fumes from the burning plastic eat at my eyes. I'm blind, as tears pour down my cheeks, and I can't blink them away. Viciously, I rub at my eyes with my healthy arm, smudging soot over my cheeks.

I spy Mia's school blazer on the back of her chair. Coughing, I crawl on my stomach towards it. Rising on all fours, I yank the blazer down, burying my face in it. The demure, crisp smell of lily of the valley hits my nose over the stench of the fire, making me angry.

Mia, you little sneaky bitch! You pray that I die in here and never meet you after this!

I take a deep breath through the fabric and then wrap its sleeves around my fist and, lifting myself up, I start beating at the edge of the fire with Mia's blazer. The blazer smacks at the fire, landing on the floor with a thump, but does nothing to bring the fire down. I haven't made a dent in the deadly wall around me.

Another coughing fit wrings me to the ground.

I bring the blazer back to my face, covering my nose and mouth, but the raging fire has burned out the oxygen. I'm struggling for air as my lungs collapse on themselves.

I can't move anymore.

The sound of a fight comes through the other noises and I feel vibrations of hits through the floor. I hear crashes of broken furniture and shattered glass, the buzz of a whip and the heavy thud of a weapon meeting concrete and metal.

I fall sideways, gulping for air like a fish on a river bank, scratching at my throat.

Red dots buzz, spreading in front of my vision, growing with every empty breath. Blood thunders in my ears, taking over all other noises as my mind goes black. My thoughts are sluggish and empty as I slowly lose consciousness.

* * *

I slowly stir and stretch.

I'm cosy and warm, swaddled in soft bedding under a fluffy quilt. My limbs are heavy from the sleep. I roll onto my back and rub my eyes.

With my eyes still closed, I remember a new, weird dream of a fire, crazy Mia and 'Sam the Angel'. Although weird dreams have always been a part of me, I am worried that now they are changing, adding something new to the staple diet of assassination.

With one last yawn, I open my eyes and freeze mid–stretch at the sight of a high, ornate gold ceiling above me. Intricate stuccowork of wine leaves, flowers and fruits cover the entire ceiling, painted in different shades of gold, giving it stunning depth. My jaw drops at the sight of a striking crystal chandelier the size of a small car, suspended from the ceiling. Sun rays caught by the crystals split into shards of rainbow across the room.

I sit up. My head is spinning from coming up that fast. I gape at the unfamiliar room I'm in.

I turn my head from side to side, taking in the quiet, opulent gold and burgundy room. The room smells of lemon furniture polish and flowers. I'm lying on the large mahogany four post bed, with luxury burgundy velvet draped over the posts' sides, held back by gold cords with tassels.

The sun is streaming through the large window, illuminating the imperious room. The window takes up the entire wall and has a door to the side, probably leading to the balcony. The gold-stitched drapes around the window are drawn back by heavy golden cords with tassels matching the ones around the bed.

The walls are covered in burgundy velour with a subtle golden leaf design. Old oil paintings, which are clearly original and must cost a fortune, hang heavily on every wall in substantial golden frames.

A few pieces of heavy, dark furniture are scattered around this vast room. Fresh flowers in vases are standing proudly on every surface, releasing elegant sweet perfume.

A large fireplace with an ornate white mantelpiece occupies the entire wall across the room, with a hazy and haunting painting of a ship in the middle of a storm hanging above it in its elaborate gold frame.

None of it makes any sense and, just to make sure I am not dreaming, I pinch myself.

"Ouch!" I pinched harder than I thought.

A grim thought pops into my head. If I'm not asleep, I must be hallucinating. Crazy, here I come.

A soft knock sounds at the door and I yank my quilt up to my eyes as the door slightly opens and a girl's head pops in.

"Hi, I heard you're up. Can I get you anything?" A pretty child's face with small pixie features, big brown eyes and a volume of brown, glossy curls chirps excitedly at me.

"Who are you? Where am I?" I demand, as fearless as I can muster.

I want to ask her if I'm hallucinating but I stop myself, figuring that if I am, she'll be part of it and that question won't offer me any clarity.

She giggles, as if I said something funny and her bobbing head disappears as she shuts the door.

I can feel that I am in my underwear under the sheets, so I scan the room for my clothes. My school uniform is hanging over the back of the regal armchair near the fireplace.

With a quick glance at the door, I throw the quilt over and dash on my tippy-toes to the chair to grab my clothes. I shove my legs into my skirt as fast as I can, afraid of anyone else to pop their heads in the room and catching me in a half-naked state.

As I fight with my skirt with only my bra covering my top, another knock sounds and before I can say not to come in, the door swings open with a decisive hand.

Sam is in the room, stunned, gawking at me. His piercing blue eyes are open wide, taking all of me in.

With a piglet squeal, I dive behind the armchair, protectively covering myself.

I peek over the back of the chair, keeping myself covered as much as I can.

"What are you doing in here?! Get out!" I shriek.

Slowly Sam's stunned expression is replaced with one of his signature smirks. Appreciation is bouncing behind his eyes.

"Sorry", he says, without making an effort to retreat and not sounding like he means it.

"Get out!" I yell, still crouched behind the chair. "And next time, wait to be invited, unless you want an important part of your anatomy to be cut off", I hiss.

"I didn't realise I needed an invitation in my own home", he declares, as smug as usual.

"Do you mind?" I'm annoyed as hell now. My legs hurt from crouching behind the chair and I'm not prepared to have a battle of wits while I'm still undressed.

"Okay, I will give you some time and I'll be back", he says and with a last once over of the chair, he leaves the room.

I decide to get dressed in my nook behind the chair, just in case more visitors decide to burst in uninvited. My trembling fingers fumble with the buttons, struggling to push them through the holes on my shirt, as my mind contemplates the last few days.

What really happened, and was it a fantasy, a hallucination? Was the fire in the science room, Mia and 'Sam the Angel' a dream? Am I losing my mind? How did I end up here? The questions are endless and I don't know the answer to any of them.

Soon another knock sounds but this time the door remains closed.

"Come in", I yell. Fully dressed, I feel less vulnerable and scared.

The door opens cautiously and Sam steps into the room.

Sam looks effortlessly hot this morning and my heart skips a beat as I watch him entering the room.

His broad shoulders are tightly hugged by a thin navy jumper and I can just make out an outline of his pecs and a six-pack underneath it. His black jeans fit exquisitely over his long legs and his taught butt. Expensive looking black leather trainers finish his outfit.

He smells fresh out of the shower and his usual smell of moss and undergrowth is now mixed with a tingling smell of the mint and rosemary. His hair is still damp, falling in waves over his clear forehead.

"Is it safe to come in? Is everyone dressed now?" he calls in a sing a song voice, with his hand covering his eyes, spinning on the spot. He is mocking me.

"Yeah, everybody's dressed", I grumble, annoyed at myself that I'm finding him so attractive. "Listen, can you please explain where I am?"

"You are in my home", he smiles, looking at me. He spreads his arms wide, inviting me to take in the grandeur of this place.

"Yes, not bad, thanks. But I really need to get back to my house", I say, moving towards the door, walking around him. "I don't want people to start panicking and call the feds on my arse". Although I don't remember how I ended up in here, I most definitely am not going to tell him that.

"You can't go back. Well, not now, anyway", he says. His sober voice is calmer and quieter than usual.

"What do you mean?" I stop midstride gaping at him, hoping for a "gotcha" any moment now. I'm just a few steps away from the door.

"It's just, you need to stay here for a bit", he says, "for your own safety".

As I gawk at him, not saying a word, he continues.

"Do you remember the fire in the science class?" he asks.

"Yes", I stretch out the word, looking at him, waiting to see where he's going with it.

So the fire did happen?

I try to keep my face neutral as my mind is churning, spinning, trying to process the fact that the fire wasn't my imagination.

"And do you remember *everything* that happened during the fire?" He asks me, placing the emphasis on "everything". His gaze is locked on mine. He is expecting something from me.

"Well", I answer, keeping my voice measured. "Here's your reason why I need to keep going, everyone at the house had probably heard about the fire by now and are trying to contact me. Thank you for your hospitality, but I'd better go", I say as I take another cautious step, skirting around, while keeping my eyes on him.

"And do you remember Mia?" he utters and I stop, frozen to the spot.

I spin to face him. My stomach pulls at the memory of Mia, of my burning blistering arm, and I'm petrified to hear what more he will say about Mia.

"What do you mean?" I croak. I need him to say the words. He needs to vocalise them. I don't trust my mind any more.

"Do you remember Mia starting the fire in the science class and trapping you in? She was trying to kill you", he cautiously starts.

"And do you remember me?" He takes a step closer. I'm watching him, afraid to speak and desperately wanting him to shut up. It's never good for me when I'm reminded of my past, of things that I've done, of things done to me.

He takes another step towards me.

"I've saved you". He is now next to me. I crane my head up, our gazes are locked. His smell of moss and the forest undergrowth envelops me.

"Thank you", I whisper.

His lips lift into a smile, his perfect dimple is back on his cheek. He bows his head slightly in acknowledgement.

But I'm silent, waiting. I feel that he's going somewhere with it but, for now, I don't know where to. Or maybe I just don't want to know.

"I'm an angel and so is Mia. And she will try to kill you again", he says.

Wow. That is not what I expected.

He said he's an angel. An angel! He is nuts. That or one of us is nuts!

Wait. Could we both be nuts? Maybe we both inhaled something during the fire, toxic fumes or something. I remember the smell of burning plastic...

My mind is racing. My thoughts are like galloping horses on a racing track, sprinting, overtaking each other, falling back. I'm struggling to process it all.

And then a clear winner rushes forward. It carries only one thought: *He said that he's an angel!*

I repeat it in my head on a loop. I remember his wings, but I thought at the time, that it was my oxygen deprived brain working overtime, cooking up something crazy, like when people who have experienced a clinical death claim they saw a tunnel filled with a white light.

But he's saying it so calm, so matter of fact...

That's impossible. He's crazy. Angels aren't real! I need to get out of here.

The thoughts are pouring through so fast that I'm struggling to catch and formulate all of them. But I know for sure that he must be crazy and I need to get out of here.

I take a small step away from him, forcing my face to form a calm polite smile.

Feeling nauseated, I decide to go with it, treading a thin, constantly changing and fluid line with a psychopath.

"Okay, Sam. So the fire was real. Mia was trying to kill me and you're an angel, but I remember burning my arm. I had blisters all over. How is it possible for them to disappear? Where did they go?" I look at my perfectly healthy arm.

"I healed you", Sam answers matter of fact, shrugging his shoulders.

"Sure", I say. I can't help it. My careful reasoning is all forgotten as sarcasm drips off my tongue. "No doubt, with your heavenly powers".

Shit. Calm and nice with a psychopath. Remember the movies, you need to agree with him.

That's a downfall of mine, when I'm scared, I utilise sarcasm as my defence mechanism. The problem is that I usually annoy the hell out of people, aggravating them even further instead of keeping them calm and placid.

I take another step closer to the door. "As much as this is a very fascinating conversation, I really have to go".

Trust me to befriend someone crazier than me.

"You can't go", he says quietly.

"And you can't hold me here against my will". I'm by the door now, turning the handle.

"Will this help you make up your mind?" He says behind my back.

I glance over my shoulder, handle in my hand.

Stunned, I let go of the handle and the door closes again with a soft click.

I turn on the spot, pressing my back against the door. If I could go through the wall right now, I would.

Glorious angel wings are unfurled behind his back, shooting up to the ceiling, swallowing the space in the room. The chandelier chimes with a soft, crystal sound as droplets hit each other when his wing brushes over them.

My mouth agape, I take a step back away from him, sliding along the wall. Then another one. Then one more.

Stunned, I lose my footing and land painfully on my butt. My mind spins, taking in the magnificent, imperial sight of a real to God angel in front of me, with pure white wings.

Who's nuts now?!

He has *four* wings although I only remember seeing two in the science class. Two larger ones are spread wide behind his back, shooting up to the ceiling, while the smaller two are facing down, growing from his lower back, half hidden behind each leg, their tips brushing the floor.

I sit and stare. Seconds are trickling by. He doesn't say a word, doesn't rush me.

My eyes are still locked on him. I raise my hand and pinch myself.

"Ouch", I protest weakly. It does hurt. I really need to stop doing it or my arm will be covered in bruises. Or, more accurately, I need to stop finding myself in situations where I have to question my sanity.

"It's a trick. Your fake wings are just strap-ons", I whisper in an accusing shaky voice. "You've probably nicked them from one of those half naked Victoria's Secret models".

He throws his head back and laughs, a bewitching, irresistible, musical sound.

"You are welcome to inspect them", he says with a charming smile. His blue eyes are hooded, looking at me. "I can even take my shirt off for you". His smirk is back on, now with a challenge.

I ignore his remark about the shirt, mesmerised by the sight of his wide white wings, gently moving around him, taking up almost the entire space in the room.

Okay, let's take stock. I'm not asleep and my pain is real. But is it possible to feel the pain, corresponding with the hallucination and still be hallucinating?

I'm so confused and I don't know what to think, as my mind is going into overdrive.

Clumsily, I scramble myself up off the floor.

It takes a few moments and dozens of heartbeats for me to command my feet to carry me closer to Sam.

The ever so familiar scent of pine needles, forest and moss shrouds around me. I close my eyes and take in a deep breath. I don't care anymore if I look stupid, needy or too girly. I need something to calm me, to ground me, and right now this scent is as good as anything.

I open my eyes and lift my head up at him. My eyes are seeking permission. He answers me with a nod.

I'm confused and scared. Not scared, petrified. The possibility of him being an angel, of me being here or of another set of species being real. All of it can be confirmed with one stroke of my hand over his wing. But what if I've finally lost my mind? What if I've finally fallen through that rabbit hole, through the black hole of no return? The prospect of my final demise scares me more than the discovery of celestial creatures.

"Go on", his relaxed smirk is back on. He dares me.

I take two sidesteps to the left, behind his muscular body. His pure-white angel wings move slow and steady. Close up, they have the luminescent glow of a pearl. I can see individual feathers making up the wing as I reach out.

The moment my fingers make contact with the silky softness of a feather, his wing jerks away from my touch, starting to beat like wings of a butterfly caught in a net.

Startled, I drop my hand.

The chandelier above chimes wildly, when it's hit by his thrashing wing.

"Sorry", he grits through his teeth. "Give me a second. Nobody's touched my wings in a while", he mumbles apologetically.

He tightly shuts his eyes.

"Okay. I'm ready. I will keep still", he exhales.

"Are you sure?" The strangled, stammering whisper doesn't sound like my voice at all.

"Yes", he snaps. "It's fine. Just do it".

I look at him. His eyes are tightly shut, his lips pressed in a decisive line.

I slowly reach again.

His wing jerks again once my fingers make contact with his feathers. I pull my hand back as my gaze jumps to his face. His jaw muscles strain under the skin, as his eyes close tighter than they were before, if that is even possible. But his wings are pushed back into their original position and frozen in place.

Tentatively, I move my finger up to meet the feather, slowly stroking its silkiness.

And as his wings stay still, I feel braver and I want to touch more of his wing.

I take a small step closer to him, closing the distance between us.

I'm next to his body. I lay my open palm on his wing and stroke it upwards as far as I can reach up on my tippy toes and then bring my hand back to the base of his wing and stroke it again.

The feel of his feathers under my palm is strangely satisfying. It's soft and silky, fragile yet strong, and very graceful. I'm in awe by the sheer divinity of it. The shape of his feathers is uniform but the size of them differs, depending on the area of the wing. Some feathers are as long as my arm, while others are of the length of my hand. I marvel at the feel and the look of them – they are magnificent.

I turn my head, looking up at him. My wonder struck smile shrivels under the intensity of his gaze on me.

I drop my hand, swallow, and take a small step back. I turn my gaze back to his wing and watch it for a bit before I speak again.

"How is this possible?" I croak, bewildered, needing to hear something, I don't know what, but something to tell me that I'm not losing my mind.

"Everything is possible", he replies in a coarse, throaty voice. "Remember, Mr Shaw said once in his class, that just because you can't see something, doesn't mean it does not exist". The side of his mouth lifts up into his usual smirk. "Wise man", he winks at me, "for a human that is".

His face sobers, relaxes, his unseeing gaze stares into space. I don't know what he is thinking, but now I have this nudging feeling that something else is happening behind those eyes, something more, that's not shared with me.

His gaze sweeps back to me.

It locks on mine and then, guided by his thoughts, it leisurely travels around my face, taking in my features, lingering on my lips, as if drawn to them by a magnet. I shift uncomfortably under his gaze, unconsciously wetting my lips with my tongue.

I clear my throat.

"But if you're an angel, what were you doing in my class? Why were you there?" I ask, filling in the uncomfortable silence.

"I was there because Mia was there. I had to protect you from her", he answers.

"Like my personal guardian angel?" I snort out an unamused, sarcastic laugh.

He shrugs his shoulders.

"Well, I still don't see why I can't go back to my house?" I demand. Now it's my turn to shrug my shoulders.

"Mia is still out there. She is after you and it's much harder for me to protect you out there", he says slowly and patiently, as if he's talking to a toddler.

I hate to be patronised like that. Like I'm too stupid to understand the enormity of the situation or the gravity of my decisions, which only wise people, like him, should make for me. Sure, I haven't been that smart until now, but that doesn't mean an automatic void on my input on any of my wishes or needs.

And just like that, my annoyance and irritation spikes up.

"But what about my family, school, people who know me?" I stammer, appalled. "They will worry about me. Can't we just go to the police and tell them about Mia, about how she did set the fire to the class? With the fire damage to the room and thirty witnesses that had to flee it, it'll be valid enough evidence. I'm sure they'll be able protect me".

"Unfortunately, police can't protect you from *her*. I told you, she is an angel, just like me", he cuts me off.

He is a picture of a calm determination. His arms are folded over his chest, his jaw is set and he is clearly not going to budge on this one.

I inhale a shaky, angry breath, and I am about to tell him what I think about his totalitarian and obnoxious attitude, and where he can shove it when the door creaks open again.

The young girl from earlier with bouncy curls pokes her head through it.

"I've got her breakfast", she chirps, giving us both a wide smile. She nudges the door wider and comes in with a tray in her hands, laden with food. A pair of silvery-grey angel wings flutter behind her back, opening and closing in time with her bouncing steps. Unlike Sam, she doesn't have an extra pair of wings growing towards the ground. She only has two regular ones, shooting upwards.

Look at me, talking about two angelic wings as if it's a norm!

The girl bounces across the room with a tray towards me, and then abruptly stops a few steps away, looking at me expectantly. I don't think she is usually a servant: she doesn't seem to know what to do with the tray and is too excited by such a simple job.

She looks like a ten year old child and is dressed like a one. She wears a dark grey sweatshirt dress with a picture of the Empire State Building in New York on the front. Colourful tights in a crazy red and green swirling pattern cover her skinny, twig like legs. Red high tops, laced with acidic yellow laces finish her outfit.

Unsure, she sweeps her gaze around the room, turning slightly on the spot, but then shrugs and places the tray on the floor in front of me, beaming at me with a gorgeous, bright and open smile. This girl is really pleased with herself.

"Thank you", I say warmly, smiling back at her.

She is cute and quite entertaining, and just because Sam had annoyed the hell out of me, doesn't mean I'm going to take it out on her. She reminds me of my sister.

"My name is Tabbris, but you can call me Tabby", she chimes, giving me another bright smile.

"Nice to meet you, Tabby. I'm Ariel", I reply, smiling at her. Her smile is contagious and I find that I want to smile back at her when she beams like that.

"I've heard so much about you", she says as she darts her gaze at Sam.

"Ariel, I think you need to eat. I think it might help you", Sam interjects into our pleasant exchange, souring my mood instantly.

"Don't you think that you're thinking too much?" I snap, turning to him. "People will be worrying about me. I need to get back to my home, to my life, to my family. I can't just disappear like that", my voice is rising.

"And you will get back, once I take care of Mia." The determination in his voice confirms that he won't budge on this.

"And how long do *you think*, this is going to take?" I snap.

Irritation and anger are my 'go to' emotions when I'm confronted or cornered in a desperate situation and right now I can feel the crippling tide of fear coming over me, already touching my toes, threatening to consume me whole.

My useless therapist at the house always preached that I needed to learn how to control and 'manage' my emotions, my anger and rage in particular. That I need to take time out, to take myself out of the situation, to calm myself and to think before running head forward, but... it's easier said than done.

I feel almost a physical pain in my gut when I walk away, suppressing the release of my emotions, blocking them in. It's like trying to stuff the morning fog into a bottle and my anger and rage hate that. They are like a poison grenade, like a Molotov cocktail – ready to explode the moment it's created, slowly dissolving, leaking its toxic poison, not caring who's going to get hurt in the process.

But sometimes, I found comfort in my rage.

She is real.

She kept me going like kindling stoking the fire. She kept my back straight and my determination focused. Rage and the promise of revenge have kept me better company than my family ever had. She led me to the other side though horrors and she will serve me well again.

"I don't know", he says with a finality which really means 'I don't care'.

I swallow the toxic poison back into my gut for now.

"But what about people who know me?" I ask him calmly, stamping hard on the panic in my throat, trying to be calm and logical as I try to reason with him. "They'll report me missing tonight if I'm not home after school. If they haven't reported already".

"They haven't and they won't", he answers. "I cleared your room in that house where you were residing. I cleared up any evidence of you from the school. All that's left behind is a fire-damaged classroom, with some broken furniture and glass, but even that will be passed as a result of an accidental fire and the stampede that followed it. I altered people's memories of you, so nobody in the school or that residence of yours will be looking for you. All their memories of you were pushed to the back of their minds and only occasionally, if they come across something of yours, it might rise up like a sense of déjà vu, but then they'll get back to whatever they were doing before, like you were never there. That's it", he shrugs his shoulders.

"So I have been wiped out of their minds?" I stammer in disbelief. "Everyone's? Like I never existed? And they'll not even be looking for me?"

I'm incredulous. I can't believe that there's a truth in what he says. How could it be? How is it possible?

My own personal sense of déjà vu is catching up with me. My fear hikes up a notch.

I might throw up.

Again I feel hidden away, at the mercy of someone else. Powerless, voiceless, forgotten. Only this time nobody is looking for me.

I look up at him.

"You have to take me back. I'd rather take my chances with Mia. I'm not afraid of her. If she kills me then so be it", I say, steadying my body and forcing my voice to sound strong.

"I can't do that", he shakes his head slowly.

He is a stone statue, unmoving and unwavering. My fists curl up at my sides. I desperately want to hit him.

"Fine", I snap. "I'll find my way out. Thanks once again for your hospitality". Sarcasm is back with a vengeance.

Screw the therapist.

Rage is back, skipping in after the sarcasm, whistling a happy song while polishing her blood stained talons.

I step over the tray, marching past Sam and Tabby, surprised when allowed to reach the door. I'm even more surprised when the doorknob turns in my hand and the door swings open for me.

With a final glance over my shoulder at him, I step into the hall.

I hesitate for a moment, deciding whether to go left or right down the hall and, concluding that the 'eeny meeny' method is as good as any, I turn left.

CHAPTER 8

A s I set upon my escape, I don't hear footsteps behind me.

My pace is set to a 'power-walking' as I march down this dark, creepily quiet corridor, which is dimly lit with identical rich crystal wall candelabras, fitted at even intervals.

The only noise down here is the strangled echo of my muffled footsteps on the dark plush carpet, bouncing off the regal walls.

The walls are covered in blood red velour, with a golden panel dividing the wall at waist height. It's like a long tunnel ahead of me, stretching for miles on end and there's no light at the end of this one.

After a few minutes, fear stirs inside. It grips my gut, rising, and by the time it squeezes my throat, I'm running down the hall looking for a way out.

Only the balls of my feet are touching the ground. My arms are working in time with my legs, pushing me forward. My heavy breathing echoes in my ears.

I've been running for a while now, but the hall hasn't turned, twisted or split even once.

Over time, my feet grew heavier, weighing me down now with every step. Salty beads of sweat bloom on my forehead, pooling on my body, streaming down my back, soaking my clothes and then running down my face, stinging my eyes. My heart is throbbing in my chest and I'm trying to swallow against my parched throat.

I grab hold of my side, now I have stitch. My pace slows to a pathetic limp and after a few more painful meters, I stop.

I double over, pushing my hands on my knees, trying to get some air into my burning lungs.

I slide down the wall, fighting with my lungs and my terrified heart. I need to find the cool in me, to think logically and composed on what to do next.

The sound of light skipping footsteps, muffled by the carpet, upsurges from the darkness of the hall. A bright crystal voice sings something in a strange language. The stride is short and the footsteps are light and fast as they could only belong to a child.

I claw at the wall behind me, rising unsteadily, ready to bolt when Tabby comes into view, slowly emerging from the shadows. Her grey wings are folded behind her back, protruding above her shoulders. Her wings look darker in the dim corridor light, hidden in the shadows behind her.

She stops a few steps away from me, silent, studying me with the seriousness young children are known for, and killer psychopaths.

"Why did you run?" she asks me after a while. Her brows are drawn, pretty eyes are gazing at me.

"Because I don't want to be here and I want to go home. My sister needs me and I need to be there for her", I reply, sliding down the wall again. The carpet is soft and plush under my hands.

"I don't have a sister, or a mother", she offers. "What is it like to have a sister?"

She plonks herself on the floor right in front of me. She sits, cross-legged, gazing intently at me, eager for a conversation. Her wings are open behind her back so that the bottom corners are streaming over the carpet.

I don't think this girl has ever heard of personal space. I shift uncomfortably, sliding on the carpet away from her, giving myself a more comfortable space between us. But not so much that I offend her.

"It's like having a best friend forever", I say, thinking about my sister. "You love each other, help each other. You look after each other, and you know, that no matter what, someone will be there for you. Always. Now my sister's in a hospital and she needs me." I'm trying to explain the concept that is so easy for siblings to understand and so hard for the 'only child' to fathom.

"I've failed her already. I wasn't there when she needed me, I didn't look after her and now I need to be there to help her", I say, simplifying mine and my sister's problems.

Tabby's studious gaze lingers on my face and her head is cocked to the side.

"I want to have a best friend forever too", she supplies. "If I had a friend like that, I would want to be with her all the time. We could play dress up together and play with my dolls, and do colouring together and I would show her my collection of colourful rocks...", she chatters excitedly as her gaze turns dreamy, her face lights up at the possibility of having a friend. Then her gaze snaps back to me.

"What is your sister's name?" she asks, cocking her head at me again.

"Jess".

"J-e-s-s-s-s", she tries it around her mouth, stretching syllables. "Do you think you and I can be sisters as well?"

Tabby's innocent question catches me off guard.

I turn my gaze to her. Her bright eyes are unguarded and earnest as she waits for my answer.

"Sure", I hesitate. I don't want to offend her but I don't think she understands what sisters are, but nonetheless, she wants us to be friends and I can appreciate that.

She jumps up and hugs me tight, startling me. She smells of fruits and sweets. Once my surprise dies, I raise my arms to hug her back.

Her wings open up wider, shooting up, away from my embrace. Her wings are now beating faster behind her back, creating a soft gust of wind, which moves my hair and caresses my face.

My hug is awkward and unsure. My arms are wrapped around her back, below the wings.

She is a soft little child in my arms, just like my sister always was. Sadness and guilt tug at my heart as I think about Jess. If only I was there to protect her; if only I had found a way to stay.

Tears begin to stream down my cheeks and I can't stop them. The stress of the last two days has finally caught up with me. It pushes at the walls that I built so carefully around, to protect myself, to keep everyone out.

But there is a crack in the wall and the misery is here, swallowing me, pulling me down under its weight, reminding me of everything that I was so eager to forget. And I can't hold it in any more. I'm crying for mine and my sister's lives, so powerless, broken and abused.

Sobs escape me, but Tabby doesn't pull away. Tears run down my chin, darkening the top of her head.

Now she's holding me.

I wail. The ugly sound of unchecked pain echoes along the walls, pouring out for everyone to see. Tabby strokes my back, not rushing me, not asking to stop. She comforts me and I grab hold of her, afraid that this tide will take me with it and I'll never come back.

I don't know how long I've been crying, but I'm out of tears and completely dehydrated. Soft hiccups escape between my lips. When I press my lips together, trying to keep them back, I sound like a frog in a pond in the evening.

"Sorry... about... that", I hiccup as I pull away, and Tabby lets me go.

My nose is blocked, snot pools underneath it and I have no tissue. I wipe my face on my sleeve. My face is probably blotchy and red – I'm an ugly crier.

"What can I –", hiccup, "… do?" I say to myself, not really expecting an answer.

"Sometimes you only do what you *can* do", Tabby says, looking up at the dark ceiling. "Sometimes surviving is all that's left, but it can be even more than you thought you are capable of", she declares, like she is reciting someone else's words.

She turns her gaze back to me.

"Mia is out there and she's going to kill you. For sure", Tabby offers, all practical and rational like discussing a dinner menu. "And your human 'palees' couldn't protect you from her, but Sam can. You have to stay here for now."

"But for how long?" I'm desperate.

"I don't think for that long. He is a good hunter", she nods confidently. "But Mia is very good too", she mumbles. "So maybe not that fast, but definitely not that long." She smiles at me again, happy with her appraisal of the situation.

She is open and candid like a child, and I feel that I can trust her 'truth' more than others.

"Cause if you're dead, how are you going to help your sister and play dress up with her?" she asks, dramatically spreading her arms.

Then she leans in closer to me.

"The dead are not allowed back into the human world", she whispers, looking around, sharing the secret with me. "Sometimes they sneak in, but *you* will never be allowed".

"Why not?" I mumble, shocked. It's not like I plan to come back from the dead to look after my sister, but I want to know why I would never be allowed.

"You've already crossed it", she whispers, smiling with excitement, her bright eyes bulge out of their sockets.

"What? How? When?" I'm so shocked that I can't seem to formulate sentences longer than one word. It doesn't help that Tabby is not making much sense either.

"Your Qal did". She nods her head urgently, willing for me to believe her.

"What is 'Qal'?"

"It's inside you".

Dear god, give me strength. She must be delusional. She's not making any sense.

"How?" I ask again, praying for patience, taking a different route with her.

"Through the passage", she nods proudly, sharing the knowledge.

Oh, boy. That might take a while.

"What passage?" I try again.

"There", she points her finger up to the ceiling.

I crane my head and look up at the ordinary ceiling above us, covered in thick grey shadows from the candelabras nearby. I see nothing, no passage, no hole, not even a crack.

I look back at her. Tabby smiles wide at me, her open eyes are unguarded and earnest.

For God's sake! She doesn't make any sense.

I sigh. I don't think I'll get any more from her following this road so I try a different angle.

"But why me?" I search her face for an answer, but she just shrugs her shoulders.

"And angels? I always thought that you guys weren't real. You know, like a legend or a fairy tale and stuff", I say, shrugging my shoulders in return.

"I'm not a fairy", Tabby huffs, folding her arms at me. The hurt is clear on her lively face. "We are primordial beings and not basic elementals, who are tied up to their area and birthing element. It's like comparing a mammal to an insect".

Oops. I think I've just offended her.

"I'm sorry, Tabby", I gently touch her arm. "I didn't mean to offend you. It's just all of this is very new to me and up until two days ago, I didn't even know that you guys existed".

Tabby unfolds her arms, gazing back at me with a renewed adoration.

Wow. This girl's mood changes so fast that it makes my head spin.

"You know, once Sam took me to one of your safari parks. A big one, in Africa", she says. "I really wanted to see a giraffe. When we found a mummy and baby giraffe, they were standing next to a ve-e-e-ry tall tree and the mummy was eating leaves off of the top of that tree. But there were three naughty hyenas nearby and one jumped up and bit the baby giraffe on the leg. Mummy giraffe came to the rescue and kicked the hyena away, but later she told me that she didn't see the hyenas".

She looks at me, checking if I'm following her story. But I don't know if I am.

"You see, her head was high up in the sky and she didn't see anything that was happening low on the ground, hidden under the leaves", she explains. "So I think you, humans, are like that mummy giraffe. You only can see your section of the tree", she says, "but your section of the tree is down below, next to the ground, and not high up in the sky".

She beams at me, pleased with herself and with her explanation.

Only one sentence sticks in my mind. "Mummy giraffe *told* you?" I ask incredulous.

"Yeah", she animatedly nods, her glossy curls bouncing around her pixie face. "Straight after those naughty hyenas ran away".

"So you can speak to animals?" I ask, trying to sound cool and composed.

Tabby's baffled expression answers my question better than any words.

"Can't you?" she replies, confused by such possibility.

I slowly shake my head at her. Here's another piece of this crazy jigsaw to wrap my head around.

I sit quietly for a minute, digesting the latest revelation.

"Maybe you are right", I mutter. "At the end of the day, lots of things in this world still remain unexplained. Maybe angels are just one of them, like an undiscovered species in the Amazon or something. I spoke to Sam, touched his wing, felt it and it felt real", I mumble to myself.

"You touched Sam's wing?" Tabby breathes out. Her frightened eyes rapidly blink at me. "By accident?"

"Well, no. He wanted to show me that he's real, that he is not a part of my crazy imagination, so he let me touch his wing and I stroked his wing for a bit", I say, shrugging my shoulders. "It was very soft and silky" I add.

She stares at me, blinking her big eyes in stunned confusion.

"What's the big deal?" I ask, irritated by her mute shocked face.

"Angels *never* let anyone touch their wings", she whispers, bug-eyed. "Unless they are married".

The next second a fresh thought crosses her mind and her face blossoms with a beautiful smile.

"Are you and Sam married now?" she chirps. Now her eyes are wide with excitement. I wonder if this girl is even capable of calm restrained emotions.

"What? No!" It's now my turn to wear "the incredulous face" mask.

"I hope not!" I blurt out.

"I'm sure we are not! What a ridiculous suggestion that is. I just touched his wing to make sure that he's real. That's it!" I ramble, shaking my head.

"Oh", Tabby's face falls.

"That's okay", she says, lightening up the next second. "You're still my sister".

We sit in silence, while I try to think of other alternative options out of my predicament, consistently coming up empty handed. I don't see any other way out of this mess.

"We need to get back to your room. I can take you there", Tabby offers.

"Great", a bitter sarcastic laugh escapes me. "Just my sodding luck". I adjust myself to the idea that I'm here to stay, even if it's just for a short while.

CHAPTER 9

S am is still in the room where I left him. He's comfortably reclined in the armchair near the lit fire in that enormous fireplace. The logs are crackling like miniature fireworks going off celebrating the 5th of November, relaxing me somehow.

Sam's wings are folded behind his back, spilling over the back of the chair. His long legs are stretched in front of him, crossed at the ankles; his hands are folded over his taut stomach. A half-empty mug of coffee sits on the small table in front of him.

His hair is dry now and the waves on top of his head are more defined, falling over his forehead.

Somewhere along our way back, Tabby vanished, so now it's just me and Sam in the room.

I expect to hear some mocking from him of my pathetic, failed attempt to escape, but he says nothing, just looking at me, waiting, so I speak first, breaking the silence.

"I can't get out of this place, can I?" I ask him.

"No, you can't. And I'm not going to help you. I need to keep you safe. That's what I'm here for", he says quietly.

I walk further into the room, sitting carefully on the edge of the bed. My bed is made now, leaving no signs of anyone sleeping in it last night. The heavy, gold-stitched throw is spread on top of it, with an array of cushions of different shades of red arranged at the head of the bed.

"Why me? How did I get in the middle of this mess?" I mumble, shaking my head in disbelief.

I'm at a loss at how someone like me, who made so sure to keep their head down for the last few years, ended up here.

"How about I'll answer your questions if you eat your breakfast", he gestures to the tray full of food on the small table and an armchair across from him.

"Okay, but I need all the information", I warn him.

I decided to keep an open mind. Whichever way you slice it, I'm stuck here and I need to find a way out of this situation. And for that, I need the information. All of it.

"If I know the answer, I'll give it to you", he simply says.

I walk over and take a seat in the armchair across from Sam.

The food on the tray looks inviting and smells delicious. Cafetiere, filled with freshly brewed coffee, spreads its steamy aroma around the room. Croissants, jam in a crystal vase with a tiny silver spoon, slices of ham on a plate, all of it looks fresh and smells divine. I'm hungrier than I thought.

"Is there poison in the food?" I ask, eyeing the tray, before touching any of it.

I want Sam to know that I don't trust him. My show of mistrust has very little to do with the food. I'm not naïve to think that even if it's spiked, he'll fall to his knees under my suspicious stare, cry and beg for my forgiveness. But I doubt he would stoop that low, there's no reason for that, as I'm already trapped.

"I'd never do anything that might hurt you", he says, sounding sincere. His wistful eyes gaze openly into mine.

"Whatever", I mumble, pouring the coffee into a clean mug. I scoop out some jam from a crystal vase, spreading it carefully over a croissant and taking the first bite of it. The croissant is freshly baked and melts in my mouth. As I close my eyes and chew, the little hum of appreciation escapes me.

"Nice?" Sam's low, hoarse voice interrupts the enjoyment of my breakfast and I open my eyes, suddenly aware of his presence. Sam's gaze is on me, hot and intense. I gulp uncomfortably, pinned to my seat under his gaze. His soft gaze from under his hooded eyes is stroking my face, caressing me.

"Do you know that I like you?" he asks, as his warm gaze lingers on me. A little smile lifts the corners of his mouth, producing that irresistible dimple.

"No. I don't", my squeaky voice betrays me. I sound all girly, scared and excited at the same time, and I want to kick myself for that.

"You are not very observant", he chuckles. "But please eat. I'm not going to distract you anymore".

He gets up, walks over to the burning fire and places a few more logs in it. His wings are folded behind his back with the lower ones only an inch from the ground.

My appetite is now gone, so I sip my coffee, following Sam's movement with my eyes over the rim of my mug.

"What were you doing in my school?" I ask his back.

"So I guess we're ready to start the quiz", he chuckles, as he turns around. The side of his face and body are illuminated by the soft yellow glow of the fire, changing the colour of his wings to an orangey gold.

"I was sent to your school to find and protect you from Mia and Rafe." He moves to stand behind his armchair. He leans in, resting his folded arms on the top of the back rest.

"Rafe? Is he an angel too?" I pull the mug away from my face. I'm surprised by how calm and matter-of-fact I'm discussing the possibility of one of the students in my school being an angel.

"Yes, he is."

Sam doesn't expand on it, doesn't give any more information. But this dry minimum feels cautiously measured, managed. I feel like *I'm* being managed, like all the information that currently is being given to me, is given strictly on a 'need to know basis' and there's more, much more, hidden in the shadows.

I tuck this suspicion away for now, deciding not to confront him just yet, and try to gather more information by myself. Knowledge is power and information its ultimate currency.

I decide to start from the beginning.

"Okay", I sigh. "What do they both want with me?"

Sam steps around his armchair and walks over to me. He kneels in front of me and takes my hands in his. His smell envelops me and I'm fighting with myself not to close my eyes again and melt like a finishing school debutante, as I'm inhaling his glorious scent.

His hands are big and warm and exciting tingles spread from my hands up through my body.

I can see how every girl would want a caring and loyal boyfriend, a boy who only has eyes for her, who looks after her, protects her. I would have loved one too, but I know better than to rely on someone else to save me. That will never happen.

I remember seeing an old-fashioned poster in a local museum once. It was from the thirties and it was made to promote the safety on water in coastal communities and to encourage children to learn how to swim. A basic, bold drawing of the sea, the sky, a bright and perky sun and a little boy who's submerged deeply in the water with only his head poking above the waves, gasping for air. Lazy seagulls hover above him and a colourful Ferris wheel twinkles in the distance on the pier. The boy is clearly drowning in the sea and the big red round letters at the bottom of the poster are formed into a sharp and powerful slogan: *'It's your job to stay afloat'.*

Bold and to the point. Maybe it's a bit morbid and somewhat unsupportive, but I certainly appreciate the no-nonsense importance of that message: "Don't expect to be saved, make sure that you can save yourself". And that was the best advice anyone has given me, better than my mother's usual: 'Pray for forgiveness, you little sinner!'

I took that message to heart. Later, life taught me that it was the soundest advice ever, that relying on someone else makes you weak, makes you an easy prey, makes you a victim. I'm done being a victim.

"Can we please agree that you need to be open-minded with all the information I give you?" He asks, gazing into my eyes.

I nod, ready to play the game.

"You need to be extra open-minded about this one", he pauses, gazing at me.

But as I say nothing he speaks again.

"You are an angel", he utters, cautiously studying me.

Flabbergasted, I stare at him for a minute. That was not what I expected, at all.

The universe must have shifted somewhere between the fire and me waking up in his house or I've crossed into an alternate one where an average girl from a boring sleepy coastal town is an angel and a hunk, like Sam, likes her.

Giggles escape me. I can't help it.

At first it's only a few but soon they're pushing up to the top, like a million of bubbles in a shaken can of fizz. I'm laughing, head back, a loud rumble rising from my throat, shaking my body, tears gathering in my eyes.

He lets go of my hands and pulls back, sitting on his heels. Confusion is showing on his face.

My laugh rises, picking up volume and pace. It's getting hysterical, even I can hear it. Tears overflow and start rolling down my face. I slap at my thighs and wipe at my face, as I throw my head back and laugh some more, freely, to the full, like I haven't laughed in a while.

It's very liberating to laugh to the full and not care who is watching.

I laugh out loud, until I'm all spent, until my throat is dry and sore, and my jaw hurts.

It takes me a while but eventually I sober up and, with a final giggle, I wipe at my eyes, looking back at Sam, searching his face for a suppressed laughter or smile, but he sits there, in front of me, stiff and uncomfortable, unsure of himself and maybe, even afraid of me.

A quizzical expression is marring his perfect face, setting two deep wrinkles between his eyebrows. He is looking at me, lost and silent, searching my face, not knowing what to do or say.

Sticky silence stretches between us.

The longer I look at his confused face, the faster I sober up.

"You aren't serious, are you?" I stammer, pulling myself back away from him, deeper into the chair as he nods.

"Whoa. And I thought I was open-minded before", I mumble.

"Are you completely sure that I'm an angel? Maybe there was some mix up somewhere?" I ramble on. "Maybe you got the wrong girl? I don't even have wings", I gesture over my shoulder. Petrified chatter rolls off me, desperate to show him that I'm not an angel and shouldn't be here. How good that would be if I was allowed to leave? Just like that. Back to my ordinary life.

"And my parents are absolutely normal. Well, maybe not exactly normal, but human for sure. I'm not an expert in heavenly reproduction but I do understand genetics. Shouldn't at least one of the parents be an angel for this kind of stuff to pass down?" I babble.

He puts his warm hands over mine, covering them with his completely.

I stop talking. He should stop doing this, I lose my train of thought when he touches me.

"There's no mix up, Ariel. You have an angel's Qal, or essence if you wish, hidden in you – I can sense it", he says. "When your soul was forming, an angel was assassinated. That angel's followers reached out to the Ophanims, the keepers of universal laws, and asked them to intervene in an effort to preserve the essence. The Ophanims decided to save the essence of the angel, mainly for the balance of forces, but they placed it in a mortal child for safekeeping until they investigated the matter and decided what to do with it. You were born with that angel's essence in you", he utters carefully, keeping his gaze fixed on me.

"I grant you, nobody thought that the essence would manifest itself so fast. The Ophanims probably thought that they easily had until you died of old age. It would've been almost a century for you, but it would've been only a day for them. Then, the essence would have naturally separated itself from your life source, without affecting you. So your essence waking up this early is a shock for them and pretty much for everyone in our realm, and now everybody is scrambling around, trying to figure out what's going on".

For the first time since I've known him, information is flowing out of him instead of the usual smirk as a standard means of reply.

"Hold on. But how can you make sure that I have that essence inside me? I can't see it. Can you?" I ask, dubious.

"Not right this second. Your essence is currently only active when you're asleep or unconscious. It was seeping from you earlier when you were asleep. I saw it then. The essence is still suppressed, small and weak, like a flicker of a candle in a wind, very faint to see, especially from the angel's realm, and easy to blow out.

"But whoever wanted that essence extinguished was looking for you and so was I. Over time, they narrowed it down to your town and I followed them. I knew that Rafe was an angel, I could smell it on him, but Mia had covered her essence perfectly. Mind you, she is an assassin and I wouldn't have expected anything less from her. I didn't know who you were, but neither did they. However, two nights ago your essence erupted like a volcano, shooting like a beacon through yours and our realm and, in that instance, you were in play. From that moment, Mia knew who she was looking for, so she went in for a kill".

He falls quiet. I sit, staring into space, digesting all that unbelievable information.

I wanted the information currency to grow my power, but I didn't expect that currency to be fluffy pink unicorn droppings.

"Whatever happened that night was a very strong catalyst for the essence. It allowed for the essence to take over. What happened to you two nights ago?" he asks gently, stroking my hands in his. His thumb softly follows over my fingers and my knuckles, sending shivers down my spine.

"My sister got hurt", I reply. That's as much as I'm prepared to give him at this time.

I scramble in my brain, trying to arrange and prioritise this steaming pile of magic nonsense.

"But why do they want to kill me?" I can barely make my tongue to turn, to put words like 'kill' and 'me' in the same sentence.

"They are the ones who assassinated that essence in the first place, so they are coming for you to finish the job", he says gently. I imagine it is how a doctor might deliver a terminal prognosis to his patient.

"You said that the angel was already assassinated. What's the point in all of it now? I'm not an angel. Why kill me?" I whisper. I try to wrap my mind around this news and the fact that somewhere out there walks a bloodthirsty 'they' who are plotting my demise.

Memories of Mia's pitiless, homicidal cold stare, the blisters on my arm, and the surrounding fire pushing at me is a crude reminder that 'they' are no longer plotting. 'They' have moved into an active stage of their "kill Ariel" plan.

"Essence is..." he flickers his fingers in the air, "essence. It's vital for any angel and keeps our core within. With the essence intact, an angel has been known to be resurrected. You extinguish the essence, you kill an angel forever. No turning back. Their assassination didn't go to plan and now they're here to clear up the mess and finish off the job".

"So they're trying to kill me for my essence? Can't I just give it to them?" I'm struggling to be comfortable with the idea of someone trying to kill me for something that I didn't know I had and don't really want.

"No. The essence is now to stay with you. It's now connected to you and intertwined with your life source. You now feed off each other, it's replenishing your substance and you are nourishing the essence. No one can separate the essence and you. Now, it can be only extinguished with you. You're tied up to each other. If the essence dies, you will die".

He stops for a moment and I know that there's more to come.

"And as it has awakened and some of it has come to the forefront, it will start changing you", Sam says softly, as he strokes the top of my hands with his thumbs. "An essence transforms the host, irrelevant of the species, into an angel with the previous owner's powers, memories, abilities, the lot. It's carrying the powers and abilities, almost like your human DNA. It will change you, slowly, over time. It will evolve as it takes on more of its host abilities. It's expanding. The essence slowly takes control".

He sees something in my face as he adds in a rush, "But ultimately, the essence can protect you as well. It will give you powers to fight them as equals, to have even chances against any of them, including Mia. The essence will give you enormous powers. Powers you would have never thought existed in this world. Your world will change but it will open up to you in different colours and experiences that you never knew. One day, you'll even learn how to fly, and I promise you that, one day, you'll be happy that the essence landed on you".

Bewildered, I can't hear much of what he is saying. His words "if the essence dies, you will die" are playing in my head over and over on repeat, like a needle, stuck on the same terrifying song on vinyl.

His face sobers as he speaks again.

"They lost the element of surprise for now but that doesn't mean they gave up on the job. It would've made their work easier if they'd killed you before the essence had woken up, but the final goal is annihilation and nothing has changed that", he remarks.

"So, no matter what I do, they'll try to kill me?" My small scared voice sounds pathetic, even to my ears.

"I'm afraid so", his sympathetic eyes are on me. He looks at me like I'm damned, and I want to cry.

My hands are shaking in his. He feels sorry for me and I can't stand his pity.

I pull my hands free and get out of the chair.

He lets me go, effortlessly rising to his feet, but I still feel his eyes on me as I stand confused, scanning the pompous room.

My throat feels dry and full of choking sand. I would love to have a glass of water, but all I can see on the table is coffee. The cafetiere clanks against the rim of the mug as I pour coffee with my shaking hand. I gulp it down, wishing it could be something stronger.

I turn to him. "Where can I get some water?"

He rings a small silver bell next to the mantel, which I hadn't noticed earlier.

A few seconds later, a gorgeous tall girl with the face of a model and the fluid movement of a dancer saunters in, carrying a tray with a crystal jug full of water and a beaker, angel wings flutter behind her back.

Now I'm paying close attention to her wings. She only has two, like Tabby, and unlike Sam's hers are slimmer, more elegant and not white, but ash-grey.

She places the tray on the table, turns and leaves without a word, keeping her eyes professionally fixed in space.

Once the door closes behind her, I narrow my eyes at Sam. "Is this room bugged?"

He looks at me confused, probably thinking that I've finally lost my mind. His forehead creases as he silently studies me and I almost can hear cogs in his brain turning.

"Bugs? Cameras? listening devices?" I prompt him.

"No", he stumbles, slowly shaking his head. He clearly doesn't understand what I'm on about.

"How did she know what to bring?" I demand.

His face relaxes a bit.

"I spoke to her in my mind and told her to bring you some water", he gazes openly into my eyes, with the sincerity of a child telling the truth. Just like my sister when she used to tell me about her imaginary friend and couldn't comprehend why I couldn't see him. With everything I've learnt so far, maybe her friend wasn't that imaginary after all.

Of course, he can communicate telepathically!

I think that the part of my brain, responsible for reactions to surprises, has died off. I pour myself some water, pleased that my hands are less shaky, and gulp it down.

He moves back next to the fireplace and now he watches me, waiting for another outburst. His body radiates the pressure of a tight guitar string. I think about giving him another tantrum, but I'm so shell shocked and tired that I don't know if I have the energy for one.

I drain the beaker and place it on the table.

"Okay. So let me sum it all up, please do correct me if I miss anything out. Angels are real. You are one and so is Tabby, and Mia and Rafe, and even that one", I gesture to the closed door, "And apparently I'm becoming one, according to you, as I have the angelic essence in me, which is changing me, which I can't take out or stop. And a few assassins are now after me, wanting to kill me because of that essence and because they couldn't finish that essence off when they had their bloody chance. And you can communicate telepathically. All correct? I haven't missed anything?" My voice rises with every word spoken and I practically yell the last question, glaring at him, leaning over the small table.

I'm angry. Livid. I'm in deep shit, up to my neck and none of it is of my making. An unexpected thought hits me.

"And why are you here? What's in it for you?" I narrow my eyes at him.

He is more comfortable with my attitude and clearly, that's the question he was expecting from me, as his body relaxes a bit, with his face taking on his usual smirk.

"Well, let's say I'm playing for the opposing team", he says, as he folds his arms, leaning his shoulder on the fireplace's mantle.

"And how is that?" I demand. "Are you the angelic police or something?"

"Not exactly", he chuckles. "I just don't believe that annihilating the essence is the answer to a disagreement and neither do the angels who I'm working with. We think that there's a need for every essence out there and we feel that your essence should be protected".

"And have I mentioned that I like you?" His quiet, velvety voice brushes over me. His smirk is coy and playful as his eyes stroke me.

Heat pinches my cheeks as I drop my gaze. He said it again. Never have I had a boy say it to me, so I'm really unsure on the etiquette on this. Do I say 'thank you' or is 'I like you too' compulsory in these situations?

I clear my throat and shift in my chair while keeping my eyes down. But I don't know what to say, so I decide to change the subject.

"So what am I supposed to do now?" I ask, looking down at my clasped hands and my fingers intertwined on my lap.

Intertwined together, now inseparable like that stupid essence and me, I think bitterly.

"For now, *you* need to sit tight. Here. And *I* need to find Mia and Rafe and get that threat eliminated. Then you can go back to your old life, if you still decide to do so", he instructs.

I hesitate.

"I want to ask you a question."

"Anything."

He takes a seat in the armchair.

"Your wings. Can you fly?" I lift my head, gazing at him.

"Of course", he answers with a patient smile and I feel like I'm three again when I was told about the magic of a rainbow.

"Can you show me?" I slide closer in my seat, eager for a demonstration.

"Later, if you still want it. I'd need more space", he sweeps his arm around to say how small this room is for him.

"Oh, of course. And telepathy. How does that work?" I'm fascinated. "Can you read my mind?"

That possibility unsettles me.

"No, I can't read minds, but I can speak *to* minds. It's like a radio frequency: you need to know the wave frequency of your recipient. And it's good manners to ask for permission first, before establishing that kind of contact. We are using it mainly for communicating between ourselves, but sometimes it's been known to be used to communicate with humans. But there you just open the sequence, send your message out there, not knowing if anyone will receive it, who is the recipient or what he might do with it.

"It was more common thousands of years ago to deliver the 'Word of God' to the humans", he says and rolls his eyes, "but now humans are more cynical and with the help of pharmaceutical advancement, you're now able to block those messages, so we rarely do it nowadays".

"And your wings? How come you didn't have them when you were in my school?" I ask.

"Who said I didn't have them?" His lips lift into a playful half smile. Mischief dances behind his eyes. He wants to play.

I roll my eyes and take a patient breath, settling in to play a 'guessing game' with him.

"Okay then. So you had them at school", I look at him and he inclines his head at me, confirming my words.

"But I still can't see where you could've hidden them. You weren't wearing bulky clothes, no big coat", I muse to myself. "It must be some sort of angelic magic..."

A sudden thought hits me.

"Or maybe they're detachable. You know, like the hood on a coat – a couple of poppers and, hey presto, you've got a coat with a hood", I'm grinning at him, well chuffed with my detective skills and logical thinking.

A wide unguarded smile spreads on his face as he starts chuckling. "Poppers... Like a hood..." He shakes his head as he laughs. At me!

With a huff, I fold my arms over my chest and, settling deeper in my seat, give him one of my most threatening glares, annoyed that he is lifting his spirits at my expense.

"I don't know. Can you just tell me and quit laughing at me?" I narrow my eyes at him.

"Please don't be offended Mermaid, but it's funny, "poppers on a hood". Maybe we should look into engineering something like that", he is beaming at me with his glorious smile and I realise that I'm smiling back at him.

"It's a lot simpler than that. We always have our wings on us. They're attached to us just like our heads. We are not hiding them because we *can't* hide them. But you, humans, are choosing not to see them. You are born with the ability to see a lot more of this world, to see beyond your reality, to see us and our wings but, as you get older, you choose to block out anything that doesn't fit into your simple little world.

"And you're taught by the people around you, time and time again, that all that you see is just your imagination, that it's not real, it's not possible. They show you the fabricated proof, ramble on with the evidence and statistics and they're so convincing while doing so, that slowly you start believing them. But we're always there, all of us. Humans are like little scared children playing hide and seek. They cover their eyes with their hands and because they can't see the world, they think that their trick has hidden them from the world as well".

He gazes at me, relaying something important and willing for me to understand it.

"Just because you refuse to see us, doesn't mean that we're not there", he says.

I'm sitting here, looking at him, digesting all that unbelievable new information.

"Well, I need to go", he says, getting up from his chair. "Mia is still out there and she is not going to eliminate herself. You didn't eat anything, so I'm going to send you some more breakfast. Please try to eat and try to get some rest. I thought you might want to change out of your school uniform, so you'll find some clothes and shoes in the wardrobe. I believe they're all your size. Take a walk around the gardens if you wish. Tabby can show you around, and later we have dinner to attend to in your honour. Everyone is excited to meet you."

"And what if I don't want to go?"

He takes a small step closer.

"I hope you decide to join me", he says, his soft low voice caresses me. "I would like the opportunity to dance with you."

And before I can think of an answer, he picks up and rings a silver bell and the earlier supermodel waltzes in with another tray. She places that one down, picks up the old one and leaves without a word or glance at either of us.

"Don't miss me too much, Mermaid", his arrogance is back and with it the Sam I know. "I'll see you later", and with a last wink, he walks out, leaving me alone in the vast imperial room.

I make a mental note to talk to him again tonight. He can't possibly be serious about my indefinite stay here.

CHAPTER 10

I try to eat, but my appetite is gone and I can't push down more than half of a croissant. I finish my breakfast, wipe my fingers on a napkin and decide to check out the clothes in the wardrobe. I'd love a pair of jeans, trainers and a sweatshirt. A school pencil skirt isn't the most comfortable thing to wear if you need to run or fight, and right now I'm not excluding either possibility.

Of course, there's a strong doubt in my ability to fight Sam for example and win, but I'm trying not to think about it right now.

My bedroom has three more sets of doors, apart from the entrance doors. The wide double doors with glass tops, surrounded by wide windows on either side, must be leading outside as the sunlight streams through them into the room.

I slowly come closer and peek out.

I huff as I strain, pulling open the heavy door and step out onto an enormous balcony. The room I'm in is suspended high in a tall building. It is easily the twentieth floor, maybe even higher. A thick and intricate stone railing encircles the entire balcony. It's like the balcony is surrounded by fat upside down stone vases. A black wrought iron gate with a simple latch is fitted in the middle of the stone railing and the confusion is replaced with the appreciation for angelic attention to detail. If I needed extra proof that 'Sam the angel' is not a product of my imagination, the gate in the middle of the railing of the balcony on the twentieth floor must be it. I wouldn't have such a detailed hallucination. I guess that gate saves angels climbing over the railing to take to the sky or to come back to land.

I come closer to the railing, resting my belly on its stone top as I look down.

Below spreads a park with large, perfectly green lawns, rolling far into the horizon like posh golf retreat grounds. Shimmering ponds speckle the endless enormity of the lawn, reflecting the piercing cloudless blue sky above. A few small forestry areas are dotted around, interrupting the perfect stretch of grass. A warm summer breeze strokes my face, bringing woodland smells, mixed with a sweet hint of cherry blossom and cut grass.

Although 'picture perfect', something bothers me and it takes me a minute to realise that the sky is unnaturally still and quiet. The bright sunny day isn't interrupted with the usual hustle of wildlife in the sky, birds aren't singing and insects aren't buzzing in the vastness of it, the air is totally silent. This sky and grass look like the photographic backdrop for a TV show. This unnerving silence unsettles me and with a final glance over the silicon perfection, I rush back inside, closing the doors tightly behind me.

I try the next set of doors and freeze on the spot as the door swings open to a large brightly illuminated room, organised with mahogany wooden shelves, hangers and drawers, all filled with neatly arranged clothes and shoes. This room is a shopaholic's heaven.

I gawk, open mouthed, at the substantial palatial walk in closet, as I take a few tentative steps in.

Shelves full of shoes are taking up the closest wall on the right. Shoes, boots, and sandals of all colours and styles are lined up precisely on the shelves, like soldiers in a parade. I bet if they had arms, they would be saluting me now. The shelves reach to the ceiling and I wonder how you're supposed to take the shoes down from the top shelf. Maybe there is a ladder or some rotating mechanism built into them?

The farthest half of the right wall is taken up by a ceiling high large mirror in a gold opulent frame.

The opposite wall holds a single, long rail, offering an extensive collection of silk and sparkling evening dresses on wooden and padded hangers, some jackets and long coats hang towards the end. The single mahogany shelf is suspended above the rail, holding the collection of hat boxes, mixed with a mouth-watering selection of handbags of all shapes, colours, sizes and styles.

The remaining walls are holding clothes on hangers, interspersed by closed drawers of polished mahogany wood, decorated with intricate gold handles. Sweaters and jumpers, trousers and skirts are arranged in their private sections with care and precision.

A circular, cream leather "Chesterfield" couch, like a fat cat is nestled in the centre of the room.

I take a few more steps inside the 'wonder room'. It smells of orange peel, lavender and wood polish.

Now inside, I can see a mirror, covering the entire ceiling with a smaller copy of the main room's crystal chandelier, suspended heavily from it. The light catches off the mirror, bending through the edges and corners of the crystal droplets of the chandelier, fanning the rainbows over the room. Rainbow speckles are sprayed over the ceiling and walls. Spot lights above the clothing alcoves add to the brightness of the room.

I stand there in awe, taking in the sheer wealth of it all. Hesitantly, I turn and close the distance between me and the parade of shoes. With a shaking hand, I reach out and stroke the black patent high heeled pair next to me. They are an absolute beauty. "Gucci". Wow!

I don't know who the owner of these beauties might be or if I'll be slapped on the hand for touching someone's treasures but, unable to stop myself, I reach out and take them in my hands. They are my size. With a quick glance over my shoulder at the door, I put them on. They pinch my feet and I'm very unsteady in heels, but catching a reflection of myself in the mirror, I like how I look in them.

I know Sam said that the clothes and shoes are for me, but I'm sure he meant that I can borrow someone else's stuff for a bit.

I put the shoes back and scan the shelves for the cheapest pair of trainers I can find. One shelf is filled with trainers, each pair is more expensive than the next. After scanning for a while, I decide to bite the bullet and take something black and conservative looking, but even these are "Moschino".

I move to the next wall where I spy neatly folded jeans, nestled in four box-like shelves. I pick a pair, deciding this time not to even look at the label and hope to be alive after the lending owner discovers what I took. Next I pick a vest and pull a sweatshirt off a hanger.

Now I need to find a bathroom to have a shower and get dressed in privacy, because let's face it, this room is busier than the bathrooms in an airport with someone barging in through the door every second. I wonder if the privacy is alien concept to angels and if they live like one big, happy, hippy community here?

I leave the 'every girl's dream' room and try the last set of doors. Sure enough, I'm in a luxurious bathroom, dazzling with shiny white tiles, mirrors, gold taps and handles. A few white orchids are placed around the room, adding the sophistication to the room.

A white Jacuzzi, the size of a medium pool, occupies a further corner of the room, while a large high-tech shower stall with a small white bench inside takes up another. I've never seen a shower stall big enough to house a bench and still have enough space for three people to comfortably have a shower. A white fluffy pyramid of towels is stacked up on the wooden bench nearby. A white leather armchair is in the corner next to the door. I lay my new clothes on it.

One wall is taken by two large sinks with golden taps, with white glossy cabinet doors underneath and a large mirror above. The glass cabinet next to it holds a stockpile of posh looking toiletries, toothbrushes sealed in packets and even some make-up items.

With an unsure hand, I open the glass door and take a bottle of shower gel and a bottle of shampoo.

I lock the door to the bathroom and yank it to check that it works. Although the door is locked, I feel less than secure, so I strip, take a shower, wash my hair, dry myself and dress in record time.

Once my sweatshirt and jeans are on, I exhale with relief. Covered, I feel less exposed and less vulnerable.

As I come out of the bathroom, I stop in my tracks.

Tabby is sitting in one of the chairs with my breakfast tray on her lap, littered with crumbs and leftovers, while she is busily stuffing her face with my food. Only the coffee jug remains untouched on the table.

"Hi Tabby", she looks very cute and my lips stretch unwillingly into a smile, as I come closer to her.

"Hi", she mumbles with a mouth full of food. I'm gifted with a wide smile and a glorious view of the half-chewed breakfast in her mouth.

"What are you doing in here?" I ask as I approach her.

"Sam said you needed company, and he asked me to show you the park."

Swallowing her food, she wipes her mouth with her arm.

Tabby is wearing a denim dungaree skirt with a black punk style t-shirt underneath. Black knee-high socks and the earlier red high-top trainers finish off her rebellious look.

"We can go when you finish your breakfast". I will pay for the missing breakfast later, but I'm not angry with her.

"I'm finished anyway". She places the tray on the table, hops off the chair and crumbs and food bits fall from her lap onto the carpet like autumn leaves.

She steps over the semi-circle of mess she made and we turn to the door, ready to go, when the door swings open.

Again.

For crying out loud! Does anyone know how to knock in here? I'll have to speak to Sam about it.

A striking supermodel with waist-long blonde hair lazily saunters into the room, swaying her hips as she walks. Shimmering blonde hair, perfectly formed face, sparkling green eyes and luscious red lips, only one sentiment pops into my head as I watch her approach: 'sex on a stick'. A pair of pale blue wings moves lazily behind her back. Her tight grey mini dress accentuates every curve of her gorgeous figure. This one knows that she is gorgeous and isn't afraid to use it.

I stand there, gawking at her.

With a charming smile, she comes closer.

"You must be Ariel". Her voice is soft and melodic and she smells amazing. I can't put my finger on the smell but I can bet that it's something expensive, designed to be as sensual as possible.

Languorously, she sweeps her gaze over me, from the top of my head to the tip of the trainers I'm wearing. Her mesmerising bright smile lightens her face but doesn't touch her venomous cold eyes. It's like her eyes belong to another person entirely. And I feel like I've been slapped.

I take a step back, surprised and shocked by such raw malice.

"I have to say, I expected something better". If anyone saw her through the glass without hearing her, one might've thought that she'd been nice and pleasant to me.

I slam my mouth shut. I straighten by back, jerk my chin up and narrow my eyes at her.

"And you are?.." I ask with my best acidic voice. *What the hell is going on? I don't even know you.*

"How rude it is of me not to introduce myself. I'm Lis, Sam's friend", innuendo drips off her tongue.

"And what do you want, Lis?" I square my shoulders and fold my arms over my chest.

"To see the famous Ariel everyone's talking about. To see what the fuss is about", she answers with a sly smile.

That must be some talent, to say polite things but sound totally insulting.

"Well now you've seen me. Anything else I can help you with?" With every spiteful word she utters, I'm getting more and more wound up.

I want to roll my eyes and scream. Another one of Sam's groupies. Why am I always in the middle of it? I don't even want to do anything with him. I've got nothing to do with him, so what's their problem with me? Daisy and now her...

"No. That's it. I've seen everything I needed to see", she replies, pursing her lips tight like she's eaten a lemon. "I sincerely hope that they do have a back-up plan, if that..." she waves her hand loosely at me, sweeping from my toes to my head and back, "is what we are relying on".

Who the hell does she think she is, talking to me like that? This bitch had better think again if she thinks that she can take me on.

"Listen, Lis."

Now it's my turn to dispense the poison. I take a few steps closer to her, now only a tiny step separates us.

"I don't know you and you don't know me. Don't think even for a second that you can come here and try to intimidate me. That's right, "try". I don't know what you're relying on me for", I make an air quote marks gesture, "but I don't owe you anything, so you need to drop your expectations, attitude and leave. I'm not interested in dealing with a rancid skank like you, so if you'll excuse me, I'm late for my walk with Tabby."

I glare at her, waiting for her to move out of my way but she doesn't budge. Any earlier pretence has peeled off and discarded like yesterday's tarantula skin. The sides of her mouth lift, exposing her perfect white teeth, which are now grinding with hate. Millions of tiny wrinkles cut through her forehead, across and around her nose. She no longer looks pretty, elegant or sexy. Her face is the gruesome mask of loathing and detest.

A pang of sadness stabs at my heart. Why do I get those feelings? Why am I the subject of hate? I never did anything to her. I've never done anything wrong to anyone... *"Maybe that's the reason", Rage whispers inside me. "You were too good to some. You let them believe that you're weak, that you can be broken"*.

Rage is back. She is stretching her muscles, gleefully jogging on the spot and punching the air, like a boxer in a ring waiting for his opponent. A loud Metallica song plays around her and my Rage is smiling. She is finally pleased.

Okay, let's continue our little showdown.

"I would've thought that Sam kept better company than that". Now it's my turn to wave my hand over her, while pursing my lips in distaste. "Don't you have a spiteful bimbo convention to attend or something?" I say folding my arms at her.

"Sam will never be interested in someone like you", she snarls, bending down, her face inches from mine. I'm itching to slap her stupid face, but Tabby might get scared and I don't know how strong angels are and what will be my chances in a fight with one.

But I cannot afford to back down in this new place. Survival 101: Never show fear to your enemy.

"Get out of my face or we are going to find out what Sam thinks about your conduct here and hospitality skills", I hiss, narrowing my eyes at her. "I'm here as his guest and I don't think you were announced in the programme planned for me. I bet he doesn't even know that you're here", I leer at her, my acidic smile is on point. "Tabby, do you think Sam would like the way Lis is talking to me?" I say over my shoulder at Tabby, keeping my eyes fixed on Lis' vicious face.

I glance over my shoulder and see Tabby, mesmerised, shaking her head without uttering a word, her big eyes on both of us.

I take a step around the blondie and with a glance at Tabby I say: "Come on Tabby. Let's go for that walk", and I'm out of the door.

CHAPTER 11

I'm out of the room, but still reeling. Rage is pouting at me in disbelief. The boxer skipping rope lies limp on the ground. My Rage stomps off and turns off the Metallica. She is no longer pleased with me.

I'm livid and boiling inside. I take a few steps down the hall, but I can't suppress that feeling any longer. I swing my leg and kick the wall. Once, twice. I feel a bit better, Rage winks at me.

I hate you Sam! Nothing good comes out of knowing you. Nothing! I kick the wall once more.

I feel the adrenaline fleeing my body like a tide, leaving behind the cold and tired body. I lean my shoulder on the wall, waiting for Tabby.

She catches up with me. She's not saying a word, not looking at me, taking the open lift's doors on the right and I follow her.

I step into a mirror and steel cubicle, which looks like that boring office lift in the tall office building in the centre of London that I used to ride occasionally when I had to go to see my mum's solicitor.

The panel on the left is covered in gold, shiny buttons, embossed with some ancient looking symbols, maybe hieroglyphs. Every single one is unique and I cannot spot any repetition in them.

Tabby takes a step around me and to my surprise, reaches on her tippy toes and presses the top right button on the dial. Maybe there's a garden on the roof or pool or whatever else rich people or *angels* might have there.

I catch myself on the thought that I no longer gawk at Tabby's or Sam's wings. I see and notice them just as much as I would notice someone's arm or leg. I even wonder if the absence of their wings would bother me now and I would be automatically searching for them, expecting a relaxed bobbing behind their back.

We don't speak during the short ride, standing awkwardly in separate corners, while the lift takes us up. I don't know what to say, uncomfortable with my earlier outburst.

After a short ride, the lift stops, pings and opens its doors. Tabby steps out first and I follow her.

We are in a spacious and grandeur foyer. It smells of wealth and money. Clearly "wealth and gold" is the theme of this building. Gold, glass, crystal and marble catch the sunlight, which is streaming through the windows and doors, spraying across the room, blinding visitors. The chandeliers that I know so well are hanging heavily off the ceilings, adding to the blinding dazzle of the place.

Two opposing walls of the long foyer are covered in celestial themed murals, with female and male angels flying, dancing, laughing or kissing each other. These murals are like propaganda of the benefits and perks of an angelic lifestyle although I haven't seen any dancing and laughing yet. The plants the size of an average tree grow in large ceramic planters, which are placed along the walls between the murals.

As we get closer to the door, Tabby relaxes a bit and eventually her cautious footsteps turn into skipping bounces. Our footsteps on the marble floor are echoing in the empty and silent foyer.

"Where is everybody?" I ask Tabby, as I turn my head from side to side, looking at different murals along the walls.

"Who?" she asks back, without looking at me. Tabby is busy skipping ahead of me while humming something to herself, her arms swinging in time with every skip. That girl is in a world of her own.

"I don't know", I mumble. "Other angels, I guess. It's such a large building and the foyer's so massive, I thought more angels would be here", I muse.

"Oh. No, it's Baza's building. He lives here, plus some of his malakhims and that's it", she answers over her shoulder, still busy skipping.

"Mala – what?" I stop to look at her.

It takes Tabby a few more skips to notice that I'm no longer next to her. She stops and walks back to me.

"Ma-la-kheem-s". Tabby spells it out for me, carefully forming her mouth and stretching her syllables as she looks at me. "Not malawots", she giggles.

"And what are those "malakhims"?" I ask, trying to absorb and classify another bit of information and fit it into the little shelf inside the safe deposit box in my head.

"Malakhims are his angels. They work and fight together against the common enemy. Like a family... or an army", she grins, pleased with her explanation.

"And who's Baza?" I ask her, as the automatic doors silently slide open, letting us through. The park I saw from my window stretches in front of us, brightly lit by the blistering sunshine.

Taking a few steps out of the building, I look back, craning my head up, taking in the tall glass and metal high-tech skyscraper, with long and short balconies and ledges circling every floor of the building. The sun catches and reflects off the building's polished metal and glass. The green shades of grass and trees reflect in the building's windows.

"Is my room up there?" I point to the top of the building.

Tabby twitches to keep on moving. This '20 Questions' game clearly bores her. With a heavy resigned sigh, she stops and follows my finger with her eyes.

"Yeah".

"How come we came *up* in the lift but we're now *down* at the bottom of the building?" I quiz her.

Tabby shrugs, "I dunno".

She spins back, resuming her skipping and humming. Clearly there's nothing more to discuss according to her. This girl is seriously frustrating. One moment she takes time to sit down and talk to me, giving out mature and sound advice and the next minute, I can't get two words out of her, so I decide to ask Sam later.

I follow Tabby into the park, plodding down the footpath between manicured lawns and flower beds, looking down at my feet and thinking about my predicament. I'm still struggling to accept the reality of it all: the angels, Mia, Sam, angels wanting to kill me for an angelic essence that I, apparently, possess. I think about my sister, wondering how and when I'll be able to get to her. I feel disjointed and trapped.

I squint into the horizon as I notice a male figure slowly coming our way. I shield my eyes with my hand against the bright sun and I see a stout male angel in a suit, walking our way, leaning on a cane in his left hand.

As he comes closer, I spot four wings, like Sam's, folded behind his back, only his are bigger than Sam's, with folds rising well above his head and, even when folded, at least a third of the wing is protruding to the sides around his chubby body. I bet he can wrap himself in his own wings like a bat. His black wings glisten with a blue sheen when they are hit by the sun's beam, shining like a magpie's tail. He wears an elegant grey pinstripe suit with a waistcoat underneath, buttoned tight over his round stomach.

This angel isn't as tall as Sam, but he is much older. His silver grey hair is cut in a short and conservative haircut, and his grey beard is round and neatly trimmed. His walking cane makes a clacking noise every time it hits the gravel, giving some weird, repeating soundtrack to his walk.

"Baza", Tabby squeaks, spotting the man and sprinting towards him with the full speed of her young legs. She runs into him and hugs him tight.

He bends to her, stroking her hair, speaking softly to her so only she can hear. She looks up at him with a beaming smile, nods and they both start back to where I stand.

An open and kind smile softens his face, deepening the wrinkles around his eyes further. He looks like a Father Christmas from an old Hollywood movie, all cosy, warm and sweet. On its own accord, my face stretches into an answering smile.

"You must be Ariel", he says in a deep, velvety baritone, which suits his Father Christmas look so well. He stretches out his hand to me for a handshake. His wrinkly hand is dry and surprisingly soft. He smells of a clean soap, rosemary, mint and sandalwood. "My name is Baz, but everyone calls me Baza here. I think it's something to do with a new fashion in your world." He smiles kindly as a grandfather would, while describing his beloved grandchildren's shenanigans.

I always feel uncomfortable when a stranger knows my name while I'm in the dark about them. My strategy in changing this misbalance is always to quiz them in return with as much arrogance and brusque as I can, but today I cannot bring myself to be so rude to this Father Christmas, so I stand there, smiling politely, as if meeting an old, distant relative, waiting for whatever more he has to say.

"Sam and Tabby have both spoken highly of you and your resilience. It is truly a compliment to your character, the strength with which you have taken on the news and your current situation. I know that Sam is working hard on resolving our predicament with Mia", he says, sounding like a man from old times, so articulate and well spoken. His baritone is soft and velvety.

I stand there, mute, unsure of what is expected of me here, a polite smile plastered to my lips.

"Would you kindly grant me the pleasure of your lovely company on my walk?" he offers me his bent arm.

"Sure." I hook my arm through the loop of his and we start our stroll, following Tabby's earlier chosen direction.

Tabby clearly isn't interested in our company or conversation. She goes back to her skipping, speeding ahead of us, her denim dungaree skirt bouncing away. I walk slowly, measuring my pace to Baza's.

There's an awkward space between us as I'm careful not to step on his lower wings, as the tips of his wings are sweeping over the ground.

"How do you like it here, Ariel?" Baza sweeps his hand over the park.

"It's very beautiful in here", I agree.

"And how do you find your rooms? Do you have everything you might need?" He turns to look at me.

"I do have everything, thank you. And my room is lovely". I can see that he is doing some polite chit chat before coming up to a real conversation and I inwardly brace myself.

"I hope you'll like it here and perhaps, in time, you will see us as your family and maybe, even when the situation with Mia is resolved, you'll choose to stay with us", he glances at me, gauging my reaction.

I keep my eyes firmly on the ground.

"Thank you very much for such a kind offer", I mumble to my trainers. "I already see Tabby as my sister and I think the world of her, and I'm very grateful to Sam for saving my life back in school and to you for giving me a place to stay but I'd rather go back when I'm able to do so. I have my family out there, my sister. She needs me now and I need to be with her".

He stops and turns to me, releasing my arm. I stop with him.

"Oh, yes. I've heard of your sister's plight. I think it's very unfortunate what has happened to her", he remarks in his soft voice. "It saddens me deeply when such horrible things happen to such young and innocent souls. I just would like you to know that we are all here for you and if you need anything, please don't hesitate to ask."

He takes my hand in his and I can feel his gaze on my bent head. "We are a family here and we look after our own, no matter what."

I hesitate.

"Thank you very much. It's very kind of you", I mumble. I've mentioned my sister to Tabby, but how much about her *plight* does he really know?

"I know a lot of things, my dear child", he says with a sad smile, meeting my eyes and answering my unspoken question as if reading my mind. "I am old and have been around long enough to know that there is nothing new to human nature. It's predictable. It is always kill or be killed, victim or assailant. Human nature is a gruesome one, violent. The yearning to dominate everything in one's demesne is as strong as one's basic needs and desires."

He turns and starts again down the path, leaning slightly on his cane with every step and I follow, lumbering behind.

I want to turn around and walk. Walk away from him, from this place, from Sam, from everything. But I force myself to keep my feet moving, one in front of the other, while sitting hard on my Rage, as she gives me her sly smile.

"I know a lot more about you than you might think." His voice is soft and tender as I reluctantly catch up with him. "I know about the suffering you have been enduring for years, the hardship and misery that you encountered at such a young age. Everything you went through."

He gives me a glance at *everything*.

I stumble and almost fall. My face heats up and my heart picks up the pace as I stare after him.

He tells me that he knows *everything* and I'm petrified to even ask *what* he knows.

I don't know how he could possibly know. But even that doesn't concern me as much as how I'm supposed to handle it. How do I react to his disclosure? What does he want from me after that kind of statement? I never advertised it because I didn't want anyone to know. I didn't want judgmental, pitied or speculative looks. I desperately wanted to be me or even better, to be me as *before*.

He keeps on walking, slightly ahead. Silent, giving me time to digest. I say nothing as I follow him. My head is spinning.

He stops, turning around, facing me again. "You have nothing to feel shameful about. This was not your fault."

"No", I choke out, cutting him mid-sentence.

Rage is awake and doing a little cha-cha dance.

"*No*", I croak through the brittle glass in my closing throat. My back straightens, shoulders squared, as I meet his gaze.

"NO", I say, my voice growing stronger.

"We will *not* be talking about it", I snap. My voice is coarse and I struggle to push the words out through the choking sense of exposure.

I glare at him, expecting him to push further. But he doesn't. He nods. Thank god for small graces!

His soft Father Christmas smile is back on, but now with a hint of sorrow and understanding.

"You're absolutely right, my dear child. It is not my place to discuss it." He isn't flustered by my outburst in the slightest. His eyes are soft and kind.

"The only reason I dared to approach such a delicate topic is the fact that I believe I might be of assistance of sorts. You see, my life was always a colourful one. I'm shameful to admit, but I have been known to fall victim to many very human emotions. I have been taken advantage of and was wronged by many, but what I was careful to do each time is to give each and everyone their dues. I am a very old fashioned man and believe in an *eye for an eye*", he shares, inclining his head. And looking into his steely eyes, I have a feeling that he followed through on these promises more than once.

"You are infinitely more special than you think. You are no longer a powerless creature, at the mercy of stronger ones", he urges. "You are an angel with an army standing behind you, which will not hesitate to repay your debts and to make reprisal to everyone who wronged you. And I will help you avenge everyone who ever wronged you", he calls.

His voice is young, strong and clear and I know that he is offering me something big and life changing. I feel that buzz of power behind his voice, behind him, and I know that he can deliver on every promise he makes. His earnest gaze penetrates me and I feel like he is speaking to something deep inside me.

"You have an interminable ability in you to change the world, to make things right, for yourself and for everyone who wrongly suffered, and I can help you with that. You have an immense power in you and I will help you come to your powers in full, to become superior, formidable, the being you were supposed to be. I'll teach you everything you need and you will always have a rightful place near me in my council, next to Sam. I am offering you a family, which cares for one another, fights for one another, cries for one another, protects one another", he urges. His eyes are glistening, excited, looking deep into mine.

An uncomfortable silence falls over us once he stops his speech.

"Are you completely sure that I am the one?" I whisper unsteadily. Everyone keeps repeating that I'm one of them, repeating that I am an angel, but how could I be if I don't even have wings and I have been human all my life?

His face softens with a kind smile. He reaches out, gently patting my arm.

"My dear child, I don't make mistakes. Ever. I make decisions", he shares.

"And I know exactly who you are", he whispers conspiratorially. "I would like you to consider my offer and everything that I just shared, but in the meantime we have arranged a family dinner in your honour tonight and I would love to see you there, to welcome you into our family, amongst *your* kind. I hope you will choose to join us."

He lets go of my upper arm and takes a half step back.

"I'll leave you in Tabby's care and hopefully we will see you tonight". He reaches his hand out to me. I place my hand in his and instead of the earlier handshake, he gently kisses my knuckles and releases my hand.

"It was a pleasure to meet you, Ariel." He does an old fashioned bow to me, then turns and walks off, into the direction he came from. His cane is beating a slow pulsating rhythm on the gravel. I'm left standing alone on the footpath, surrounded by bright sunshine in the sparkling blue sky and silent air.

CHAPTER 12

For the second time today, I step into the wardrobe. Apparently the dinner, planned in my honour, is a formal black-tie event. I don't quite see the need for all this fancy-shmancy stuff or the pretentious debutante ball with a view to introduce me into society, but if everyone there will be dressed up, I really don't want to stand out like a sore thumb in my black jeans and a sweatshirt.

Maybe I won't go at all? I muse hopefully in my head.
Maybe I'll speak to Sam or Tabby. Maybe I'll say that I'm unwell?

Filled with dread, I take a few steps closer to the wall, filled with silky and glittery dresses. I never had the chance to touch one, let alone wear one, so I'm out of my depth here. I feel nauseated at the prospect of choosing and wearing one, and the idea to 'throw a sickie' sounds more and more appealing.

I stroke the silky fabrics and pray for inspiration to hit me. Do I wear a dress with sleeves or without? What fit am I looking for? How long a dress to go for and if I pick a long one will I manage to walk in it at all? What colour to choose?

I remember once overhearing the popular girls discussing prom dresses and mentioning something about some colours 'washing you out', whatever that means. I have no clue where to begin.

A delicate pale blue colour cuts through the sea of colours, catching my eye. The colour is muted and subtle with a grey hue and reminds me of a summer sky in Northern England. The silky fabric falls to the floor and as I pick it up it looks like I'm holding a waterfall in my hands.

I lift it for closer inspection and I'm immediately confronted by my fear of overexposure. The dress has two practically symmetrical V-shape cuts at the front and the back, which I swear will go to my belly button.

Although I do like the dress, I'm not brave enough to flash so much skin. I put the dress back and check out every other dress on the hangers. I decide to try two others: a conservative-looking black dress with sheer sleeves and a yellow fine cotton one, which reminds me of the 50-s with big and wide skirts.

But both have their faults. In the black number I will look like a young widow, while the yellow one looks like an expensive, artistic costume of the 'sun' for a local school production. The widow it is. At least I'm not going to get stuck in a doorframe.

"Ariel", Tabby calls in a sing-song voice from my room.

"In the wardrobe", I yell back.

She opens the door and skips in. Her skipping stops and a wide smile dies, turning into a studious frown as she sees me.

She tilts her head to the side.

It suddenly hits me that almost every encounter with her, she's been looking at me, studying me as if I'm a monkey in a zoo, where she is on a school visit to learn about primates' odd behaviour.

"What are you wearing?" she asks cautiously, stretching the last word longer than necessary, like she is afraid of my answer.

"Don't you like it?" I try to sound chirpy, giving her a little twirl. I know too well that these types of questions never bode well for me.

"You look like a nun. Or a headmistress", she scoffs.

Ouch. That hurts.

"There's nothing else that looks any better", I object weakly. "Maybe I can wear jeans and a T-shirt?" I propose, pleading with my eyes, but Tabby furiously shakes her head.

"No. You're supposed to look dressy. Like me", she chirps.

Tabby's face blossoms again with a wide grin. She picks up the hem of her bright red elaborately embroidered knee-length dress and does a few little dance moves and twirls. She is clearly chuffed with her choice of attire.

"Yes, Tabby. You look very pretty", I smile at her.

She stops mid-twist, serious again.

"Don't you have any other dresses? You need a dress and it needs to be a good one", she reprimands me, putting her hand on her hip, glaring at me.

She marches across the room and stops by the dresses. She pulls out silky and glittery fabrics one by one, rummaging through them, and my heart stops when she pauses by the pale blue number.

Oh no; say hello to the 'peek-a-boo nipple' game.

"What about this one?" her face lights up as she looks at me over her shoulder. She likes this dress.

"It's a very beautiful dress, Tabby, but the cut is too deep. It's just too revealing", I'm trying to reason with her.

Tabby glares at me.

"Have you tried it?" she demands.

"No, but–"

"Exactly! How are you supposed to see how it looks if you haven't tried it?" This child is clearly exasperated with me and isn't hiding it. "And Lis will be there. You don't want her to make fun of you." She looks up at me, batting her eyelashes, a picture of innocence. This girl knows how to work people.

She is not tall enough to reach the hanger, so she stands there, holding the side of the dress, staring me down, waiting.

"Okay", I resign myself to it. Maybe once the dress is on and I do a few jumps, she'll see just how likely it is for my boobs to pop out, and she'll leave me alone.

I put the dress on. The silk is weightless. It's cool and smooth against my skin, like I've stepped into a pool, minus the stench of chlorine. I stroke the fabric, loving the feel of it against my skin and hating the fact that I like it so much. I shouldn't get used to all these nice things, they'll be gone once I'm out of this place. Everything that surrounds me now will disappear, including Sam.

Hate him!

"You see. You look beautiful, like a princess", Tabby is jumping in front of me, clapping her hands; her grin is back.

"Thank you", I walk to the nearest mirror ready to bounce myself, to prove my point, when I halt to an abrupt stop, as I catch a glimpse of my reflection.

The stranger in the mirror stares back at me with an awed and frightened expression. She looks elegant and sophisticated in this dress. My hair is swept to the side of my face, falling freely and looking unexpectedly well. The dress hugs my figure perfectly. Thin like thread, a silver chain holds both sides of the fabric in place over my chest.

I love this dress and now I don't have any valid excuse to take it off. Not that I want to.

It falls to the floor and I need to pull it up slightly when I walk.

"What shoes do I wear?" If Tabby started dressing me up and offered her stylist's services, she'll have to finish it off.

"How about those silver ones?" She points at the wall of shoes behind me.

My gaze follows her finger. Shiny, silver, pointed shoes stand out among the others. I come closer, relieved at the sight of a small and sturdy heel and an ankle strap. In these I could walk.

Like all the other shoes in this massive wardrobe, they fit perfectly.

"And the hair?" I ask her.

"I can brush your hair for you". Her face lights up at the prospect to play with a real, life sized doll.

"Thank you. That would be great".

With a small squeak, she runs out of the wardrobe to get a brush. I take a seat on the couch and wait.

She comes back, a few minutes later, holding the hair brush and a small tube of lip gloss, proudly waving both high above her head like a captured enemy's flag.

"I got you lip gloss as well", she babbles. She is so excited, that her words come out of her in a rush, gabbled out, half of the vowels are swallowed.

She climbs up on the couch behind me and gets to work.

I enjoy my hair being brushed, enjoy being tended to. It reminds me of the good times, when mum still cared for me and when she would do my hair every morning while singing the latest pop tunes to herself. She loved me then.

"Why are you sad?" I don't know when the brushing stopped and how long Tabby studied me in the mirror on the wall.

I blink through the pain, past the memory. "I was thinking of something. Everything's fine, Tabby, don't worry." I stretch my lips into a smile. I don't know who I'm trying to fool, but Tabby is not buying it. Her intense gaze is on me, readying for further interrogation.

"Ariel", Sam calls from the room.

"We're in here", I call out. "In the wardrobe."

It strikes me how weird it sounds to be 'in the wardrobe' and even weirder to have a party in one.

He opens the door and takes a few steps in. His bright blue eyes are on me, taking in everything from the tips of my shoes, poking from under the hem of my dress, to the top of my head, with my hair brushed to the side.

For the first time, I see his eyes widened and unguarded. Unexpectedly his face looks younger and more vulnerable. His hankering gaze rakes over me, consuming, taking all of me in. I fidget on the spot, uncomfortable under his gaze, smoothing invisible wrinkles on my dress.

And just as suddenly as it came, the spell disperses. The energy has shifted, the moment has passed and his stance is once again relaxed and casual. His usual arrogant smirk is back on, stretching his lips. His thumb is hooked over his trouser pocket as he leans on the doorframe with his shoulder. He lets out a long whistle.

"Not bad, Mermaid, not bad. You clean up very well, in fact", he offers.

"Thanks", I scoff, relieved and upset at the same time. I'm afraid of the return of that energy, but somewhere deep inside, where I don't even want to acknowledge it to myself, I want that moment to come back.

Sam looks like a movie star in his perfectly fitted black tuxedo, putting to shame my feeble attempt at sophistication. His bow tie is still hanging untied around his neck, adding to his irresistible 'Hollywood star gone bad' look. His hair falls perfectly over his eye and now and again he raises his hand, casually sweeping back his glossy waves.

"Now we need to put on some lip gloss and we're done", Tabby sounds pompous like a professional make–up artist. Then she smears the lip gloss over my lips. Thank god it's a light colour, otherwise I'd look like a clown.

"Done."

She jumps off the couch and takes a few steps back, assessing her work like a true artist.

Sam takes that as a cue and strides over to me, offering his hand. I take it and he gently pulls me to my feet.

"You look beautiful, Mermaid", he murmurs into my hair. He is so close to me. He is not taking a step back, not making a move to release me. He just stands there, holding my hand in his, hovering above me.

I lift my head. I'm so close to him that our breaths mingle. His gaze is hot, searching. I can smell his aftershave, laced with his usual scent of the undergrowth and a tang of mint on his breath and, surprisingly, I like the proximity and warmth of his body next to mine.

"Okay, shall we go?" Tabby's chirpy voice cuts into my foggy mind. Reality comes back, flooding in, crushing the dream rudely, reminding with a slap that guys like him never have anything to do with girls like me. I fiercely blink to disperse the spell, angry with myself, and take a step back, pulling my hand out of his and adjusting my glasses on my nose to hide my discomfort.

"We should go", I tell him. He nods and follows me out of the dressing room.

The lift ride is uncomfortable, but luckily for me, brief. Tabby seems to be oblivious to any of it. She is busy chatting, speculating about the food and entertainment planned for tonight.

The lift pings. The doors open and I'm immediately deafened by the noise of the band playing and hundreds of guests talking, laughing and clinking their glasses. The party is already in full swing.

Sam offers me his bent large muscular arm and I take it, grateful deep inside for this lifeline.

The immense banquet room is lit with hundreds and hundreds of candles in chandeliers under the ceiling and on the walls, in crystal candle holders on the tables. Everything glitters and sparkles in this room, the people, silverware, crystal chandeliers, glasses and jewellery. The walls are covered in deep blood red velour, interrupted by an array of large and tall windows on both sides of the room, now black with the darkness outside.

Red velour is clearly the theme in this building and I wonder if they got a bulk discount on the purchase. The high, glistening white, dome ceiling above me is covered in large artfully painted and intertwined gold hieroglyphs, somewhat reminding me of the ones on the panel in the lift. They intertwine like branches of an old tree, flowing, dancing on the ceiling, becoming a perplexing, beautiful work of art.

Wings of different shades, colours and sizes are neatly folded behind guests' backs. Only a few guests here have four wings like Sam and Baza while most of them have just two wings behind their backs. I'm the only one in this vast room without wings and oddly enough, I feel naked.

The air in the room is filled with the smell of jasmine, freesias and a melting wax.

A half moon stage is raised against one of the walls. A group of two winged male angels in white tuxedos are playing soulful and brooding Blues on their instruments. A gorgeous blonde with a luminescent pair of white wings and dressed in a pure-white dress is in front of the band, crooning something seductively into the microphone in a language I can't understand.

As we walk farther into the room, the crowd parts in front of us, giving way as guests turn in our direction. Some angels smile at us and a few salute me with their drinks while others just watch with scathing glares. Some gazes are assessing and speculative. There are even some with open scowls on their faces, directed at me. Not everybody is pleased to see me here, that is for sure.

With every passing minute and with each new hostile glance, I feel more uncomfortable, more out of my depth, vulnerable. Even Sam's presence and warm strong arm does nothing to settle me. My hands are clammy. I feel hot and sweaty, as I'm trying to keep my feet from bolting back through the entrance door.

Sam turns his head to me, taking in my flushed face.

His gorgeous face is a peeved stony mask. His lips are set into a thin line. He is angry. And for a moment I think that he is angry with me, and I take a surprised step back, pulling my arm out of his hold.

But his face warms up the second his eyes meet mine. He places his warm hand over mine, threaded through the crook of his arm, and gently rubs my knuckles, and just like that I feel better. He smiles encouragingly at me and then gives me a playful wink. I know my answering smile is weak and pathetic as his forehead wrinkles at the sight of me.

And then I trip. Lost in his eyes, I miss the step, tripping over my long skirt, but before I can start my flight across the room and humiliate myself further, Sam's arm locks me in place, holding me up. Then his arm releases mine, snaking around my waist, keeping me close to him. His arm is like solid warm metal, anchoring me in place.

"Are you okay?" he whispers above my head, leaning in closer. His breath strokes the top of my head. His lips are like a butterfly, fluttering above it.

"Yeah, I'm fine. Thank you", I raise my face up. Our faces again are just an inch away. My eyes are locked to his. Curtains are falling around us, blurring my vision, leaving only Sam in it. My head is filled with his smell, his warmth and pull of his eyes. My eyes slowly slide down his face and lock on his lips.

I swallow.

An invisible power pulls at my body, urging my face closer, against all the reasons and doubts that are muffling something important somewhere deep at the back of my brain. My toes are itching to stretch, to push my body for the last inch.

But he just stands there, not making a move. But not pulling away either. I can't read his guarded expression.

I wrestle with myself, for a long minute or maybe an hour, I don't know. I reluctantly pull my gaze away from his only to slam into the deadly iceberg of Lis' eyes. She could kill and freeze at the same time. The Titanic would have no chance against her icy stare.

Oh, for Christ's sake! I inwardly roll my eyes. That's just getting old.

Fine. You want the drama? I'll give you the drama!

I narrow my eyes at her in a challenge and before I get cold feet and change my mind, I spin around to Sam, reach out and lay my trembling hand at the back of his neck. His big shocked eyes are fixed on me, searching my face for an explanation.

Sudden fear, brought in by the common sense at the back of my mind and the possibility of public humiliation, punches at my chest, shrinking my lungs, filling my head with vivid humiliation scenes. But I'm already in the game and leaving it now would be just as humiliating as to see it through. Taking in a shaky breath, I decide to take a chance and jump into that abyss. Maybe that's the problem with my life? Too much 'chancing'?

My mouth is dry and I hastily run my tongue over my lips.

With numb fingers, I gently pull his head down, towards me, towards my lips.

My decision is made. I'm about to kiss a boy. For the first time, ever. And I only hope that he feels the same way about me or at least is willing to kiss me now. My hand is shaking on his neck, my eyes darting between his eyes and his lips.

I'm so out of my depth here and don't even know how to do it. I'm starting to hyperventilate, instinctively licking my dry lips over and over again, desperately trying to think what to do next. My heart beats a jumpy tempo.

Finally, understanding lights up behind Sam's eyes. His lips are leisurely stretching into a knee-melting smile as he bends down, closing the last inches between our lips.

His soft lips are on mine, gentle and tender. His arms bound me, pulling me closer, fingers rubbing the nape of my neck. He is not pushing, not rushing anything, letting me set the pace.

He is letting me know that I'm in control.

I reach on the tips of my toes and entwine my hands around his neck. His smell fills my nose, exploding in the kaleidoscope of blinding shards in my head, cutting through reason, morphing the reality.

I don't want to let go.

"Ah, young love", Baza's soft voice like an upcoming train, rushes through to the surface of my fogged up mind, grounding me, waking me with its blinding beam. "I remember being in love once. Although that was eons ago."

My face heats up as I pull away from Sam, keeping my eyes down, reluctant to look at anyone. But Sam's hands are on my waist, steadying me, not letting me go.

"Ariel, I hope you are hungry", Baza says to me. "I have been told that I have the best chef in the universe." He winks at me, his soft smile deepening the millions of wrinkles around his eyes.

Baza is in an exquisite tuxedo today, his bow tie hiding under his round beard. As he stands, he's leaning on a black, shining walking stick with a silver intricate handle.

Baza turns to the crowd, raising his arm with his cane in the air. The music dies down and so does any chatter. Silence spreads over the room.

"Friends, it's a remarkable day today. We welcome a new member into our family. She is eminent, strong, extraordinary. Her arrival will mark the beginning of a new era for us all. We will take back what has been taken from us, and we will show that we are a force to be reckoned with. Our family is now formidable. We are joining forces. We are finding allies and we are growing. We are growing in numbers and in power, shaping our own future. Now we can make the world our own", he calls to the room, a powerful and charismatic leader igniting his followers.

"But that's tomorrow. Today we drink, eat and enjoy the lovely company. So let us show our guest of honour a good time and welcome her warmly into our family."

An uproar of applause, whistling and cheering takes over the room. Some wings shoot up towards the ceiling. The floor is vibrating under the stamping feet.

Baza offers me his arm. "Shall we?"

I hesitate for a minute, but Sam releases his hold on me and I take Baza's arm and he leads me to the table. Baza is taking the seat at the head of the table, gesturing for me to take a seat to his right. Sam takes the seat next to me.

Baza's speech has confused and unsettled me. The outcry for a battle, where I seem to have been assigned a side already, doesn't sit well with me. I decide to push Sam for answers after dinner.

Our extremely long table is flanked on each side by two mile-long tables, creating an entertainment space in the middle, which is promptly taken by the earlier singing angel. She is singing a broody ballad in that strange language with an accompaniment from one of the male angels in a white tuxedo, playing a miniature harp. Her voice is pure, bright and haunted.

The tables are covered in white, crispy linen, with candlelit candelabras placed in a highly organised fashion. A ridiculous volume of cutlery and crockery in front of each seating starts another wave of perspiration on me. With so much stress, I will need to have another shower soon.

About twenty pieces of cutlery are fanned around and above my plates, six different glasses and a few ceramic bowls to my right. I frantically turn my head from side to side, scanning the plates' settings on either side of me, hoping for some clue on this poncey setup. How am I supposed to know what all these things are for and when to use any of it?

Sam's warm hand comes over mine, which is shakily strangling a napkin on my lap.

"Just follow my lead", Sam's warm breath tickles my ear.

I lift my eyes to his and nod.

At that moment, the doors open to let in an army of waiters in scarlet red suits with crispy, white shirts underneath and black bow ties. Each waiter is as handsome as the next, with beautiful faces and a muscled physique, but behind their backs flutter a set of large butterfly wings in different shades and patterns.

The waiters are carrying trays heavily laden with food and pitchers of drinks. But I barely pay any attention to the food and drinks appearing in front of me, as I sit there, mesmerised by a colourful show of the moving butterfly wings, which flutter in time to each owner's move. Their wings are thin as rice paper, letting the candlelight through, illuminating and changing the colour on them.

I seem to be the only one gawking at the waiters, as the room slowly fills with the noises of a ravishing party, with hundreds of voices talking and laughing, cutlery scraping on plates and glasses clinking.

I lean over to Sam.

"What are they?" I whisper, jabbing my chin in the direction of the nearest waiter.

"How much do you know about ancient civilisations?" he whispers back, leaning in closer.

"Very little", I admit. The school curriculum is filled with Romans but nothing older than that. I watched some TV programmes about Ancient Egypt and Tutankhamun, but that's about it.

"They are 'istana'", he whispers back at me. "They've lived here with us since their Sumerian goddess visited and left them as collateral".

"Sumerian. Wow. So is that the language she's singing in?" I turn my head in the direction of the space in the centre where the singer is still serenading to the guests.

"Yes. All of us speak old languages but some relics", he carefully inclines his head to a group of older-looking angels at the nearby table, "still stubbornly refuse to learn modern languages. But come on, Mermaid, this is a party in your honour, so eat, drink, and be merry", he grins.

I pick a spoon and start on my first course, which, thankfully, I can recognise as soup.

CHAPTER 13

Hours and countless courses later, I sit between Baza and Sam and listen to the pleasantries of a group of angels with a military stance, dish out to Baza. Something about the latest plan of advancement and the decision he forced through at the last council.

I fight sleepiness and debate whether it would be regarded as appropriate to leave this party in my honour. By now, the singer has stopped singing and a trio of angel-musicians have taken to the stage, playing haunting melodies on their string instruments.

A very large and mean looking angel with two dark grey wings enters the banquet hall and marches to our table. At the sight of him, the politicking warriors bow down to Baza and disperse into the crowd, sheepishly glancing over their shoulders at the newcomer.

The newcomer wasn't invited to the party but, in all fairness, he doesn't look like he belongs in here.

His massive frame is covered in a thick and rigid black leather tunic of a butcher, laced on both sides. I bet this tunic can stop an arrow or maybe even a bullet. His bare massive arms, thicker than my waist, are laced with old and new scars. Thick leather wristbands are strapped to both of his arms and I spy handles of weapons tucked into one.

Two wide belts criss-cross his torso, another circles at his waist, holding up his weapons. He looks like a walking armoury. Like your average Terminator assassin. The arsenal of his weapons is so vast and varied that I can only recognise a few: knives, small swords with wide blades and a whip. All his weapons look menacing and the 'real deal'. Black leather trousers cover his legs, while a military grade, black, laced high boots encase his feet.

His face carries a mean scowl. A weird-looking necklace bounces on his chest with every step. When he leans over to Baza to whisper something into his ear, I almost pass out at the realisation that his necklace is made of human teeth of different shapes and sizes.

Baza listens intently to the newcomer and gives a short nod in approval and the mean butcher leaves the room.

Baza rises from his seat, raising his arms, calling for silence. Swiftly all conversations die around the room. Hundreds of angelic faces are now watching him, ready to take in every word he'll deliver.

"Dear friends, our quest for justice begins today", he announces to the crowd. "Today we take the first step toward righteousness. Our new sister has suffered injustice and maltreatment, just like we all have. Higher power did not protect her, did not stand up for her, did not intervene, allowing the scarring of an innocent soul. She was powerless against her adversaries then. But now, she has us!" He calls to the guests, his voice steadily rising.

"We will fight for her. We will deliver vengeance for her. We will help her rectify it all, deliver everyone's dues by their deeds, because we will not stand idly watching as one of us suffers. We will stand up for our own!"

He turns to me. "We are your family now and we will deliver vengeance for you".

With every word he utters, drowsiness evaporates and panic sets in. My face is on fire, while the rest of my body is cold, as if suspended in an ice tank. One by one faces turn to me.

I sit numb, frozen in place, unable to scrape the energy to get up and leave, afraid of what is to come.

In the ringing silence, the entrance doors swing open to let in a group of tall and muscly male angels, sealed in black leather.

The earlier 'butcher' is leading the way and is clearly in charge. He is the tallest among them, a head and shoulders above the others. The three angels behind him carry mean scowls on their faces, while scanning the crowd of partygoers with disdain. All four wear the similar black leather tunics, worn out to a different degree, the weapon belts crossing their bodies. They all look like battle weathered warriors.

Two bloodied prisoners are staggering between them, shackled and chained, with warriors on both sides, yanking their neck chains now and again. The prisoners are not angels, or at least they don't have wings behind their backs.

I'm mortified as I watch their treatment. The abuse, torture and humiliation they've endured, paraded like a safari trophy. I draw the air in my lungs, leaning slightly to Sam, about to speak up for them and find a way to stop this gruesome show, when a fat chavvy chain on the neck of one of the prisoners catches the light on its unsoiled side.

The chain has a round pendant and vaguely reminds me of something. The faint memory tugs at me, but I cannot seem to pin it down. And then he moves again, takes a few more steps. Then another.

The world is tilting, spinning. Or maybe it's me?

I feel afloat, disconnected, violently spinning in a vacuum.

Silence. I can't hear anything around me. I can't see anything but *him*. The world has darkened and fuzzed around him. He fills my vision, my head, and I can even smell his aftershave in my nose after all these years.

Dread squeezes my stomach with an iron hand and I'm about to vomit.

I repeatedly swallow, as hard as I can, forcing the vomit back down my throat, burning it with acid on the way down. I grip the napkin on my lap until my hand hurts. I look for a way out of this room but there's only one way out, and now it's blocked by something I pushed so hard to hide, to bury in the deepest grave.

The group reaches our table.

My sluggish brain livens up, and in an urgent petrified whisper begs me to run, but my frozen body is unable to obey. I'm about to push my stiff muscles to respond and to bolt, when Baza turns and addresses me.

"Ariel, we promised to stand strong with you and we promised to avenge anyone who wronged you. Now we keep our promise." His voice rings in the silent room. "This is your chance to deliver vengeance and put things right. We all know that nothing heals old wounds better than revenge, so let the healing begin!" He yells the last five words to the crowd.

The guests roar in approval.

'Butcher' keeps his gaze on me as he comes closer. He takes the enormous hunting knife off his belt and unclips the coiled whip. He stops in front of me, only the dining table separates us. His thugs and the prisoners are behind him, replacing the Ella Fitzgerald of the angelic world.

I guess this is the new entertainment now.

His hands reach out to me across the table, offering me the whip in one hand and the knife in the other. His cold gaze meets mine as he waits for me to take either weapon, to make a decision. I don't understand why the Butcher would offer this to me so, baffled, I just stand there, blinking at him.

My shocked gaze travels to the prisoners. They've been beaten long and hard; their faces are a swollen black and purple mess with dried blood crusts in places, their shirts soaked with blood, dried, then soaked again. One prisoner's arm is swinging at a weird angle, clearly broken. The stench of urine, vomit and dried blood surrounds them.

I gulp, shaking my head at Butcher.

And then *he* raises his head. His gaze meets mine and my world tilts once more. A familiar arrogant, sly half smile stretches his broken lips, revealing newly missing teeth. Blood starts to trickle from the corner of his mouth.

"Ah, isn't it our sweet, innocent Ariel", he lispers with his coarse voice through broken teeth. "I have to say, I am surprised to see you alive. Thought you would be dead by now, overdosed more likely. Shame that our arrangement didn't last as long as I would've wished. My associates used to love your innocence".

He drops his voice to a loud conspiratory whisper for everyone to hear, "And I know deep down *you* liked it too".

A hand touches my arm. I jump in my seat, startled. It's Sam. He's looking at me with sad and worried eyes. Muscles are tense on his jaw and neck. He's not saying a word, although I can hear his realisation and pity loud and clear.

Rage floods me. I'm blinded by her. I don't feel anything but her pulsating energy. She's back, and she's as strong as ever.

I shake off Sam's hand and snatch the whip out of Butcher's hand. An approving smirk stretches his lips.

It's a long way around the tables. Hundreds of eyes are following me. Pitiful, gloating, lustful and blood thirsty. Rage is screaming inside me, blazing with the heat of a wild fire, blinding, hot, scorching, death-wielding.

I stop in front of *him*. Watching.

"Looking good", he chuckles, eyeing me. "Inviting some more?"

With a hurt bellow, I throw the whip in. Whip uncoils, biting me hard on the side but barely touching him.

He chuckles, spitting blood on the floor. "Slug as ever".

I clench my teeth, grinding them with a screeching noise. Tears pool in my eyes. I raise my arm up with the whip again, this time above my shoulder.

The tail flickers in front of my eyes, flying ahead, biting, slicing across his face, through the skin and muscle, leaving behind a bloody track. Blood pools and runs down his face from the split wound.

I raise my arm again, above my shoulder, sending another flick of the whip towards him, slicing across the face and chest. His bloodied shirt rips, exposing his chest. An ugly blood line sprints from his chest up to his face, gruesomely dividing his face in two. He wails. My tears spill over, eroding my vision, blinding me.

I raise my hand again. The whip flies. Again and again. The rusty smell of blood fills my nose.

I don't count, don't feel the time, suspended in my own memory. I can smell his aftershave again, the same as years ago. My foggy drugged, up mind crying like a child locked in a wardrobe. The aftershaves of his buddies after him. The chaffing of the metal cuffs on my wrists and the screech of metal on metal when the cuffs slid along the headboard.

I hear that deafening rhythmic squeak of the metal coils of a cheap and dirty mattress underneath me. I feel the heavy weight of a sweaty and smelly body on top of me. The basement's smell of mould and mildew with the stench of yesterday's curry, and the spidery cracks on the low dirty grey basement's ceiling in front of me, with flakes of old, peeling paint hanging off it.

And lucid moments of terror when my mind didn't have the blessed numbness of the fog to hide in. And the beating. Regular, repeated daily, with cold calculation to break me, to push me into absolute submission, but sometimes just vicious, punishing and sadistic.

I see nothing but a bloodied pile of meat, his deformed face and body, ripped apart by the whip, now on the floor, coiled like a snake, crying for mercy. Pleading, like I was once. Blood pools underneath him and the puddle slowly gets wider, filled by the fruitful rain of my rage.

But I keep going, desperate to appease the ravaging animal inside me, who refuses to be silenced who's raging, demanding more wrath.

The sobering barrage of applause and cheers cut through me, roll over me like a frigid North Sea wave, waking me up. The raging fire inside me is flushed down, exposing the charred ruins of what's left of me.

Suddenly I feel infinitely tired and alone. Disorientated, numb, exposed.

I can't take it anymore. I don't want to do it anymore. I don't want to see anybody.

I open my hand. The whip slides out of my hand as a strangled dead snake. It drops to the floor with a soft swoosh.

In an exhausted haze, I walk to the door, stumble unsteady around his limp body, around the guards. Away from him, his grotesque tortured body, from my public exposure, from the assault of the animal in me. Away from everyone, without looking back. My legs are taking me out, living a life of their own.

CHAPTER 14

I'm curled up in a ball on the floor. The carpet in this hall is surprisingly plush and feels soft under my cheek, like one of my teddies used to be.

I don't know how long I've been laying here and I don't know where I am. Ornate lights along the walls dissipate the darkness with puddles of a soft glow. I lay and stare at the gold and olive green leafy design of the wallpaper in front of my face.

At some point my mind awoke to me running, heaving through my burning throat, down the unfamiliar hall. I was barefoot and I couldn't remember where I left my shoes.

Now I lie here, in the cool and silent hall, wishing I could become invisible and be allowed to lie down and die here. What peace that would be.

Rushed male footsteps are coming down the hall, approaching me. I close my eyes, childishly hoping that if I pretend to be asleep, they'll walk away and leave me alone.

The feet stop a few yards away, before finding a new unhurried, cautious pace. Undoubtedly, the feet were looking for me and now I've been found.

But I keep my eyes shut, refusing to be found.

The feet stop next to me and a body slides along the wall, next to my head. The familiar smell of undergrowth and moss tickles my nose.

Padded silence surrounds us, disturbed only by our breathing.

"I was looking for you", his soft words sound too loud for this hall and for my ears. I don't open my eyes, don't speak.

"I'm sorry. I didn't know Baza would do it", he says into the silence after a while. I feel his discomfort and I'm not trying to be mean, but I'm too done in and empty for anyone else's needs. I just simply don't care if or how uncomfortable he is.

"Ariel", he calls softly to me. "Please", he whispers. With a sigh, I lift my lids and turn my head to look up at him.

"I swear to you, I never knew. I would never have put you through it. You have to trust me on that." He reaches out and gently moves hair out of my face, tucking a strand behind my ear.

I want to confront him, to ask why I should trust him, tell him to stay away from me, but his touch is so soothing and I am so bone tired that I just lay there in a broken pile.

He slides closer and lifts my head onto his lap.

In the silence, he strokes my hair.

Time is ticking by. He carefully bends over me and gently tugs at my glasses before taking them off.

"I know you don't need those", he murmurs. "I've noticed at school that you have clear lenses in those and wondered why you were wearing them. I think now I know why."

After everything that came out today, this little secret doesn't even crack the top one hundred.

"I'm sorry about today", he softly whispers, playing with my hair. "I just wanted you to have a good time. When Baza suggested a party, I thought that was an excellent idea. I was hoping that it would cheer you up and might persuade you to stay longer with us. With me."

He quiets. The rhythm of stroking becomes monotonous and I know that he's deep in his own thoughts. After a while he speaks again, seeming to be talking more to himself than to me.

"I should've seen it coming. I should've looked into your past. I should've found it before him and eliminated it all. I know better than to leave such leverage for him, but I never imagined that anything out of the ordinary might be in your past..."

His hand freezes mid stroke and for a moment I can feel a sudden angry tension radiating off him before settling again.

"You are so strange, unlike anyone I've met before. Always sad. Guess, now I know why..." he mumbles.

"I'm sorry, Ariel. I'm sorry for everything. Ariel, can you please look at me?" He calls to me, as he's stroking the side of my face, gently willing my face to come up.

With my darkest secret out, I feel small and defenceless again. Cornered, with no voice and no leverage or power of my own.

Contradicting emotions are tangled in one frightening mess inside me. I feel closer to him and somewhat freer. I feel empty and numb and yet feel stronger and more vulnerable at the same time. I twist on the floor, looking up at him. Strangely, I feel hopeful as well.

"I would like you to stay with me, even after Mia", he says, gazing into my eyes. "I just want to try to make you happy, to make you smile again, maybe even hear you laugh one day. I promise I'll protect you better. Nobody will ever hurt you again. Can you forgive me?"

His face is a rigid armour of pain. His blue eyes are open wide, with emotions rippling behind them, eyes of a convict waiting for his sentencing.

I nod.

His strained face relaxes, letting a small tired smile take over his lips. "Thank you. I promise, you'll never regret putting your trust in me".

He relaxes his head against the wall.

The warmth from his body seeps into mine and I feel surprisingly cosy on the floor. The sound of his even breathing, the smell of him, his warmth, my lids are growing heavy and I decide to rest, just for a bit.

* * *

I wake with a jolt and sit up.

I'm in *my* room in Baza's place. A fuzzy memory rushes in of me falling asleep on Sam and then him trying to carry me, me fighting him off and then walking, which was more like drunk staggering into the room and then into my bed.

Sam is asleep in the armchair next to the fireplace. His long legs stretch out for a mile. His head is propped up on his arm. His glorious white wings are spread around him like limbs of a sleeping toddler or of a starfish.

I'm tucked in my bed, still wearing my evening dress. As I try to turn, a sharp pain stings at the side of my body. I roll over and throw the quilt off me, inspecting the cut in the dress with a matching crusting wound underneath. The whip made a clean cut through the dress and my skin, like a scalpel.

Well, the dress is now ruined for sure. Not like I planned to save it for an audience with the queen...

With a grunt, I rise and slowly plod my way to the bathroom, when Sam's voice catches me somewhere in the middle of the room.

"Morning, Mermaid", Sam calls, yearning, swallowing half of the second word in the process.

"Morning", I turn to him. "Have you been here all night?"

"Yes. Guarding your sleep, like a real knight should do", he smirks. His lopsided smug smile is as charming as ever.

I roll my eyes at his cheeky and sarcastic reply.

"I'm off to the shower", I offer into the uncomfortable silence. I'm not sure how to talk to him after yesterday. I turn, starting back on my route.

"Okay. And I'll get us a breakfast. Any preferences?" he calls after me.

"Pastries would be nice. Thank you". I scoot into the bathroom to take care of my morning needs.

The water burns at the cut when I climb into the shower. The shock of the first sting is replaced by the familiar memory of pain – it's not my first shower with bruises and cuts.

I decide to leave the cut alone. It's not that deep and it's crusting over already, and I don't know where to find medical supplies in anyway.

Wrapped in a bathrobe, I come out and halt to a stop at the sight of Baza, sitting in the armchair across from Sam, his black, shining wings spread behind him.

Fear washes over me at the sight of him. I desperately want to bolt, feeling vulnerable, dressed in just a bathrobe, so I tighten the belt, adjusting the sides, digging deeper into my stock of anger to replace the weakening panic.

"Morning, Ariel. I trust you slept well." He gets out of his chair to greet me. Sam rises with him, his weary eyes on me.

"Yes, fine", I'm pleased that I sound short and cheesed off, with not a drop of fear in my voice.

"I came to see how you're doing and to apologise for last night", he starts. "I realise that I should've discussed my procurement with you prior to revealing it in front of everybody or offered you privacy in dealing with such a personal matter, but I have to say I'm extremely proud of the way you handled it. You showed the strength in you to every doubter out there. Our small community is abuzz today with immense admiration of you and we are all exhilarated to have you with us", he says, all pompous, as if he's still making a speech in front of yesterday's crowd.

He theatrically leans in and drops his voice to a loud whisper. "I am a bit jealous of the way you found so many admirers here", and winks at me.

He turns and reclines back into his seat. He crosses one leg over the other, resting his right hand on the cane next to him, all business like.

"You will be pleased to know that the residual issues with procurement were handled as well", he utters. "You will never have to set your eyes on these men again. I've made sure that this issue was finalised."

I swallow. My head is spinning. Does he mean what I think he means?

He reclines back into his chair.

"Yesterday you showed everyone that you are not a victim. You showed them that you're a survivor! I could not be prouder. The steel of your character, the potential of your powers... You are a rarity, a wonder that can change the world. You are inspiring our kind and I can see a magnificent future ahead of you with us. Colossal things you can achieve. I would like you seriously to consider staying with us, even once the imminent threat of Mia is eliminated."

He finishes his speech, looking up at me, waiting for an answer.

I clear my throat.

"Thank you for these kind words. I'll think about it."

"Thank you", he smiles. "And I have a gift for you."

He reaches into the breast pocket of his elegant suit and produces a black velvet jewellery box.

After seeing his idea of gifts last night, I'm really worried about what might be inside that box, maybe a finger as a confirmation of the 'finality' of the issue. It takes me a few more minutes to wrestle with myself, but eventually I step towards him, taking the box from his palm. As if it's about to explode in my face, I carefully lift the lid.

My breath leaves me at the sight of a large clear diamond, resting on the black silk inside, spraying rays of light with its millions of facets. The stone is round and clear, the size of the fingernail on my middle finger. A thin thread chain holds the stone and disappears, folded inside the box.

I've never seen diamonds this close up.

"Is it for me?" My voice is weak and unsure.

"Of course", he smiles, "the first of many to come. Something small to show you our appreciation and our gratitude." He smiles, pleased with my reaction.

"Sam, could you please help Ariel with it?" he says to Sam, who hasn't spoken a word since Baza came in.

Sam rises from his chair, fishes out the necklace from its box and walks around to stand behind me, as I lift my hair to the side.

The stone's cold surface heats up fast on my skin. It lies heavily past my clavicle, shining arrogant and bright, demanding attention.

I turn my head to Sam: "Thank you".

He nods.

"Thank you", I say, addressing Baza now. "It's very generous of you, and it's beautiful, but I don't think I can accept such an expensive gift".

"Nonsense, my dear child", he dismisses me with a casual wave of his hand. "It's nothing to me and suits you rather well. Besides consider it an apology for last night".

"Thank you", I'm fidgeting with my bathrobe, unsure what to do or say now. I have never had anyone give me a gift. "I'll go and quickly get dressed".

"Don't worry my dear child, take your time", he smiles kindly at me and if I didn't know who orchestrated last night's horror show, I might have believed him. "I need to go, duty calls, but hopefully I'll see you shortly".

I nod and take to the wardrobe.

I dress into yesterday's jeans, a T-shirt and a sweatshirt in a record time. I wonder if I should join the army after this ordeal. I'd be the best at sixty second drills.

I come to the door and am about to turn the handle when I hear the hum of Baza's voice seeping through the door. Then I hear my name. I stop in my tracks, leaning into the door.

I can't make out a single word.

Holding my breath, I gently turn the handle, stopping every few seconds. The steady rhythm of Baza's hushed voice pushes me to keep going.

Once the handle is turned to the full, I pull at the door, moving it a millimetre at a time, praying that they service everything well in here and the hinges won't squeak.

"... Council was very impressed with her abilities. During the execution, the gates opened only a fraction, but it was enough for us to see her potential. A few daemons managed to advance onto the Apkallu plane, but the gates didn't hold long enough for the malakhims to ascend too. Ideally, we need to enlist her in full, of her own accord, but in case we can't achieve it, I have set up the arrangements for a Plan B", he commands in a hushed voice.

"I sent ibnatum to acquire her sister and to bring her back here. She'll be very useful as leverage. I've kept the scoundrels alive for now as well. Ultimately, we'll do whatever is needed to open the gate. These miscreants have shown us the depth of her ability, so I'm absolutely convinced now that she was the cause of the earthquake and tsunamis two years ago on the Apkallu plane", he says. I can hear the muffled clacks of his cane on the carpet as he takes a few steps around.

"All I want for you to do is to concentrate on her, court her, get involved with her, whatever it takes. You are still our first plan and first choice", Baza instructs with a steely note in his voice that I never heard before. "The rewards are immense at the succession of this plan. I have authorised your immediate exemption along with free access to the treasury. Use any funds necessary. As of today, you have a full Counthood, with all the assigned benefits. Remember, we count on you."

He lets out a gentle grandfatherly laugh, pleased with his pun.

Before my shaky hands give away my snooping, I nudge the door shut, turning the knob with numb fingers and slide down the wall.

I'm screwed.

We have arrived at our final destination, please remember your belongings.

I sit by the wall, staring into space. Minutes trickle by and I can't come up with any plan or way out. My mind is stuck on a loop, screaming at me to get out and drowning tentative ideas which are trying to poke their heads through the mist.

I need to get out, but how?

I don't know this place, don't know the way out. I've tried to walk off once but got lost, after running around pointlessly for hours in this overwordly circle, like a pathetic hamster in its wheel, until I was found by Tabby.

Tabby... Tabby... An idea is still forming, elusive and phantom.

What if I ask Tabby for help? Will she help? Or will she sell me down the river? What can I do to persuade her?

I'm in an angelic realm and one might think that heavenly matters are up for thrashing in here, not playground politicking on a universal scale. I feel like I haven't left my world at all. I guess it shows that angels are just like humans, honest and scheming, trustworthy and conniving.

If I approach Tabby, I might lose the upper hand, which I just gained. But for me to get out, I need someone's help and apart from Tabby, there is no one else I see who I can ask.

The careful tap of knuckles sounds on the door. I jump up with a surprise, banging my head on the wall.

"Ariel? Are you okay?" Sam's voice calls from behind the door. He sounds worried. Only a few hours ago I would've been pleased about it, would've been excited that he is interested in me. Now it's just killing me not to show him how much I hate him.

"You've been there for a while. Baza has left. He asked me to pass his apologies that he couldn't wait any longer. Is everything okay? Can I come in?"

"*No*. No, I'm not dressed", I sound panicked even for my ears, so I try again to make my voice as chirpy as Daisy's when she flirted.

"Everything's fine. I was trying all these gorgeous clothes on and I guess I lost all sense of time. I'm coming out now", my voice is so sugary sweet that even my teeth hurt.

"Ah, okay." Muffled steps disappear behind the door.

I push myself up and head for the mirror. It takes me a few more minutes to arrange my face into something less resentful and nervous before I'm able to join Sam.

He takes in the casual sight of me in jeans and a sweater. "Um... you look nice". A gentleman is always a gentleman. Manners are clearly not allowing him to say "And *this is* what took you so long?"

"Nice, right? I think I got it perfect this time", and I give him a twirl, coquettishly smiling and batting my eyelashes at him.

Sam wisely decides to change the subject.

"What would you like to do today? I have a couple of hours available but then I have to go and follow up on a few of Mia's leads", he says.

"Do you think you've found her?" A faint flicker of hope lights up inside me, hoping that maybe, just maybe, they'll let me go back home once Mia is gone.

"I hope so, but I need to check those leads to know for sure. But before then, we can do anything you like." His charming smile is back on, revealing the unstoppable force of the dimple.

I have to control my facial expression with all my will, to prevent it from morphing into a despised mask of contempt. My hand is itching to slap him and tell him that I heard everything. So instead I smile sweetly.

"You know what? Go and take care of Mia, and I can spend some time with Tabby. Is she around?" I chirp.

He takes a step closer, wrapping me in his scent. "Tabby would love to have your company", he murmurs, leaning into me. "She keeps talking about you, calling you her sister". He is smiling now like a proud papa.

"It's settled then", I answer cheerfully. "You go and find Mia so I can get back to my life, and I'll spend the day with Tabby, and in the evening we can all have dinner together." My charming smile is off the charts, holding a good competition with his.

"That sounds like a perfect plan", he murmurs, diving his head closer to mine. He's going in for a kiss.

I can't!

And just a second before our lips touch, I turn my face to the side, giving him a peck on the cheek instead.

"Oh. Okay..." he stammers. He pulls his head up, his piercing blue eyes confused and his smile withering.

Confusing emotions are intertwined inside me. I still like him so much and now I hate him, just as deeply. For Daisy, for Lis, for me liking him, for me trusting him, even briefly. For him seeing the deepest and darkest secret of mine and *pretending* that he is okay with it. But most of all, I hate him for his betrayal.

And I hate myself. I feel like a stupid, gullible little girl who fell for the wrong guy, and I should've known better.

Poker face, poker face.

I look into his gorgeous blue eyes, so beautiful and vivid against his soft tanned face. Still smiling, I fold my hands behind my back so my hand doesn't slip and connect with his deceitful face.

"I'm going to send for Tabby", he utters, still sounding lost.

He stands there for a few more heartbeats, opens his mouth, thinking of saying something, then shuts it, changing his mind.

"Well..." he shifts uncomfortably, "I'll see you later", and in a few long strides, he is out of the door.

As the door shuts behind him, the wound up tension leaves my body and I desperately want to cry. Betrayal never gets any easier, each new wound is carved just as deep as the one before. They cut deep because they cut on the soft flesh of your heart, after you've made a mistake allowing them in through your armoured shell.

Tabby is about to get here and I need my game face on.

I throw my head up to the ceiling, blinking away the tears. *I'll think about him later.*

"Hi", Tabby's bright voice pulls me back. "What are you doing?" she is curious like all little children.

"was just looking at the ceiling. Thought I saw a fly there", I answer, pulling my lips into a smile. I do a double take at her get up today.

She is dressed like a crazy goth ballerina. Today she's sporting a pink leotard with a neon-pink tutu over it and black glittery tights underneath. Her feet are wrapped in black leather 'skinhead's edition' Doc Martens with a black leather biker jacket finishing the look. Her hair is tied into two bunches above her ears with neon yellow ribbons.

"Did you?" She throws her head back and stares at the ceiling with me.

"It probably flew away", I have never seen any insect in this place, so I doubt flies will be here either, but Tabby is happy to believe my little lie, ready to chase after an imaginary fly, fairies with unicorns.

"I like your look today Tabby", I compliment her.

Her face lights up with a bright smile.

"Thank you", she proudly replies. "I chose it", and she gives me a twirl.

I'm about to lie to her and use her like Sam and Baza did to me.

Realisation squeezes my throat, leaving a bitter taste in my mouth.

She is my only way out. I need to do it. I have no choice.

That's probably what Sam was saying to himself as he was betraying me and before I can change my mind, I take a step closer to Tabby.

Here my advantage goes down the toilet.

"Tabby, I'm in big trouble and I need your help", I look at her, making sure she's listening to me, although I can't hear much over the loud drum of my heart. "I'm in big danger here, and so is my sister. I need to get out of here before anything happens to me or to her."

"You need to tell Sam. He will protect you and your sister", she pipes in earnestly. Her sincerity and trust in Sam makes me want to wail.

"I can't tell Sam. He is the one who's trying to hurt us", I reach out and take her small hand in mine. "He needs something from me, something I don't know how to find, so now he's planning to bring my sister here and hurt her, and me, until I do what he wants. I need to find a way out of this place and find my sister before Sam does."

I look into her eyes, pleading with her.

"I'm not sure if I can help you with that", she whispers; her big brown eyes are petrified.

"Remember when you asked me to be your sister, and I said yes? I meant it. I want to be your sister. Only, if I'm your sister, so is Jess", I urge her. "You can have not one, but two sisters and as sisters we always look after each other, we have each other's backs. That is what having a sister is about, you have a friend you can trust, forever. No matter what", I say, still holding her hand in mine.

"We can get out of here together and you can stay with us for as long as you want", I ramble on. "We can live together, take care of each other and I'll take care of both of you, but I need to get out of here first. Will you help me? Please?"

My hand is shaking around hers and I can taste the panic.

I need to convince her, I need her on my side. Failure here will mean a rapid shuttle to a heavily guarded prison without the possibility of parole. Baza doesn't strike me as the forgiving kind.

Tabby is quiet, looking at me with her big baby eyes and I can't make out what she is thinking, but I can't afford to let it go, to lose that option to escape, so I keep on pleading.

"You don't have to stay here. You can come with me. Where I'm from, we have lots of animals and insects, and butterflies and birds in the sky. They chirp every morning outside my window and you can feed them. And there's a river near my house and when I was your age, I used to go there to fish. And farms around us have cows and horses and sheep and chickens", I ramble.

Hot tears sting my eyes and I think they're about to spill.

"Jess loves animals. You can go and see animals together, and fish, and feed birds..." I go on, in one breath, afraid to stop, to hear her to say *'no'* and tell on me.

"Tabby. Please", I whisper.

"I can help you get to the Gates, but I can't open them", she answers, and I inhale. At least she is on board.

"Maybe I can", I sound completely nuts and my rational self rolls her eyes. Hopefully she doesn't change her mind about helping me now.

"I think I might be able to open the Gates, at least for long enough for us to slip out. I think I might have that power", I mumble, keeping my eyes on Tabby.

Tabby's eyes pop out, as her mouth forms a perfect 'O'.

"So it was you who opened the Gates last night?" she whispers, darting her glances around the room, like she is afraid to be overheard.

"I think so", I nod.

"E-e-e!" she squeals, clapping her hands and bouncing on the spot. Suddenly she remembers herself and slaps both hands over her mouth, her beautiful eyes shining over her hands.

"Then we are in the game!" She throws her tiny fist in the air. I wonder where she picked up all these expressions.

"So you're going to help me?" I ask, unable to believe my luck.

"Yeah, man", she sharply nods her head. "If you can open the Gates and I can get us there, we are outta here!

Woo-hoo!" She does some weird jig in front of me, kicking her legs and punching the air. Her tutu and neon ribbons in her hair bounce around her. But the next instance she sobers.

"I will get things ready and will pack my bag. You", she points her finger at my chest, all bossy. "Pack your backpack. Pack light", she commands, clearly setting the boundaries that she is in charge of this mission.

"I'll be back soon and we'll leave", she strides decisively and out of the door before I can even ask her what I need to pack.

CHAPTER 15

"I guess you're still packing." Tabby's voice startles me. I snap upright, half expecting to see the Butcher or Baza behind her. But she is alone.

Now she is rocking black chinos with millions of pockets, military-green Martens and an outdoorsy jacket. A backpack is strapped to her back. I don't know how far we will need to walk, but judging by her get-up, we'll be trekking through the wilderness for a while.

"Yeah, wasn't sure what to pack", I mumble.

"I got everything we need", she declares. "You need to pack a change of clothes and a toothbrush".

She is in charge and she loves it.

She marches to the bag section in the wardrobe, pulls out a small and pretentious black-sequined backpack and stuffs into it a cream jumper, a yellow T-shirt and bright pink jeans. Clearly the trekking gear is reserved only for the expedition leader and the rest of us can look like parrots.

In the bathroom I grab the toothbrush I opened earlier and a bar of soap, scooping a few underwear garments along the way, and shove it all in my backpack.

"Okay. We're all ready", she announces brightly. A wide grin spreads across her face.

"Okay, let's do this." I strap my less practical backpack on.

I follow Tabby out of the door and into the familiar lift. She reaches up, presses the top button on the panel, and I can feel the lift moving down as I feel a gentle push at my ribcage.

The lift pings and again we are in the ostentatious foyer I saw yesterday, only today Tabby leaves our lift and leads me to the one next to it.

This one looks more like a service lift. It doesn't have any frills, just a big, heavy-duty metal cage behind the lift's doors. Tabby is confident when she stretches on her toes and pushes a button on the top row of the dial, then settles cross legged on the floor by the wall.

And again we go down.

"Tabby, shouldn't we have arrived by now?" I whisper in the silence, interrupted only by the occasional grinding sound of metal behind the lift's doors. I feel uneasy in the metal cage which still keeps moving, even after ten minutes, with no end in sight.

"No", she giggles, "it'll be much longer than that".

I'm tired of standing, so I sit on the floor across from her. Tabby is completely relaxed and at ease, confident in her plan. Her confidence helps to calm my nerves a bit and for the first time since I asked for her help, I believe that maybe I have a chance to get out of this place.

The metal cage jerks to a stop, yanking me out of my sleep. I fell asleep at some point during the ride and now I'm sitting stiff and disoriented, like a rabbit dragged out of a sack. I don't know how long I've been out.

My stiff body is arguing with me, refusing to do what it's been told, and it takes me a while to unwrap my legs from the pretzel position and to straighten my back and push myself up.

Tabby is already by the open door, disapprovingly eyeing my clumsy rising.

I freeze, gaping open mouthed at the terrain opening in front of me, past the open doors of the lift.

The landscape lying ahead is bare to the horizon.

It's a burnt-out, lifeless surface of a wasteland, scorched by vicious heat. Red brownish dry soil is cracked on the top. Low, charred bushes dot the landscape. Their branches, like the broken and bent arthritic fingers of an old witch, are spread wide, ready to snag on clothes.

Further in the distance, rocky hills are jagged on the red horizon, slicing the black billowing smog, rolling over them with their sharp, broken teeth. The strong wind gusts over the wasteland, carrying dust and dirt, waiting to scratch the cornea of an unwelcomed visitor.

The black smog is billowing over the horizon, obscuring the reddish-orange sky. The orange glow that manages to trickle through the smog, dimly lights up the empty terrain.

It is an apocalyptic wasteland reminiscent of the surface Mars.

As I take the first step off the lift and onto the bare clay red ground, the stench of rotting rubbish, heightened by the sauna hot air, hits my nose. I have never been on top of a city dump in scorching mid-July, but I imagine it would smell just like this.

The hot air is sticky and scorching. It burns inside my throat as it slides into my lungs. I'm fighting for every bit of oxygen in this burning air, and when I manage to get some into my lungs, reflux, brought on by the stench, squeezes my throat and I wish I hadn't taken that breath. My stomach loudly rumbles, reminding me that I haven't had breakfast today.

Looking ahead at this post-apocalyptic horror, I understand Tabby's attempt at trekking gear. I only wish we had access to an air-conditioned all terrain vehicle with plenty of air fresheners inside or a military grade tank.

Tabby hikes up her backpack on her shoulders and decisively sets off into the wilderness without checking if I'm following her. I'm more afraid to be lost in here than to be led on the wrong path, so I sprint after her. Tabby's grey wings are folded tightly against her back.

"Tabby, are you sure you know where we're going?" I call to her after a while. The terrain is empty and quiet, only the sound of the wind carrying dust swishes in the air.

My voice is muffled by the fabric mask that I constructed out of the yellow T-shirt Tabby jammed into my backpack. My DIY mask blocks some smell and stops most of the dust and dirt.

With a nerve twisting pitch, the dirt scratches on the lenses of my old glasses that I found jammed in the pocket of my jeans and now put on my nose to serve as safety goggles. I am thankful to my old habits and that I stuffed my old glasses in the pocket, as now I can use them as a plastic barrier between the high speed dirt and my eyes. I pull off my sweatshirt as I walk, and although the impulse to dump it by the side of the road is strong, I wrap it around my waist, just in case.

We have wandered for a few miles now and I don't see any obvious path or road that Tabby might be following. The charred landscape hasn't changed a bit, only the broken teeth of the hills have moved to our left.

"Don't worry, Ariel, I know how to get to the Gates", she calls to me over the sound of the wind, glancing over her shoulder at me, still chirpy and upbeat. The smell and dirt don't seem to bother her in the slightest as her pace remains strong and steady. Her back is straight against the scratching gusts with only her head slightly bent down, while I'm stumbling, doubled over, shading my eyes and covering my mouth with the mask.

After trekking for what feels like half a day, with only two short stops under the watchful eye of the Generalissimus Tabby, where I was allowed to drink strictly half of a cup of water and given a squashed cereal bar, the skylight around hasn't changed. It is neither darkened nor got lighter, and I begin to wonder if this terrain ever gets lit by the sun.

As we trek farther, the charred wasteland of Mars' landscape begins to change, to include short industrial-looking buildings, covered in dull grey metal sheets, all one storey buildings with no frills, no signage, no windows propped on the cracked soil. Some buildings are no bigger than a garden shed whereas others are as big as a retirement bungalow.

The wind and dust are singing an orchestral cacophony around these buildings. The swoosh of dust brushed on metal, the bangs of thin, loosened metal sheets on the structures, the whistles and billows of the wind in the cavities of the buildings. It's like all the wind and percussion instruments have gathered together to make the most hideous and annoying racket.

Tabby keeps only to her visible path, marching and swinging her arms, humming to herself and not hiding, as if not expected to be seen or to meet anyone here, in spite of the evidence of a progressing industrial revolution.

Metal buildings now appear more often as we get farther ahead. Through the blackening smog, I spy a large, dark outline, reaching high into the sky ahead of us, but from that far away, I can't figure out what it is. It's slim and tall and every now and again a bright luminescent light bursts out of the top of it, like the quick beam of a lighthouse, before going dark again.

"Tabby, what's that?" I call after her, slowing down behind her, squinting through the smog at the mysterious outline. Sand and dust crunch on my teeth, no longer stopped by the mask. The stench of rotting dump is still here and as poignant as before, but I must have got used to it, as I no longer want to bring up my guts with every breath.

Tabby stops and looks back at me. I point behind her, to the dark outline.

Just as she turns to follow the direction of my pointing finger, the 'lighthouse' lights up again, emitting a glorious white light, beaming it up to the sky.

As the flash dies, Tabby turns to me with a sad face. The corners of her lips are pulled down, as the top lip is riding over the bottom one and I think she is about to cry. Her eyes are betraying the torment raging inside her. The deep grief in her eyes looks wise and ancient, and at that moment she looks like a small old lady.

She walks back to me.

"What did Baza tell you about this place?" she asks me in a stranger's voice and it feels as if Tabby grew up all of a sudden. I'm scared of her now. I don't know this stranger and I don't know what it might do.

"Um... that it's where he lives and I'll be safe in here..." I mumble, keeping my eyes on her. I don't know what she wants to hear from me.

"So basically, nothing". Her shoulders slump as she lifts her suddenly matured, wise eyes at me, looking like a grown up in a child's body. "That's one of the 'processing facilities' Baza holds in here. They are designed to extract an essence, or what you might call a soul, from beings, which end up here."

Her explanation is very cryptic, confusing me even more.

"What do you mean "extract the essence"?" My voice is rising against my will as Sam's words about Mia being after my 'essence' pop into my head.

Shit!

That's why Tabby agreed to help me. That's why she didn't tell Sam or Baza about my escape plea, she works with Mia. I spin on the spot, looking for a sign of an ambush, but the surrounding landscape is as uninhabited as a few minutes ago.

"That's how Baza built his empire for the last *GA*, it was fed and sustained by essences." Tabby's grown up voice is sad and quiet. "And those stupid sorry beings have ended up here of their own will. They agreed to come here; they traded in something infinitely more valuable than their small imagination could give them."

She sadly shakes her head.

"Tabby, I don't understand. What beings? How 'traded'?" I try to control my voice, to stop it from rising with panic and frustration. I know that I need to stay calm around her, especially if she has an on-going episode of god knows what.

I inhale and try a different question.

"Tabby, why are we here?" I ask softly, taking her small hands in mine.

Tabby sighs like a tired old person.

"We are here, because that is the way to the Gates, and it is the fastest way. And you will see soon what beings I'm talking about."

She takes a long look at me, before she pulls her hands out of mine, huffs the backpack higher on her shoulders and returns to her trekking.

I spit out another mouthful of dust, yank up my canary yellow mask over my nose and mouth and follow Tabby.

The distance between us is growing, forcing me to make another decision. Turning back is not an option now, I'll never be able to find my way back from here, but even if I did, it would be the way back into a cage, so I clench my teeth and follow Tabby.

As I walk, I shrug the backpack off my back, reach deep into it, and fish out a little fruit knife that I sneaked into my backpack earlier and hid among my knickers. With a careful glance at Tabby's back, I slide the knife into the back pocket of my jeans, feeling somewhat better and more secure.

Tabby is weaving between dried out shrubs, along the cracked open soil, leading us towards the ominous outline, and with our every step, the beam of the 'lighthouse' pulses brighter ahead of us.

The closer we get, the more I can make out a large structure in front of us with a massive chimney poking into the sky, which emits that glorious light now and again, like a large candle or a war searchlight.

I'm so hypnotised by the sight of this beautiful light that I almost miss the sound of a dozen guttural voices approaching us.

The voices are calling to each other, interrupted by sharp claps of whips, reaping the silence of the terrain, followed by weak cries.

I sprint after Tabby, grabbing her arm.

"Tabby", I whisper, warning her of the voices ahead. "Listen..."

"It's okay Ariel", she replies calmly, not trying to lower her voice. "They won't hurt us. They can't see or hear us. They are only aware of the branded ones."

She puts her hand over mine, snaked around her wrists, and I let go of her, uncomfortable and feeling childish under her gaze.

She sets off again and I'm following, staying as close to her as I can, when we come into a scene of what night terrors are made of.

Ahead, blocking our path, a large horde of completely naked and barefoot humans is stretched across the landscape. They shuffle over the cracked ground, blindly roaming around with vacant, compliant eyes, following the universal flow and bumping into each other with a fear when the whip flies. They are behaving like cattle, like a herd of cows or sheep transported over a field.

There must be a couple of hundred of them. Mainly males, of different ages, but I spot a few women and even older children among the group. Their feet are covered in the red dust of the soil. None of the humans are aware of their nudity, not one is trying to cover themselves. Each one in this herd has a bleeding, large, elaborate brand, freshly burnt into the middle of their chests. Some brands are fresh and bleeding profusely, while others are black, charred scars.

The humans are herded by about a dozen of upright, walking Frankenstein's experiments of crossing dinosaurs with humans. It's like a T-Rex with human proportions and human limbs. But maybe it's not a T-Rex. I never was interested in dinosaurs, but those dinosaur men are shit scary.

The ghastly "dinosaur men" are at least seven feet tall, covered in green-yellow scaly skin from head to toe, with steroid grown bodybuilder muscles flexing underneath and a scaly long tail dragging behind each one. Now and again, with a sharp clap, the dinosaur men throw their whips into the crowd of humans, and when the whip makes contact with skin, a little whimper comes from the crowd.

The dinosaurs' bald heads are much smaller in proportion to their bodies. They are covered in a reptile skin with three rows of horns over it. Horns start with the larger ones on top of their heads and run down their backs and over their tails.

They wear wide, gold spiky bands, encircling their thick necks and their wrists, sporting the same design as the ones on the human chests. Large pieces of fabric, or more like rags, are wrapped around their waists, serving as belts for their whips.

And I scream, from the top of my lungs, when one of them turns its head to me and I take in the full glory of its ghastly face.

These scaly things don't have *any* eyes. Their flattened faces, with three horns atop, have only *one* hideous hole in the middle of the face. I think that those holes must be their mouths as a circle of protruding razor sharp teeth surround the hole. Slime excretes from the hole, coating the front of their bodies in gunk.

I squeak and clap my hand over my mouth, petrified to be spotted, but the lizard sweeps his blind head over to the other side, ignoring me completely.

With the help of their whips, the lizards herd the humans in the direction of the large building with the 'lighthouse' attached to it.

There's no order to the humans' formation, they weakly trip over stones, unseen by their vacant eyes, and often, when one falls, he brings the nearest down with him.

And then, when the closest lizard opens his mouth, a thick and scaly like an anaconda, snake-tongue flies out of the hole with an incredible speed and whips at the group of humans.

When the tongue makes contact with the body, with a heavy slap it rips out a chunk of flesh out of its victim. The chunk then drops to the ground with a revolting wet thud. The victims whimper like small children, but then they get up and keep on walking. No one helps a fallen victim nor tries to fight the lizards off. It's like all of them have accepted their fate.

I can't pull my gaze away from the gruesome procession nor can I move a muscle. Tabby had stopped a few yards away from me, watching the group with sad eyes. Tabby's grey wings are open wide behind her back, the tips of the feathers trembling with the wind.

When the procession eventually disappears into the thick smog, I manage to remember how to move my laden legs, so I plod towards Tabby.

Tabby turns to me once I'm near. Tears, like fat slugs, roll down her pretty pixie face as her lips tremble. Our gazes meet, but Tabby says nothing. She just turns on the spot, resuming her hiking.

We need to do something. We have to do something. I can't just leave them like that.

I chase after her.

"Tabby, we have to help these people", I grab her small arm, turning her around. "We have to do something!"

"We can't do anything, Ariel. Nobody can. I told you, they are *branded*", she whispers in a small shaken voice. Her warm brown eyes are sad, looking at me with pity.

"But there must be a way, Tabby. We need to help them, we need to free them." My words are coming out of me in a mumbled rush.

"Ariel, they made their choice", she mutters, sniffling and wiping her eyes and nose with her sleeve. She looks up at me with the sadness and wisdom of the world, which doesn't fit with her little child's exterior or with her wiping her snotty nose on her sleeve. "They agreed to the trade, of their free will. It's done", she yells at me angrily, fists balling at her sides. She turns and stomps away, kicking at the small stones on the red ground.

Slowly, the sense of finality Tabby is feeling sinks in.

I blindly follow her, unsure what to do or say now, as my mind is trying to process the lizard guards and the human cattle. My mind is churning at everything I have seen. It's funny how the human mind works, you could've been told millions of times about the monsters out there, about the souls, but only once you've seen it with your own eyes, you accept it as the truth. Humans are pathetic like that, to believe that something does exist, we need to see it for ourselves, but sadly, not everything can be seen or found.

Unfortunately for me, our way is weaving towards the 'lighthouse' building, after the disappeared herd. The building grows ahead of us, revealing more details.

Now I see that, just like all the previous buildings, this structure has no windows. A tall, metal net fence surrounds the building and the 'lighthouse'. It's like a massive coal power plant with a lighthouse, like a chimney, shooting high into the sky; only instead of the black smoke of burnt coal, this one is producing a glorious beaming light.

A murmur of muffled screams floats in the air from behind the walls of that building. It's like the buzz of a bee hive ahead, and as we get closer to the building, it grows louder and louder, and now I can decipher the individual agonising voices, screaming in a sea of suffering, and every time a wave of screams begins, it's followed by a burst of that glorious light from the chimney.

The screams get louder with every step I take. I can hear a woman's voice, laced over the scream of a man, followed by the bellowing of another, and another, and another.

I clap my hands over my ears, desperate to cut out this horrific roar. I stumble and stop. I squeeze my eyes shut, but the noise is seeping through my hands, getting through to me and into my heart. I try to walk after Tabby, but my legs get heavier, refusing to obey me, weakened with every scream.

I open my eyes.

Tabby's small shape is getting farther ahead, fuzzed out by my tears which I can't even wipe off.

I am staggering drunkenly ahead. I keep my head down, watching the red soil under my feet. Wet droplets appear on the cracked soil in front of me with my every step. I can't see Tabby anymore, not that I'm looking.

I trip over something and clumsily flapping my arms I land on all fours. Screams burst into my head, ripping me inside, while the stones rip the skin off my knees and hands.

Unsteadily I rise up. Blood is dripping off my hands, leaving droplets of blood on the ground in its wake, to accompany the ones of salty water. I wipe my bloodied hands on my jeans, but the blood keeps on running.

With my hands covered in blood, I don't know how to cover my ears or how long I can take these screams before I lose my mind. I raise my head and spin, looking for Tabby, for a solution, for a way out. I turn on the spot and that's then when I see it....

My breath leaves me and with it, my lungs expel a scream as high as I've ever heard, ringing in the open, drowning the agonising screams around.

I'm standing in front of a vast field, organised for miles like a vineyard, only instead of the greenery of young emerald vines, human bloodied skins are stretched on the crossed stakes, soaking the stakes and the red soil with blood. The wooden stakes, placed in rows with military precision, are stretching for miles into the horizon.

The gruesome skins have been taken off the bodies in one clean cut: from the neck, down to the fingertips, down to the toes. It's like the human meat and bones have been scraped out, leaving a shell of skin intact, leaving it out to dry on the stakes. Each stake has a wooden plank on the top, like on the top of a shovel, to keep the skin in place, shoulders stretched over it.

The skins are flapping lazily in the wind like a washing on a line. They have been taken off different bodies: fat and slim, old and young.

All these horrifying skins are headless, making this field even more spine chilling. The smell of decomposing flesh is overwhelming, and that's the smell of a rotting dump I smelt the second I set my foot onto this red ground.

Next to me, a male's skin is hanging on a stake, moving slowly with the wind, and that horrifies me even more. His arms, once colourfully tattooed, are now shrivelled, prune corpse's prune arms. With each gust of wind, they move and rise, reaching to me. It's like this empty, headless shell is still alive and trying to get off a stake to get back to its everyday human life. Or maybe it's trying to wave to me, to get my attention, to ask for help.

I double over, bringing up the remnants of the food in my stomach.

My senses are in overload: the smell of decomposing flesh, mingled with the copper smell of blood, the agonising screams, the sting of open wounds on my hands and knees, the lack of oxygen in this humid air, the heat.

I'm heaving, bringing up bile, and I can't stop.

I feel weaker with every second. I still don't know where Tabby is. I collapse on my knees, propping myself up on my arms, but topple over to the side the next second.

I draw up my knees to my chest, wanting to disappear, but there's nowhere to hide in here. I want to call out for Tabby, but I can't find the energy to do that either. I lay on the ground, weeping, willing myself to get a grip, to get up and move on, but I can't do it either.

As I lay, weeping weakly, I feel the gentle movement of the air above me and I sense, rather than see, someone next to me, leaning in closer. *Thank god, Tabby's here.*

I lift my head.

A wide shadow is spread above me, blocking the weak glow of the sky. Through the tear blurred vision, I can make out black boots on the cracked soil in front of me. Someone's standing above me. I can't see much but I know that these boots are too big for Tabby.

Butcher.

Self-preservation whips at me to get up, but as I push myself up, strong arms scoop me off the ground.

"Let go! Let me *go!*" My voice is hoarse and barely audible as I kick and wriggle in the stranger's arms. I'm sliding out of his grip, but he's not planning to let me go, just adjusting his hands on me.

A knife.

I twist my arm, sliding my hand into the back pocket of my jeans. My knife's still there.

I close my cold fingers over the handle, yanking it out. The sound of ripping fabric adds to the cacophony of noises around me and I can feel the air on my butt through the slit in my jeans.

With as much swing as I can manage in his tight grip, I thrust the little knife blindly in front of myself. The knife slows as its metal sinks into the flesh and instantly his grip on me is released.

I drop to the ground with a thump like a dusty sack of potatoes, losing my grip on the knife. Air leaves my lungs. My back and butt are screaming at the impact.

Through the groaning pain, I roll onto my side, scooping myself off the ground, unsteadily rising on all fours. My abused body is screaming at me, joining my bruised mind. Neither is happy with me right now.

My little knife lies in the dust, not far from me, so I dive towards it as fast as I can manage. I close my hand over the handle with a relief, pushing myself up, off the ground once more. My mind is whispering warnings to me, wondering how it is that I've been allowed to have my knife and my freedom to move, but the animal instinct inside drains all the cautions with the blind adrenaline of survival.

I sway unsteadily, rubbing at my blind eyes to dislodge the scratching mix of tears and dirt as I spin to face my attacker, holding my little knife in front me.

A male in front of me is taking a shape.

Angel wings are spread behind him and with every new angry blink, I see more of him. My mouth drops when I can finally make out his face.

Rafe.

He is not wearing his usual glasses, and it takes me a while to recognise him. He stands in front of me, waiting, not rushing at me. The cautious gaze of his soft, brown eyes is on me.

His four wide open, large vivid-purple angel wings are a stunning backdrop for his all-black modern military grade tactical gear. He's sealed in it from head to toe. Black laced up combat boots, trousers with pockets and ammunition belts strapped to his thighs. Black, high tech, plastic armour covers his body. The wide belt around his waist houses large, curved and ridged knives, leather pockets, a metal ball with spikes, a small axe, and some more weapons, for which I don't even have a name.

Two large sword hilts rise behind each shoulder. The leather harnesses criss-cross over his chest.

I gulp at all this gear. No way can I outfight all of *that*, but I'm not planning to let him see that. I steady my arm with a knife at him, thrusting it towards him with a shaky hand.

I feel so weak. The smell still hangs thick around us and every few minutes the gruesome orchestral screams come back to life.

"What are you doing here?" I croak. Dust is crunching on my teeth.

"I came to get you." He lifts his arms up, showing that he's not planning to fight me, but I notice his muscles tensing on his neck as he moves his arms. The blood slowly soaks the sleeve on his shirt and a clear cut in the fabric shows the wound from my knife.

"Who says I'm going anywhere with you?" I challenge him, refusing to lower the knife.

"I hope you will. It's not safe for you down here, and I can protect you", he answers, gazing at me.

And the next second, another tidal wave of screams blankets the air, igniting the white light of the 'lighthouse'.

Despair washes over me. Their cries demand to be heard and I can't speak, listening to them, to their pain. I want to clap my hands over my ears but there's no way I'll risk lowering my knife on him.

Despair is birthing the rage in me. She's happy to be back, asking what she has missed and offering to jump straight in.

"Oh, another protector!" I retort, when the wave of screams dies down. The sarcasm seeping out me is of the highest grade. "Everyone is keen to protect me nowadays. Only then I'm worse off than I was to begin with. So how 'bout you get back to wherever you came from, and I'll get back to my life and we pretend that we never met."

I keep my gaze on Rafe, refusing to move or even to lose ground.

"Ariel, I can't do that." His voice is soft and calm, like talking to a wounded animal. His sincere eyes gaze at me.

"Sure you can. Easy. I'll show you. You go that way", I jerk my chin behind his back, "and I'll go this way", I nod my head behind me.

He doesn't say a word, just keeps watching me and I watch him, waiting for his next move, which doesn't come. We just stand there, staring each other down, not moving, frozen in our delicate status-quo.

This is just getting ridiculous!

"Tabby! Tabby!" I yell into the wilderness while keeping my eyes fixed on Rafe. I want to know where she is and that she's safe.

"Tabby can't join us right now".

I spin away from Rafe, towards the newcomer's voice. The knife spins its trajectory with me in my outstretched hand.

My heart sinks at the sight of the Butcher in his black leather tunic, with the familiar whip at the belt and his large, curved axe in his hand. Two of his goons are behind him, their weapons drawn. Butcher's menacing side smile is scary as hell. Involuntarily, I swallow.

"What are you doing here, Ariel?" Butcher speaks with a strange vowel rolling accent. "Baza wanted you to stay with us." He shakes his head, softly clacking his tongue at me.

"I don't care what Baza wants", I yell over the new wave of screams, forcing my eyes to stay open and my hand to remain steady.

Suddenly Rafe's body slams into mine from behind. His strong hands are on my waist and in a split second I'm lifted and somehow now behind his back, staring at his purple feathers in front of my nose. One of his scabbards is empty and the sound of weapons colliding and a vibration of the impact rolls off his body, pushing at me through the ground.

Rafe widens his stance in front of me. His legs move with each opponent's offence, his sword slicing the air.

I take a small step back.

While they're preoccupied with each other, I decided, it's the perfect time for me to do a runner. I don't want either of them to win. The best outcome for me would be for them to kill each other and die together in each other's arms.

I take another step back, turn and sprint away from them.

Or so I imagine.

It's more of a limp and a hop. Guttural voices shout behind, noticing me, and that kicks me into action, pushes me forward.

The rush of footsteps behind my back is getting closer. I allow myself a glance over my shoulder, only to see both goons after me, and Rafe, glancing in my direction while fighting off Butcher.

The goons are behind me, I can hear the creaking of their leather tunics and almost feel them with the back of my neck. A large hand is reaching for me and before it has a chance to close around my arm, I turn, yanking my arm out of its grip, losing my footing in the process and I go flying.

I fall with a thud, sliding on my side, shredding my face on the rocks and stones on the ground. My arms are outstretched, trying to stop the grinding slide, whilst protecting my face.

My flight stops and I feel the goons above me. Almost on me. I grind my teeth, readying for more pain and the fight that I'll give them, no matter what.

As fast as I can, ignoring the screaming pain of the shredded skin on my face and arms, I flip on my back, kicking my legs at the nearest one.

My foot lands in his knee but that doesn't do as much damage as I hoped for, it just angers him. He stretches his arms to me, ready to lock them around my throat. I pause just for a second more and land a precise kick in his groin.

The goon cries out, moans and doubles over, falling sideways to the ground in slow motion. He rocks on the ground, nursing his family jewels, while swearing in a strangled whisper, cursing me and moaning in between.

But I don't have the luxury to admire my handiwork any longer, as the other goon jumps on me and wrestles me to the ground, pulling me under him. He straddles me, sitting on top of my chest, pushing me down with his weight, and I struggle to expand my ribcage to breathe.

He swings his arm back and slaps me on the face –hard.

My head whips back, hitting the ground. I can taste the iron flavour of blood in my mouth. His slap is so hard that my ears are ringing, as if I had stuck my head in a church bell and somebody rung it.

I can smell his sweat and the stench of his breath and this, combined with his weight on top of me, is making me sick with panic. I am trying to swing my fists at him, but all that I hit is empty air.

His hand vices over mine, while the other hand dives into my hair, pulling my hair out, yanking me up off the ground with him. I cry out in pain, tears fill my eyes and I start to rise, lifting my upper body, following the vicious hand, wanting to relieve the pain.

Suddenly I'm released.

Unsupported, my body flops back on the ground, head hitting the ground again and I groan, as angry red dots spin in front of my eyes.

Rafe's furious face fills my vision. His usually soft brown eyes are black and stormy now. He is heaving. A bleeding wound cuts across his bottom lip.

He kneels next to me, both his swords back in their scabbards behind his back.

I throw my fist towards his face, hoping to make contact, but he sharply jerks his head to the side, avoiding my punch.

My other hand shoots out, aiming at his head, but it fails as it hits the empty air. He moves and swings his head with lightning speed, ducking, avoiding my every hit. Unable to get myself free, I push my legs at the ground, desperate to get away from him, to get some distance between us.

But the next second, his arms shoot out, grabbing my wrists, pinning them to my sides as he leans in. His angry face is uncomfortably close to mine.

The familiar scent of crispy ocean air and the salty wind tickles my nose, but today it's somewhat heavier, stormier, mixed in with his sweat. But in spite of that, his scent relaxes my muscles against my will, melting my spine and that makes me even angrier, as I thrash in his hold.

"Please calm yourself down and stop struggling", he barks at me. "I don't want to hurt you even by accident."

His face is an inch from mine and I can see a little white scar on his left cheek and something familiar tugs at the back of my mind, at my memory, but it's elusive and faint and I can't seem to catch it. But that's just ridiculous, why would it be familiar to me? I only met him a few days ago.

I thrash, struggling to free my arms or get myself away from him, away from his hold.

"Please let me go." I stop thrashing and plead, looking into his eyes, and I think he knows that it's not only the wrists I'm talking about.

"I will. I promise, but not just yet", he replies, keeping his voice calm and even. "I can't afford to leave you defenceless against our world again, and you're not ready to face all of what you are. I was hoping to break it to you carefully, but it seems that time for a gentle induction is over."

And as I keep staring at him he continues. "Please don't be afraid of me. I swear to you that I'll never harm you, you are too vital to me. I'm very sorry that I can't let you go now and that I have to take you with me against your will, but that's the only way I can keep you safe", he murmurs, leaning in even closer.

"Please, Rafe. I need to get out, to get to my sister. Baza's already sent after her", I whisper. "He's going to hurt her to get to me. Please", I breathe out.

"I sent my-", he pointedly looks at me, "*our* kyriotes to ensure her safety the day you disappeared. They're watching over her. She remains in your realm and absolutely safe, but I can't say the same about you. And I can't risk any more of these unexpected and dangerous situations. I'm very sorry." His voice is soft, hiding the steel underneath.

I can hear that he'll not be swayed.

His thumb is lazily stroking my wrist, drawing warm circles on my skin. My traitorous body relaxes around him, it *trusts* him. I don't understand the effect he has on me, how I'm losing control over my body around him, and I don't like it. I hate that, my weak body and him.

His lingering gaze travels down from my eyes, to my lips. It stays there for a bit before it slides, falling to my neck.

I squirm and shift under his gaze, tucking my chin to my chest, a pathetic way to protect myself, to hide my neck.

His eyebrows draw together as his puzzled gaze locks on my neck. He lets go of my wrists, reaching to my neck.

Discomfort and exposure are now replaced by the fresh waves of panic. I pull my head back, straining the tendons on my neck, away from his reach.

"Where did you get that necklace?" he asks calmly, although the stormy emotions behind his eyes are anything but calm.

"Baza gave it to me", I squeak in a weak voice, like a schoolgirl who forgot her homework and has been pulled up on that.

"That's how he found you", he barks out. "How could you take anything from him? What's wrong with you? Don't you have a drop of sense in you? How anyone can be that naïve?" he reprimands me, his eyes stormy once more.

He closes his eyes for a second, exhales and once he opens them, I can see calmer waves behind his eyes.

"You have to leave this necklace here", he orders. I weakly nod.

Rafe reaches around my neck, unclips the necklace and then hurls the expensive diamond far into the dusty horizon.

The moment of quiet raptures again with a new wave of screams and I squeeze my eyes shut, burying my head into my shoulders. I want to slap my hands over my ears, but my wrists are still caged by the iron grip of his hands.

Rafe releases my wrists, threads one arm behind my back and the other under my knees and in a swift and fluid move stands up with me in his arms. My eyes fly open and I can see his purple wings, wide-spread, all four illuminated from within, changing colour from purple to the darkest and lightest blues, before turning a sublime iridescent white, so bright and pure that I have to slam my eyes shut again.

Finally I can clap my hands over my ears, dimming the screams around me.

CHAPTER 16

I'm still in Rafe's arms, but I can feel him flying now.
I can feel the rhythmic pushes of the air by his wings, moving the hot air around us. The flight is not smooth or comfortable, and it feels as if we're being yanked forward by an invisible chain again and again.

The air grows hotter, and it burns the delicate skin inside my nose as it comes in. It's now laced with the repulsive stench of sulphur, ammonia and burning matches, as if someone left a carton of eggs to rot, then urinated around it, while repeatedly striking match after match around it. All for someone's perverted pleasure.

I take one breath of the rancid air and a coughing fit takes over. The sour taste wrings my throat, bringing up a faint taste of bile.

Rafe gently swings me around and releases my legs, pressing me tight against him with one solid arm, and the next second, the fabric slaps over my nose and mouth, and I can feel elastic going around the back of my head. The stench in the air instantly becomes bearable.

I crack my eyes open to see Rafe adjusting the mask over the back of my head with one hand while still beating at the air with his wings, but I have to slam my eyes shut again at the heat burning my eyes.

The air is unbearably hot in here. Hotter than it was in the horror wasteland, and I wonder if I might cook alive in here.

The gruesome 'end-of-life' scenarios play in my mind, like a morbid kaleidoscope, brought forward by my over, capable imagination. They reshuffle, adjust, morphing, all the colours of blood, all with Rafe killing me in this scorching oven, just like Sam said he would.

Sudden fear and panic kicks in. I turn and twist in his arms, clawing at his arms around me, at his armour-bounded chest. I want him to take me back. I want him to let go of me.

"Stop it Ariel. I'm going to drop you if you don't stop." The metal ring of a command in Rafe's voice is failing to conceal his annoyance. He tightens his grip on me, adjusting his hold, pulling me closer. "Ariel, you have to trust me. Please stop this. I don't want to drop you and you're making my flying difficult", he demands through gritted teeth.

Why should I care about making any part of his life difficult? What about me?! Has anyone ever cared about me, concerned themselves with my difficult life? And now I'm about to die and the killer has the audacity to complain to *me* that I'm not compliant enough, making his task of abducting and killing me too difficult for him.

Screw him! If I'm going down, he's going down with me.

I blindly reach higher, above his armour and once my fingers make contact with the soft skin of his neck, I sink my nails into it.

"Aargh", Rafe's surprised scream fills the air.

A string of familiar profanities, and some in a foreign language, are rolling off his tongue as he shifts to move his left arm around my waist, with his right hand grabbing both of my wrists. But he's still holding me.

Now I'm suspended like a rag doll in the air.

My body is pressed against his, my arms pulled at the shoulder sockets, while wrists are squeezed tight, guaranteeing later bruises there. My legs dangle, jeans riding up, exposing my ankles to the hot air. Blinded and bided, suspended mid-air, I feel disjointed.

Gradually the temperature around us changes. A stream of cold air brushes the bare skin on my ankles. With every push of his wings, the stream gets stronger and colder, until the ice-cold blast of the walk-in freezer blankets my entire body.

My body shivers and my teeth start beating a lively allegro chatter, with Rafe's solid body being the only source of warmth.

I crack my eyes open. Shielded by frosted lashes against the icy needles of the wind, I see a mountain peak, blanketed in virgin white snow rushing towards us.

Rafe takes a sharp turn left and down. A large opening in the mountain, like an alcove scraped in the mountain's wall, comes into view.

Rafe flies into the cave and lands on his feet a few yards in, releasing me.

No longer supported by his hands or body, I stumble and fall, and he is not even trying to catch me. My legs and feet are numb, frozen by the cold and immobility.

It's quiet and chilly in the cave.

Rafe walks away from me, deeper into the cave, as his hands probe at the scratches on his face. He then fishes out some white gauze from one of the small pockets in his jacket and wipes at his neck and face.

Next, he turns his attention to the knife wound I left in his upper arm. He examines it, and then with another length of gauze wraps it roughly over the sleeve of his jacket.

I quietly watch from my spot, half expecting an outburst of anger followed by a punishment for my failed attempts to kill him, but he is ignoring me, busy with his tasks.

He walks off deeper into the cave once again. The heavy scraping sound on the stone floor comes from there, rising, coming closer and soon Rafe comes into view, dragging a large metal crate towards the centre of the cave.

That's it now. That's definitely my coffin.

Surprisingly, this thought doesn't scare me. I don't feel the fear that I think I should feel. Maybe the stress of the last days, and in particular my last outburst, burnt me out, numbing me inside or maybe I don't really believe that Rafe is going to kill me.

He drags the metal crate closer, pushing it next to the wall and opens the lid. Methodically, one by one, he produces modern hi-tech camping gear from the crate: a neatly folded tent and a couple of sleeping bags, burners, pots, some wood tied by a rope, and climbing equipment.

He ignores me as he walks around, handling his tasks, and half an hour later the small tent is up, erected next to the opposite wall, while the burner is stoked up, warming up the cave, with a small kettle atop, ready to make some tea.

"Come Ariel", he grumbles without looking in my direction. "You need to keep warm and eat to keep your strength. It's warmer here and I've got tea and an energy bar for you."

I hesitate, unsure why he would care about me when I just tried to kill him. Twice. So I wait.

He raises his head, his brown eyes on me.

"Ariel, I promise I'm not going to harm you. I told you that before and I'll repeat it again. Never." He pauses. "No matter what you might do to me", he snaps.

I get up and cautiously shuffle towards the bright and warm circle around the burner. The hole in my jeans that I ripped with the knife lets the cold air in, freezing my butt cheek, but there's nothing I can do about this issue right now. I perch on one of the rolled up sleeping bags, stretching my frozen hands and feet towards the fire, unwrapping my dusty and battered sweatshirt off my waist and dragging it over my body, feeling a bit warmer.

Rafe hands me a mug, with steam rising from the top.

I reach for the cup and pull the mask off my face. The air smells tolerable deep in this cave, and the smell of the freshly brewed tea makes my mouth water. The hot tea and the warmth and glow of the burner loosen my muscles and I feel more comfortable with every sip. Comfortable enough to talk.

"Why am I here, Rafe?" I ask, hugging the warm mug in my hands.

Rafe settles on the other rolled-up sleeping bag across from me, with the burner heating up the air between us, resting his arms on his knees, looking tired and exhausted, staring unblinkingly into the fire.

"Right now it's the only place I can take you to keep you safe", he answers after a moment. "And even this place isn't going to be safe for long. After your very eventful weekend break at Baza's, he more than ever wants to keep his hands on you. And Mik'hael will simply get to you anywhere you go, and even I won't be able to stop him."

"Who's Mik'hael?" I snap.

I am frustrated with the never-ending stream of new information of the last few days.

"That was exactly what I was trying to talk to you about that day in school", he says, his brown eyes on me. The flames from the burner make them look like a liquid amber. Shadows from the fire are dancing on the plastic of his black armour and his folded wings behind his back look almost black, hidden in the shadows. It's funny how easily I take to seeing a winged human now.

Rafe fishes out a slim packet of First Aid cleaning wipes from one of his many pockets. With a sharp noise of pulled plastic, he rips its open, gets up from his seat and takes a few steps closer to me. Once next to me, Rafe kneels in front of me, raising his hand with a wet wipe to my face. I jerk my head away from him, my frightened eyes on him, watching his every move.

He holds my gaze and then, carefully and slowly, again reaches for my face with a wet wipe. He wants me to trust him.

I stay perfectly still.

My eyes dart between his face, his arm and the wipe, but I still jump up with a surprise at the cold sting of the wipe on my wounded face.

Rafe gently strokes my abused face with the wipe, holding my chin still with his warm hand. His touch is gentle and delicate, caressing and caring and with the proximity of his warm body next to mine and with his spine melting scent, I relax, enjoying this intimate moment.

I look into his face and I feel an uncomfortable pang of guilt, confronted by the red bloodied lines all over his throat and cheek, and before this guilt can take me any further, I mentally kick myself, reminding myself that I'm here against my will.

He lifts his eyes back to me, his gaze locked to mine. Unexpected annoyance takes over his face, pressing his lips into a thin, pissed-off line.

"You need to finally understand, and accept, the importance of what you have inside of you and how your childish behaviour and stupid decisions are affecting more than just you in this world", he snaps at me, suddenly all wound up.

He rises up, towering above me, crumpling the wipe in his hand and tossing it towards the crate.

"You're like a little child right now, convinced that the world revolves around you, thinking that you are invincible. Running around with no understanding of the magnitude of your decisions. You don't spend even two minutes thinking of the consequences and think that you'll be able to fix any mistake you make, and if not, oh well, no biggy", he is fuming, yelling at me now. His eyes narrow at me as he leans in closer, blocking the light from the stove and taking the air away from me.

"You can't act like an ignorant brat anymore. It is more than just you at stake in here, more angels than you can imagine have made sacrifices. It's bigger than you or even your world", he shouts, chastising me like I'm an ignorant toddler.

"Why are you yelling at me?" I slam the mug on the stone floor and jump up from my rolled sleeping bag, standing up, facing his wrath.

"What the hell do you want from me? Do you think *I* enjoy any of this?" I yell back at him. "Do you think I asked for this?" I'm fuming now too.

"Neither of us asked for this, yet here we are", he snaps, spreading his arms, inviting me to take in the latest mess I have landed myself in.

He closes his eyes, inhales and takes back his seat on the fat roll of a sleeping bag. He seems to be a tad calmer now.

He stretches his long legs in front of him, crossing them at the ankles.

"Neither of us asked for this", he raises his gaze to me. He is much calmer than he was just a moment before. "We are both tied to the essence, but this essence is more important than either of us. The fight for this essence is bigger than you or me, or our heartache, our wishes, our desires. This essence is the ultimate key to the end of your world as you know it and it can change our world beyond recognition."

He turns his gaze away from me, to the cave opening.

"Fate definitely has a very perverted sense of humour. To put such power with such weak and pitiful creatures, the ones who are killing each other over a book, who are killing their own environment. Destroying their own home. The ones who are burning and raping and stealing and cheating."

He raises his eyes to the ceiling.

"Thank you, An. The one time we needed you the most", he bitterly laughs, unamused, shaking his head.

He turns his head back to me.

"As much as I do sympathise with your predicament", he waves his hand dismissively, "not asking for it and all, it is what it is. You are here. With transcendent power in your hands so colossal that you can decide what will happen to all humankind, to your world. What will happen to your sister, to your family, to everyone that you've ever known. But you need to know everything that you are capable of before you make such terminal decisions, and before that, I will have to keep you with me and keep you safe. Even if I don't want to", he mumbles the last sentence under his breath and my hands itch to throw something at him.

"I don't know how much Sam has told you, or how much of it was the truth or how liberal he was with it, so I'll start from the beginning", he says, settling in for a story.

"Since the beginning of creation, our worlds were joined, your realm and ours. For millions and millions of eons, we've watched different forms of life birth and die in your realm. We never interfered, careful to keep our distance and the balance of our banded worlds. But a few million human years ago, a new form of life was born. Even to this day I don't know what possessed An to get involved with your kind, but she did."

"Wait, who is An?" I cut him, already falling behind that information wagon.

Rafe slams his mouth shut and looks at me for a second with an incredulous expression before answering.

"An is the creator", he recites like my teacher used to repeat the ABCs.

"What, like a God?"

"Yes, like a God", he snaps at me, "but the ultimate one."

"Sorry for asking", I huff, raise my hands at him, cheesed off. "I just thought that God was a man, that's all."

"Well, she's not a man", he cuts. "Can I continue?"

I just shrug my shoulders.

"She became very excited at the progress this new species was making. She started nurturing them, carefully sharing our knowledge, nudging their progress along. Over time, they became her children. But those children grew up and started to misbehave. Like a good parent, she punished them, warning them away from the shaded worlds they didn't know, but they were deaf to her pleas and one day, when more of her children were suffering, trapped in unending misery and she was prepared to end it all, risking the destruction of our realm as well, Mik'hael came forward with a solution to wipe the slate clean and save the pain for his mother. To give his essence to free the trapped.."

"Hold on", I interrupt him, "I'm not that strong in religious studies and I don't know half of these words, but even I can recognise a Biblical myth when I hear one. Do you really want me to believe that all this Biblical nonsense is real?" I practically snort out my scepticism at him.

"And do you think that *your* species are imaginative enough to come up with all these teachings on their own?" Now it's his turn to snort, only his is a dismissal. "There's a reason why all religions and teachings have core similarities, about what you call soul, heaven, hell, and higher primordial, or deities, or whatever you'd like to call them. You give them different names but fundamentally you've been telling the same stories over and over again since the dawn of time", he flashes his beautiful eyes at me. He's angry again.

"Okay, sorry. Please continue." I need him to finish his story so I can understand more of the mess I'm stuck in and hopefully get some information on how to get out.

"Mik'hael saved An's "children" but at the cost of his own essence. Unable to see her son dying for her weakness, An gave him a piece of herself, but that loss weakened her. Her weakness, in return, brought a division to our realm and two opposing factions were formed, both led by her children. One faction believed that your kind is a liability to our realm and insisted on making your kind to obey or to destroy it, which quite frankly is the same, as if you change the species to force the obedience, these species will not be the same. That one was led by grieving Mik'hael. The opposing faction, which believes in preserving the "free will" for your kind was led by Uriel, the beautiful and powerful daughter of An."

His face lights up with a dreamy haze when he says her name and a small smile lifts the corners of his lips.

"Uriel was the one who had unparalleled powers, only surpassed by her mother, even Mik'hael's powers were weaker. Uriel had infinite love in her and infinite wisdom. She was the one who could end and begin worlds, the one who will be called upon on Judgment Day." He snaps his gaze back at me. "And now you have Uriel's essence in you."

He finishes speaking and looks at me, waiting for the penny to drop. I don't know what to make of it, so I stare back at him. Whatever he sees in my eyes prompts him to continue.

"Originally, Mik'hael just wanted Uriel's support, for her to see his point of view, to join him in "wiping the slate clean" and ridding the world of your species, but as she was unyielding and continued to refuse to impose our species' will on someone else and deny them their own choices, he resolved to the final solution possible, to extinguish Uriel and her essence with it. Simplified to you, to kill her. That would be the ultimate finality for our kind."

"You know", I say, musing out loud, "always, for as long as I could remember, I had this dream. There are people in it, angels to be precise, and they hunt me and when I'm cornered, with no escape, a male angel comes into the room through the crowd of angels around me. I see his face, he's not hiding. He walks around me and then plunges his sword into my back, killing me, and I feel the pain and know that I'm dying. I always thought there was something wrong with me for having such a gruesome recurring dream, but now it makes sense", I look at him, as my words rush out at the possibility of an explanation of my craziness for all of these years.

"The essence brought you Uriel's memories, powers, wishes, the lot, and that dream of yours is the memory of Uriel's death. The man you see every night in your dream is Mik'hael", he says quietly and I think he's about to apologise, but then he changes the track.

He locks his heavy gaze back on me. "So far the essence was locked inside of you, sleeping. It was only active when you were asleep, seeping through your unconscious. But since that outburst a few days ago, the essence has come forefront and is now progressing to change you."

"Oh, I know, Sam told me", I shrug, glad to be ahead at least once.

"Oh, did he?" Rafe's pretty eyes are suddenly stormy slits. His jaw is set and I swear I can hear his teeth grinding.

"Did Samael tell you why he was interested in you? Did Samael tell you why he brought you to Baza? Did Baza tell you what he wanted from you?" He is practically hissing now, leaning in closer into the warm circle.

"Well, not exactly...." I mumble.

"He mentioned the essence and how it slowly changes me, and Sam said that he wants to protect me from Mia..." I sound absolutely gullible. "But when I overheard Baza making plans to use my sister to influence me, I ran", with the last sentence I try to sound more wise and proactive than I have been so far.

"Baza wanted you because of what Uriel's essence, now your essence, can do for him", Rafe is livid again, yelling at me.

"Uriel's essence can open the Gates of Arllu, or Hell, if you wish, and with it, Baza will have the infinite power to do whatever he pleases with your realm, and this time An won't intervene or stop him. His malakhims and ibnatums will overrun your realm. He will turn *your* world into the world you just saw and travelled through so adventurously", he bites out with sarcasm.

"Those lizards you saw will be burning, killing, and enslaving everyone in your realm, and nobody will be able to stop that army, not even us. That would be Baza's dream come true, Hell but on Earth, with seven billion souls to burn, to consume, to use. Wow, just imagine", he theatrically spreads his arms, his lips stretch in a menacing smile. "And fed on that power, he could take on Sarukh and he would probably win, and then *we* would fall."

He sobers, looking straight at me, "and Sam was just following Baza's orders. Nothing more."

I flinch, sucking in breath. It hurts and my face is burning as if I've been slapped. The bitter realisation is setting in.

The guy who I thought liked me, was nice to me only because he wanted to use me. Again. Seems to be the story of my life.

But I don't say that. I bury it in a shallow grave inside me, stamping on the trampled soil. No way will I show Rafe how much that hurts me. I've been reprimanded like a small child, and now I feel like one. I want to kick myself for being that naïve and trusting, but it's not his place to lecture me.

"And why are you here?" I hiss at him. "Everyone seems to want something from me, so what's in it for you?"

"Believe it or not, but some of us still concern themselves with preserving the balance", he snaps, his hot and burning gaze on me. "Some of us still remember that yours and our realm are connected and that an unbalanced universe can take us with it. And some of us still believe in loyalty and following the orders of your suzerain once you've pledged an allegiance", he barks.

"Okay, so maybe I screwed up. But what would you wanted me do? Stay put and wait for Mia to finish me off?" The tea is forgotten, now it's my turn to glare at him.

"And who the hell is Mia and what the hell does she want from me?" I yell at him.

Only the fire in the burner separates us as we glare at each other like two angry mountain goats ready to lock horns.

"Mia is Mik'hael's kyriote. She went to finish the job", he breathes out, his anger subdued again. His mood changes make my head spin.

He looks at his hands, uncomfortable.

"I'm sorry, Ariel. Sorry that I wasn't there when you needed me that I failed you when you needed me the most. Now I only hope that I'll be able to do my job fully and that one day you'll be able to forgive me for my failings", he says quietly, still studying his hands.

He carefully raises his head and looks at me. His beautiful hazel brown eyes are locked on mine, pulling at me. Their pull is stronger somehow, maybe the things I know, maybe the surroundings, but I feel the familiar vortex coming at me again, only this time it's gentle and soft, wrapping around me like a cosy blanket.

I hear a soft female laugh in my head and see Rafe's face, beaming and mesmerised, looking at me with utter adoration. I feel the warm sunshine on my skin and I can smell the salt of the sea, mingled with the sweet zing of fruits. I feel happy although I know that it's not me who is there. Rafe's hand reaches towards me, stroking my face with his knuckles. I lean into his caress, marvelling at the feeling of his skin on mine. At this moment I feel complete. No doubts, no regrets, no worries. He leans towards me and I stretch to him, like a flower to the sun, wanting for his embrace, eager for his kiss and as our lips are about to touch, I hear a quiet female's sigh, content and happy.

No. No.

I jerk my head back to free myself from his embrace, desperate to get some distance. I push at Rafe and he releases me.

I fall back. The sharp stone floor of the cave crushes my back, knocking the air out of me.

I lay on the stone floor, looking at the dark cave ceiling with weak yellow shadows dancing on it. My back really hurts and now it will definitely be purple and blue.

Groaning, I roll to my side. Rafe is still at his spot across from the burner where I last saw him before the vortex. Slowly, I push myself up. In a few strides, Rafe is next to me, helping me up, holding my wobbling body.

"What was that?" I croak.

"Sorry about that. That was your essence. It's connected to mine, has been for eons, and now it wants back", he answers apologetically.

I weakly push at him. He steps back and lets go of my arm.

I cough a small dry laugh.

"Very nice. Now I'm in the middle of some freaky love triangle. Perfect, just perfect."

I free my arm and put some space between us.

"I'm so sick of all this shit, you can't even imagine. My life is not my life. My memories are not mine and I'm even attracted to the guy I'm not attracted to. How nuts is that?" My voice cracks as it picks up volume.

"I'm pulled and pushed all over just because of some shitty essence. I've been locked up because of it. I had no family because of it, had no childhood because of it. Now I'm chased and threatened because of it. I was literally in hell because of it!" I'm yelling at him.

"If not for that essence, I would have had a normal childhood. I would never have had these dreams and my dad would've never left. My mum would never have had enough of me. She wouldn't have subjected me to all these therapists, shamans and healers that only made it worse! And I would've never run away from home and ended up on the streets! And then with them! Do you know what happened to me there?! Do you know?!" I yell, hysterical now and, through the veil of tears, I can see Rafe's surprised and frightened eyes on me.

I turn and walk away from him. He is smart enough to know to leave me alone.

"My life would have been different. Better", I croak over my shoulder, through choking tears. "And I wish I was there for Jess. I wanted to protect her from my life. I wanted her to be safe from my monsters and I failed her. I let them break her. And I was broken from the moment I was born."

We stand there in the cold silence of the cave.

"You know, sometimes I wish I was never born", I whisper for the first time out loud, something that was in my head for a while and I never trusted anyone, I was too busy being brave.

Tears stream down my cheeks and pitiful sobs escape me.

Rafe takes a few careful steps over and wraps his arms around me, stroking my hair, my back, murmuring something quietly.

"I just wish everything was different for me", I breathe into his chest. My tears drop one by one and roll off his armour.

"I know. And I am very sorry too. I wish I could take it away from you, but sometimes we don't choose greatness, greatness chooses us. I will help you. I'll teach you how to use the essence's powers to survive in our world and to survive what you have become", he says softly. "I promise you that I will never push myself on you or whatever the essence might want. Never."

We stand like this for a while until my tears dry out. We don't speak. He just keeps stroking my back and I feel secure and warm in his arms.

"We need to settle for the night, and tomorrow I need to teach you how to use your essence. We don't have much time. Even this place will be scouted eventually by someone looking for you", he says, unrolling both sleeping bags.

I climb into one.

Rafe strides over to the burner and turns it off. The deep darkness of the cave blankets us, but before I can get scared, Rafe's body begins to radiate a soft pearl luminescent glow, dissolving the dark around him. It's like a thin aura, like the northern lights on the crown of the Earth.

He drags his sleeping bag closer to mine and now I'm in the circle of his glow. He stretches on top of his sleeping bag, wings folded around his body, like a cocoon.

"Good night Ariel."

"Night, Rafe."

CHAPTER 17

The usual ending of the usual dream wakes me up with the usual jolt. I was hoping that once I knew the reasons behind it, it would go away. Not a chance.

Rafe is next to me, asleep and still glowing. The glow forms a halo around his head, now I can totally see where the paintings of angels with a halo around their heads come from.

He has taken his weapons, belts and 'plastic' armour off for the night and it's now just a pile next to him. But he's still fully dressed, even his black combat boots are still on. His brown hair is dishevelled and his relaxed, sleeping face looks younger and softer, not coinciding with his "assassin on a mission" get up. The red marks on his face that I gave him look less angry than yesterday and that makes me feel a bit better.

His hair has fallen over his forehead, covering his eyes. I want to move it, to stroke it away but instead I kick out of my sleeping bag and get up.

The cave is cold and dark. The smell that nauseated me earlier still floats in the air, but it's manageable deep in here. I wish I had a toothbrush and hairbrush now. Note to self: ask Rafe later if he's got any stashed away in his 'magic' crate. I shuffle slowly towards the cave opening, away from Rafe and our sleeping area.

As I come closer to the edge, the heat and smell of the outside grow stronger. I pull the top of my T-shirt over my nose and mouth, clamping my hand over as well, taking slow steps closer to the edge.

The view spread in front of me catches my breath.

I'm standing in an alcove, chiselled out in the wall of a mountain. Down below flows an ocean of hot and molten magma. The magma is alive, covering the surface of the land as far as the eye can see, but it doesn't solidify at all. It keeps on moving, creating small vortexes or standing still, bubbling, spurting hot fountains now and again. The stench of rotten eggs, burning matches and urine rises from it. I can taste the sourness on my tongue.

In the distance, three high snow covered mountains punctuate the horizon. And that's it. We seem to be the only life in here.

"That is the Valley of Hinnom". I jump up and almost slide down over the edge at Rafe's voice behind me.

"What are we doing here?" My words are muffled behind the fabric and my hand. "Wasn't there a better place we could have gone to?"

"This is the only place hostile for Mik'hael and Baza, as much as to anyone else" he answers, yawning, stretching his arms above his head. "It will be the last place they'll check in the search for you, but even that will only buy us a few days. The lakes of Hinnom, and weapons made with the lakes' fire, are the only way to kill an angel, so very few of us ever venture in here."

I take in the view.

Nice, cosy and warm; on the plus side, marshmallows will toast fast.

"If you are up, have some breakfast and we'll start with our training", he says over his shoulder at me, walking back into the cave.

"What will the training be about? How to glow?" I give his back a smug half smile, shuffling back into the cave.

"Among other things", he says, folding his sleeping bag.

He spins back to me, crossing the distance between us in two long strides, "your choice is really simple right now, you either learn how to fight and stand strong and independent among our kind, or eventually be consumed by the essence, completely. There will be no you anymore. If you decide upon the second route, I need to know now. I cannot afford to leave this essence unprotected in your fragile body anymore, not now, so I'll help you make the transition as gentle as possible. But these are your only options."

"I have a feeling that these were my only options from day one", I snap at him.

"Not really. The essence could have stayed dormant for years, potentially until the day you died, released painlessly from your body back into the ether, for the Ophanims to deal with it. But what happened that night, what happened to your sister, must have been the trauma your soul couldn't take. Great emotions were breaking you from within. Maybe you felt guilt, maybe anger, I don't know. But in that instance, your soul was breaking, ruptured from within, so the essence rushed to the forefront, protecting its host. If not for that moment, you could be still living your life. You always had the chance to have a peaceful life", he informs me.

"Yeah, right", I mumble under my breath. "Okay, so how do we do it?"

He walks back into the depth of the cave and I follow after him, grateful to get away from the stench.

"You have one of the five strongest essences inside you", he looks over his shoulder at me, "so instead of learning how to grow it..." He stops, reaching the sleeping area, and turns to me, "you shall learn how to instate it and take control of it, before it overtakes you."

He gazes at me, waiting for my reaction. I pull the shirt off my nose and shrug. "Okay".

He throws his head up to the ceiling, frustrated, raking his hair with his hands. "No. You don't understand", he snaps at me. His eyes are on me, exasperated that I do not comprehend the severity of all that he's saying. "It is not going to be an "oops" moment here! You will need to let go, totally. And then find the strength to take back control. There will be *no* second chances. Once it's done, it's done", he announces in a grave voice like a commentator on a radio, informing the nation that they're at war.

"I really don't understand what you are stressing about. You'll probably only be happier to have your lover back, won't you? It's me who should be worried about the process, not you", I shrug.

"It's not that simple", he grunts through his teeth, flashing his angry eyes at me.

"Okay, okay", I raise my hands up. I walk around him to my sleeping bag and start rolling it up.

I'm at a crossroads again. Sometimes it feels like my entire life is made up of crossroad after crossroad without a break, with no straight line ever. I'm about to make another decision, although my choices are slim and the odds are not that great either. I've got no way to get out, Rafe, wanting his lover back, has a very strong motive to sabotage this 'training', so I have to just blindly trust him here. My choice is between 'to trust, maybe get screwed and die' and 'don't trust and definitely die'.

But I'll be dammed if after everything I went through I just roll over and not put up a decent fight. I owe it to myself and to my sister.

"Listen, before I start my potential death trip, can we please have some breakfast?" I sit on my rolled up bag, looking at him. "A toothbrush and hairbrush right now would be much appreciated as well. Thanks."

He exhales as if he's just pushed a car. "Sure", he nods.

He is back at the burner, starting it up. The crate has a water canister in it, so the kettle is filled and back on the burner in no time. Rafe produces a pouch with a new toothbrush, toothpaste and a comb, a very minimalistic a-la Spartan travel kit.

I huff at the sight of the comb. A typical male way of thinking, to bring a comb for a girl with long hair, but I guess it's better than nothing. Once my teeth are brushed and a good portion of my hair is yanked out, Rafe calls me for breakfast.

He hands me a mug with hot tea and an energy bar. "Sorry, it's all we've got."

"That's okay." I take a bite of my bar. "So how are we going to do this whole essence training thing?" I mumble with energy bar in my mouth, crumbs spraying out. Rafe pointedly stares at my mouth, letting me know that he's waiting for me to finish chewing.

I swallow the bite, wipe the crumbs from my lips with my sleeve and take a sip of tea.

"Okay, I'm ready."

"First, we need you to find the essence inside. Then you will need to connect with it. You need to allow it to flow freely and then bring it under *your* control", he announces the course of action.

"How are you expecting me to do all of that?"

"I'll help you to connect with your essence, like when your essence reached out earlier to mine. I'll be able to guide you, but the final step is up to you. I'll be there to guide you and help you prevent it from consuming you."

He gets up, turns off the burner, and moves it next to the crate, against the wall. He moves his sleeping bag out of the way as well, leaving me sitting on my own in the middle of the cave. I giggle. It looks like he is clearing the room for a dance practice.

He kneels in front of me. His large purple wings are folded behind his back, the lower ones spread on the floor behind him. He takes my cup out of my hand, placing it on the ground next to us, his intense gaze on me.

"Are you ready?" he murmurs and I sober instantly.

The pull of his eyes is strong, hooked somewhere deep inside me, pulling me towards him. The idea of breaking this hold frightens me. I want to drive that hook deeper, to keep him connected to me forever. And slowly that pull increases, grows, vibrates somewhere inside me.

My mind is screaming at me, demanding to reach out and touch him, to stroke his face, to kiss him, to bathe in the warmth of his hold, and somehow I know that his embrace will make me happy, protected, whole again and found. A warm liquid unfurls inside me, spreading along my body, pulling heavy at my belly, and before I can reason with myself and remember that it's not actually me wanting it all, I reach out and caress his face.

His skin is soft and the smell of an ocean air fills my nose and my head. I stretch my neck, my gaze hooked to his lips. I can't seem to blink or pull my eyes away from his beautiful lips and my body stretches to him. Closer. Closer.

Our lips touch and all my senses explode in my head, scorching my mind blinding white. I lock my arms around his neck, but my hands are restless, my fingers are stroking his neck, diving into his hair, tugging, demanding him to get closer.

My sluggish brain registers the chorus of content female sighs, two females, two voices, completely in sync, completely content. Pictures in my head are rising and bursting like bubbles, opening, changing like a montage, me and Rafe in the bright white hall from my dreams.

We're kissing, laughing, in the middle of a circle of angels, who are celebrating with us, stamping their feet in a musical chanting rhythm. Their wings open and close in time with the beat, as Rafe lifts and spins me inside the circle. He is happy and so am I. I feel wings flutter behind my back, moving my waist long hair.

I feel strong and invincible and not because I'm next to him but because I know I'm more powerful than anyone else in this great hall.

Then the pictures in the montage change again and I'm somewhere else. Something ethereal shines with the rainbow of colours when the light hits it. It surrounds me. The creatures, thin and immaterial like a morning fog, float around me, but I know that they're scared and upset, and they want me to protect them. I feel something darker coming towards us.

The montage then changes again and I'm standing in a wasteland with a white fire sword drawn, sealed in my white armour from my dreams. I am standing ready to fight and I know that Mik'hael, Rafe and the others are ready for my signal, but it's up to me to break the swallowing blackness that is coming our way, to get us a lead.

Then short, almost ripped out, pictures of the battle flash inside my head, pitch black darkness around me as I swing my sword at it, and as my sword connects with something, a large gruesome, familiar looking lizard head rolls to my feet.

The bone deep knowledge and power course through me. Somehow, I know how the universe came to be, how the Earth formed and cooled off, and I was there watching it all and as this power and knowledge spread inside me with a white heat, it scorches me and I scream.

It feels like I'm ablaze, on fire, and I can feel my skin blistering, peeling off, turning to ashes. I want to run, to jump off the cliff, anything to relieve the agony, but I can feel Rafe's tight hold on me and I can't even raise my arms to shake the fire off my body.

"Shh, shh. Ariel, it's okay. You are okay. You need to find a way to control it. You have to", Rafe's calm voice commands over my fear.

I feel his presence again in my head, on my skin. He holds me, murmuring something in my ear.

My head fills with pictures of me now, and it feels like I'm watching my family's home movies. I see my first birthday, from the sidelines, like a guest. I watch my mum, glowing with happiness, laughing. She's the most beautiful and radiant I've ever seen her. My dad is there, filming me, the child, wonder struck by the sight of a large birthday cake with a big "1" candle alight. My mum blows it out for me and they both clap, laughing, kissing me on both cheeks. I don't have memories of them like that. I don't think I have ever seen them that happy.

Then I see a small wrinkled baby face, swallowed by layers of cotton. The baby is asleep, nestled in my mum's arms. My mum is tired and I can feel her sadness through her stretched smile. My dad stands by the window, his back to us, more interested in what he sees out there than his wife and his children.

And as I watch it all, I can feel Rafe next to me. He is silent, watching. He wants me to see my family, my sister, myself. He wants me to remember that I'm here as well.

A new piece of the montage comes in, the day I was taken away. I see Jess, screaming, kicking her little legs in our mum's arms, trying to get free. She reaches for me, bawling. Tears are running down her face, soaking her favourite unicorn T-shirt. She is desperate. She wants me, she wants me to stay.

And I'm there, being dragged away in the opposite direction by a woman in a suit and I push my feet at the floor, trying to hold on. She's trying to restrain me as I'm fighting her, refusing to leave my home, my family, my inconsolable sister, as the two of us, desperately trying to reach each other, are dragged in opposite directions by adults who 'know better'. And as the distance between our outstretched arms increases, I scream from the top of my lungs.

My sister's desperate face stains my mind. The image burns deeper in me than the raging white fire, that's taking over my mind, and I know that I'll never leave her again.

A cool blue wave comes over me, washing over the white blaze, pushing it back. And then they collide. Not like two fluids mixing, immersing in each other, but like two iron-clad solids, like a wall and a hammer. Stone chips are flying off the wall with every new strike of the hammer, and although the arm wielding the hammer is getting weaker, the wall grows weaker too.

The white blaze is weakening. It still blankets my mind, but now it's cool like a morning fog. It lets the blue wave wash through it. Now they're mixed together like a rain in a foggy morning up North, like elements of the same season. Both are stirring, floating, intertwined, getting to know each other.

CHAPTER 18

I open my eyes to the twilit darkness of the cave. I lay on the stone floor, my head resting on Rafe's thighs. He sits on the floor, his back against the wall next to the crate. He is asleep. His purple wings are wrapped around us and I feel cosy and warm against him.

Shadows from the camping lantern play on the cave's ceiling.

My muscles are weak, like after a long training session, and I am thirsty. I slowly raise my head, trying to sit up without disturbing Rafe.

"Hi", Rafe croaks next to my ear.

"Hi", I get up, not as gracefully as I wish, stumbling away. "Sorry, I didn't want to wake you. I just wanted to get some water."

I walk around Rafe to the crate. Surprisingly, the lid on the crate is featherweight, which doesn't seem to coincide with the size or thickness of the metal. A metal water canister is nestled inside the crate, in the corner, with its lid shut.

Unsure, I turn to Rafe. He's watching me.

"Go on. Try to lift it", he says, jerking his chin to the crate.

"You're crazy. This canister's at least what...forty litres", I reprimand him.

"Seventy. There's the nozzle at the bottom of the canister. If you take it out and then put it on the lid, it will be a lot easier to get the water", he says, reclining leisurely against the wall, his arms folded behind his head now.

"You *are* nuts", I glare at him.

"Go on. Try", he nods again at the crate.

I dive into the crate, my body bent in half over the side. I grab the canister's handles, prepared to break my bent back in half, and gently give the metal canister a cautious tug. The canister leaves the crate with ease, like an empty cardboard box.

I take it out and turn to face Rafe, mouth agape, still holding the canister by its handles, staring at him.

"You can put it down now", he chuckles.

I release the handles like they are on fire. The canister drops to the stone floor with a wall vibrating thud, narrowly missing my toes.

"What? How?" I can't seem to come up with anything coherent or to finish the sentences I start.

"I'm pleased to inform you that your transformation is complete", he gives a small old fashioned bow. "The strength you just demonstrated tells us that you are a fully-fledged angel now."

He effortlessly gets up and strides to where I stand.

"How do you feel?" he asks, studying my face.

"Okay, I think. Just thirsty and a bit weak, but otherwise fine", I say, side glancing at the canister, as if at any moment it might turn into a lion and bite my leg off. I'm still thirsty but I'm not sure about touching the canister again.

Rafe follows my gaze, picks up the canister and takes it back to the crate. He fills a mug with water and brings it back to me. I drain it in a few thirsty gulps and hand it back to him.

"More?" he chuckles.

I nod and he fills the mug again, bringing it to me. Once the mug is emptied for the second time, I feel that I can formulate my question.

"Okay, so I'm an angel. But am I still me?" I ask him.

"I think I am", I mumble to myself.

"You are", he smiles. "You still remember your family, right? Your life before?"

I nod.

"And besides", he lowers his voice, leaning in, "when you woke up, you didn't jump up on me, so I know for sure that you're still you."

I pull back.

"Good", I snap at him.

I chew on my cheek for a bit, thinking about what I'm supposed to do now.

"So apart from freaky strength, what else can I do now?" The thought pierces my mind. "Do I have wings? Can I fly?" I look at him in awe at the sudden mind scrambling possibility.

"Yes and no." His face is stern again. "You do have wings now, but they're underdeveloped and you can't use them yet. They won't hold your weight at the moment."

Once he utters the word 'wings', I start spinning on the spot like a cat chasing its tail, trying to see behind my back, and when I catch a glimpse of a transparent, membranous section of a dragonfly wing with bluish veins running through it, I stop spinning and reach behind my back. Sure enough, I can feel the fibre of the wings behind me.

I drop my hand, gaping at Rafe, unable to hear anything over the shock and the sensation of a pile of cotton wool wrapped around my pounding head. I watch Rafe's lips move but I can't hear a word, like we are divided by thick invisible glass.

"Ariel", he touches my arm and I jump up.

"What have you done to me?" I move my lips but cannot hear a word.

"What have you done?" I push it out of me louder, closing that short distance between us. My words come out of me in a strangled whisper.

"What have you done?!" I screech from the top of my lungs, but I can't hear anything. Blood is pounding in my ears, pumping through my body by my overworking heart, beating a deafening killer rhythm. I cannot see anything. A pitch black blanket of frenzy covers my vision, numbing everything but the rage.

I jump on him. I punch, kick, hit, claw at him in a blind frenzy of rage. Some part of my sluggish mind registers an animal howl around us, and before it has the chance to process the presence of a rabid animal in the cave with us, I realise that the howl is escaping from me.

But that is unimportant because the raging animal takes over. It doesn't want to stop. It only wants to kill. I can't stop. I don't want to stop. I punch and punch, grip and rip apart.

But suddenly I am squashed in a vice. With my arms bound to my sides, my legs have no ground to move. Only my head is still free, so I try to head butt anything that might be near, but it doesn't connect.

The trapped animal screeches and thrashes in the vice. Its echo bounces off the walls. The thrashing slowly exhausts the animal within and slowly it settles inside its cage, angry and resentful but calmer than before.

"If you are quite done", Rafe's composed, admonishing voice of a stuck up highbrow comes into my head.

As the red veil clears and I manage to focus my eyes on him, I immediately feel remorseful, his bulletproof vest is ripped apart, its chunks sprinkled under our feet. His T-shirt is torn, showing bloody scratches underneath, and now fresh new scratches mar his beautiful face.

"I'm getting increasingly tired of your outbursts", he reprimands me, fairly cheesed off, glaring at me.

"I'm not me", I sob, "I'm no longer human."

"You were never human", he cuts me, short and commanding. "You were born like that. You are finally seeing on the outside what you are really inside and you need to deal with it. It's a very simple choice, you either live or you die.

But either way, you will live as an angel and you will die as an angel."

I weep with his every spoken word.

It is one thing to be told by many people that you are something else, unique, unnatural, a freak, and quite another to be confronted by it with such finality. Only now I've realised that since all this hell has begun, I was running away from it and I was looking for my way back to my family, to my sister and even to my mum. Now everything has changed. With an absolute brutal clarity, I can see that I'm no longer human and if I'm to believe Rafe, I never was.

"Ariel", he calls to me and I jump up, startled. "The transition has given you wings, but they're still not ready. They're fragile at the moment. You need to work with your essence to complete the transition in full", he instructs, waiting for me to look back at him.

"How?" My voice is so weak that I wonder if he can even hear me. My gaze is frozen to the back wall, as I watch the black veins of the pigmentation run across the rock.

"The essence is coursing through your body now. It has become you. Now you are becoming your essence. You've opened the essence in your core and you were strong enough not to let it consume you, to not lose yourself. Now you need to draw on your strength and on the infinite resources of the essence, on all that's inside you and to use it how and where you need it most. You've managed to unlock the door to the library, now it's time to learn how to read. And I promise you that this part will be easier. At least a failure won't mean the end of you." He smiles, trying to lighten the mood.

I'm still standing there like the salt pillar of Lot's wife, studying the black volcanic rock. He comes closer, his face stern, as he gently lifts my chin up, gazing into my eyes.

"I don't want to pressure you but you need to do it fast", he mutters. "We have been here for three days now and its three days longer than we have. You need to at least grow your wings before we can leave this place, and you need to tap into your essence to access the powers of the essence and to be able to do everything that it can do."

"How do I do it?" I almost cry. He is telling me all these things he's expecting me to do, and very little about how to do them.

"Close your eyes. Try to relax". He reaches for my hand and puts it flat on my belly, covering it with his. "Here. Just above the belly button. Can you feel the heat and a vibration? Right here. It's where your essence has bound itself to you. Now try to find and to see it inside. It should look like a spinning wheel of sparkling white energy. Can you see it?"

As he speaks I feel a delicate vibration seeping into my hand from my belly and I strain to see 'inside' with my closed eyes.

I'm about to tell him that his nonsense doesn't work, when slowly through the murky darkness I can see a flicker of light coming closer. I gasp and open my eyes.

"Close your eyes", he barks and I slam eyes shut. "Find it again and stay with it."

And I look for it again, a weak glimmer through the fog.

The hum and vibration grow inside me, together with the brilliant light that approaches me, and I can make out the outline of a wheel, with energy and shine reverberating from it. I brace myself to be trampled under its ferocity and might, but when it fully emerges to confront me, it slams itself around me, trapping me inside its ring of power.

And the next second I am amongst the havoc of a violent earthquake.

People, in ancient clothes are running for their lives, screaming, looking for a safe place, while magma streams down their streets, catching up with the slower ones, trampling them, dissolving their bones, while they scream for mercy under its heat.

The buildings shake, turning to rubble, burying people underneath. Waves, higher than the tallest buildings, are rolling onto the city, crushing everything on their path, solidifying magma on contact with a sizzling hiss, drowning everyone who survived the earthquake.

The destruction and chaos is everywhere, cries of women and children, howls of men and pleas for mercy and me.... floating above it on my powerful wings, orchestrating the destruction, with no mercy to give. I'm not enjoying it. It's a cool detachment, composure from a job that needs to be done.

I wave my hand and the ground immediately settles under the feet of the survivors, waves collapsing on themselves as they gently lap at the survivors' feet and the corners of the buildings. The wave retreats, leaving behind glistening pools and puddles of standing water.

But the quiet doesn't last long for them and with another wave of my hand, the ground rips apart everywhere, like a straining fabric, releasing a horde of eyeless lizard-like creatures, similar to the ones I saw during my detour in the wasteland, but these are more feral and beastly. They don't have any weapons on them or gold neck collars. These are the wild creatures of the abyss.

And again, the air is filled with terror and screams.

The bare, greenish brown scaly bodies of the lizards move fast on all fours, crouched, darting from side to side, invading the landscape. From high above, it looks like the ground moves and sways like the ripples of a wheat field. Each lizard is the size of a large human, but these creatures are as far removed from humans as a fly from a bird.

Large and heavy muscles tense under their skin. The skinned, blind faces have only one hole, surrounded by uneven, razor-sharp teeth, which serves these creatures as a mouth. Slime and blood ooze out of them.

A set of horns run down their heads. Neither of them has eyes and that total blindness infuriates them, it's a weakness that controls them, making them vicious and bloodthirsty.

The tails behind the lizards are moving, whipping from side to side, looking for victims. Once a tail has found one, it coils around its prey, and accompanied by the lizard's victory screech and the human's cries for help, the lizard darts into the nearest rip in the ground with a surprising speed, dragging its victim down with him.

But some lizards are struggling to catch victims with their tails. Those raise their blind scaly heads, let out an angry piercing screech and a thick snake of a tongue leaves their teeth guarded mouths.

Their tongues are as thick and slow as lazy anacondas, dancing unrushed, swaying from side to side, seemingly uninterested in all the commotion, but the second they lock on the victim, they shoot out with a lightning speed, coiling around a human limb or torso and not letting go.

No one can escape them.

The expanse slowly quietens down. Only the occasional lizard's victory screeches are heard with fewer and fewer human voices left above the ground to cry for help. The eerie silence settles over the rubble of the now empty, but once great city.

I'm still there, floating above, overseeing the pandemonium I've created.

"Try to bend those powers to your will", Rafe's commanding voice cuts through the vision. "Send the power to your wings, finish the metamorphosis. The essence has shown you what you're able to do, now you need to show it what you *want* it to do. Will it, control it. It's your chance to turn the balance around."

With a low hum the ground vibrates under my feet like an overheating pressure cooker. The rumbling sounds of falling rocks cut around Rafe's voice.

"Control it", Rafe's voice grows urgent. "Send the power only to your wings."

The violent push sends me flying across the cave.

I open my eyes to a glow coming off my body, as came off Rafe's body last night.

Rocks, snow and ice fall past the cave's opening. The floor is shaking under our feet.

"Are you okay? Are you hurt?" Rafe kneels in front of me, but he doesn't touch me. His perfect marble forehead is creased as he darts uneasy glances over his shoulder to the rain of boulders past the cave opening, listening to the throbbing of the earthquake shaking the mountain.

Fear and agony must be showing on my face as Rafe tries for a reassuring smile. It's unsuccessful though.

"That's okay. Your essence controls all natural phenomena, including earthquakes, so just try to stop it. Calm it", he orders over the splitting sounds of cracking stones, the deafening boom of rolling boulders over our heads, and the deep rumble in the ground below us.

"I've killed them. I killed them all", I whisper, staring with unseeing eyes into a taunting, winking oblivion. I'm afraid and petrified of what I am and what I can do. "I killed them all", I whisper. "I killed them."

Is that what I am now? Is that what I'll become? A killer, a murderer of the innocent?

I'm rocking myself. My heart thumps a sprinting rhythm in my chest, sending drumming pulsations to my ringing ears and down to my tingling fingers. I can't seem to get enough air in my burning lungs, like someone's choking me, squeezing my throat with their iron fingers. I want to puke to relieve the expanding burning ball inside of me, but I can't even get enough air to do so. The world closes around me, pushing me into a small tight ball, leaving me with only the agony inside.

"I killed them", I whisper over and over again. "I killed them."

Suddenly I'm zapped, as if I touched an open electric wire, although I haven't moved. I cry out in shock and my eyes fly open to see Rafe on his knees in front of me, grinding his teeth and nursing his left arm. He swears under his breath with a long list of intricate and imaginative profanities.

I stare at him, woken by the shock, but my mind is clear.

The floor is vibrating under us. The rumble of the falling rocks is thunderous.

"Ariel, you are not a killer", he says through his teeth, catching his breath as he raises his eyes to me. "Well, not cold-blooded, anyway."

His gaze is locked with mine.

"These people were following Baza in pursuit of the power and the gold. They were selling their own children to him, invading neighbouring cities, murdering, burning, raping. No one could have stopped them but you. You have done what you needed to do, to warn off anyone else who decides to follow Baza's promises. You can't plant an orchard without getting your hands covered in manure", he heaves through his teeth.

He's still on his knees, nursing his arm, but his jaw slowly relaxes.

"Power isn't easy to handle or to live with, but it is always up to you, how you decide to use it", he says, gazing at me.

A new tremor violently shakes the mountain.

"Ariel, you need to calm this earthquake. Now", he commands.

"I can't. I don't know how to", I cry over the new mountain vibrating quake.

Spidery cracks are spilling out of the rock veins and over the cave's walls, breaking the rock. They are shooting up and down, zigzagging down the floor under our feet. The stench of the rotten eggs is getting stronger with every new tremor, slithering into the depth of the cave, and I start to cough.

A new tremor pushes the cracks on the walls wider apart, like shutters pushed open by a giant's hand. The grinding noise of moving stone lifts the hair on the back of my neck. The crack along the opposite wall is now wide enough to push a fridge through.

Under my horrified gaze, the cracks widen and while I'm still thinking on what to do, Rafe rushes at me, scooping me in his arms. The next second, the crack shoots down and splits open the floor, just where I stood a second ago.

And Rafe doesn't slow down.

He runs, with me in his arms, as I hold onto his neck for dear life. In a few long strides he reaches the edge of the cave and without a pause, takes to the air.

The second his foot pushes us off the cliff's edge, the face of the mountain which sheltered us for the last few days, slides down into the magma ocean below with a deafening roar.

As I look down at the ocean of molten lava below, I see all the way to the horizon, that the earlier, perfectly still and calm ocean of magma is now disturbed and unsettled, moving erratically, creating high waves and large vortexes.

Rocks are falling behind Rafe's back into the lava below. His wings pushing the air, desperate to get the distance between us and the lethal mountain. But we are not fast enough.

Another quake sends the entire mountain down. A large cloud of dust shoots up in the air, engulfing us, blanketing the faint light, blinding and suffocating us.

We are surrounded by the noise and turbulence in the air. Rocks are shooting and flying around us and once the large boulders start falling into the lava ocean below, toxic pillars of magma shoot up around us, like deadly cannonballs of fire.

We are bombarded by the lethal missiles from above and below, toxic lava shooting from below and boulders falling from above. Occasionally they collide and then a rock, embraced by magma, dissolves into it with a tiny hiss like those dissolvable aspirin tablets dissolve into water. Both of them, now as one, fall down, called by gravity.

Rafe performs the miracles of aerobatics. He ducks and swings, swerving erratically, turning at an angle and bending at the waist, dodging the lethal missiles while pushing at the air with his four purple wings.

I can feel Rafe's grip on me slipping.

I tighten my arms around his neck, and before I can change my mind, I push my back at his arm and swing, hooking my right leg around his torso. His eyes briefly meet mine, but he is too preoccupied to question my shenanigans.

I wriggle on him and hook my left leg around his waist. Now I'm straddling him, my face to his, my legs hooked behind his back, my chest to his.

I duck my head in, closer to his chest. His breathing is laboured next to my ear.

"Okay, we have to move to Uras now", he yells over the sound of the commotion. "It's still not ideal, but we have no choice now."

I just nod.

Suddenly, the tall fiery pillar ejects from the depth of the magma ocean below, shooting high.

It shoots behind Rafe's back. I feel the heat of the fire on my face as I tuck my head behind Rafe's chest.

And then Rafe screams.

Raw agony of pain billows above my head and we suddenly drop. We freefall, like the stones around us and now I scream, desperately clinging to Rafe's body, which is falling down with me.

My throat is raw from the screams. I feel the rush of the air past me, which pulls at my clothes and pushing my hair above me and I think for the first time in my life, really believing, that I'm about to die.

Rafe is still howling above my head. Our agonising screams are joined by the surrounding cacophony of death. I feel the jarred movement of Rafe's left shoulder under my face and hear the swish of his two left wings still cutting the air, but that does nothing to slow our drop and we're still falling.

People who tell you, that you can come up with a rescue plan when you are about to die, that your brain comes up with clever solutions, driven by adrenaline are lying to you. All that your brain allows you to do is to accept the inevitable while still trying to grab hold to something around you. And that's it! No calculation, no schemes or plans, just the knowledge of impending death and mind numbing terror.

The fall is so rapid and jarring, and the shock is so great that it has wiped my mind blank, leaving only animal instincts behind. I slam my eyes shut.

Suddenly, we are both yanked up, like a fish snatched out of water. The pull in the opposite direction is so strong that my hold on Rafe loosens and I slide down his body.

I open my eyes.

The rainfall of stones around us died down and now only the dust cloud lingers heavy in the air, reminding me of the collapse of the mountain just a second ago.

The ground still rumbles and vibrates below us like the empty stomach of a hungry giant, but the magma below us is settling down now, bubbling and simmering.

Rafe is no longer screaming above me. The quiet has settled around us. In all that chaos I slid all the way down Rafe, now holding onto his waistband, my legs wrapped behind his knees, face pressed against his rock-hard stomach muscles.

I raise my head, warily looking up at him as I make my careful attempt to climb up his body. I never was good at PE and the skill of climbing a rope always eluded me. The highest I've ever managed to climb was to the level of the glaring, disappointed PE teacher's eyes.

"Sorry", I say looking up at him apologetically. "I was afraid I might fall holding onto you like that."

"That's okay", he grunts through gritted teeth.

Rafe's eyes are on me, watching me closely. He is in pain and he cringes with my every move but he says nothing as he regards my pathetic wriggles up his body, as I slowly make progress.

If we were on the ground I would be mortified by my position on him, now wriggling there, but for now I ignore any thoughts like that and keep on with my climbing. I'm so afraid of the fall and of hurting him that my clumsy arms and legs take forever to bring me up.

Once my face is next to his again, I can see large beads of sweat covering his face and rolling down his temples. Only his two left wings are moving the air behind his back.

"How do you feel? How are your wings?" I wonder how long he will be able to hold us mid-air with his injured wings.

"Hurts... like crazy", he stammers. Trying not to hurt him with any more of my movements, I peek over his shoulder to see his injured wings and gasp.

There are no wings there, at all. The two black charred stubs are poking from behind his back where a pair of glorious purple wings had been.

We float quietly, each preoccupied with our thoughts. Minutes tick by.

I feel horrible. Guilt claws at me for what happened to his precious wings. I don't know what that will mean for him now. Will he be left without his wings forever or will he be able to heal and somehow re-grow them? I sure hope so.

"I'm so sorry about your wings", I whisper. He says nothing. His eyes are closed as we float in the air. "Thank you for keeping us alive", I murmur, dazing up at him. "I really appreciate what you've done for us."

"Thank *you*", he mutters, pushing words out through the pain. He lifts his tired lids slightly, gazing at me. "It's you who saved us."

"What are you talking about?" I try to smile at him. Bless him for his gallantry. He doesn't want me to feel guilty and useless.

"*You* are flying us right now, not me." He looks at me with his soft brown eyes, all serious and matter-of-fact.

His spoken words are ever so slowly churning in my head, sinking into my brain like through a quicksand. I wonder what is showing on my face as Rafe gives me a short confirming nod.

Oh. Shit. Now what happened?!

Somewhere at the back of my mind, the little composed part of me, rolls her eyes at me, telling me to finally get a grip and to get used to all 'out of this world', an unbelievable fairy tale shit that I've been bombarded with since that fire at school. God, I only wish I knew that morning that it would be my last 'normal' morning. I would have taken longer shower, had Paula's fried greasy breakfast. Okay, maybe not that, but something just as normal. I never thought I would miss an ordinary day of my ordinary life.

'*You are not in Kansas anymore, Dorothy*'. No shit, Sherlock!

Carefully, I turn my head, craning my neck, desperate to see behind my back, while still holding on to Rafe.

But I don't even need to turn my head far to be able to see immense purple angel wings behind my back. I watch, mesmerised at the steady and measured opening and closing of my wings behind me.

The feathers are the deep purple colour with a touch of gold shimmer, like they've been brushed over with golden glitter. They are much bigger than Sam's or even Rafe's. I think they are even bigger than Baza's. I'm sure I can shelter both of us in my wings.

We are floating in the air, held above the ocean of death by *my* wings. I can't take my eyes off them. I want to touch them but I'm afraid to let go of Rafe. Although Rafe said that it's me who's holding us above, I still can't comprehend it.

I turn my head back to look at Rafe. I should say something. No doubt there are questions I should ask, but my head is empty, and only one thought is rolling with a rattle in its vast emptiness: *My wings are very pretty.*

"You're doing really well", he stammers after a while, watching me. "I'm very proud of you. Even if it means that you had to destroy one of only four mountains in Hinnom." His white lips strain into a small smile. He is really in pain.

"I'm so sorry about your wings. What can we do? How can we get you some help?" I ask. I spin my head left and right but all that I can see is the ocean of magma to the horizon. Two of the three remaining mountain peaks are barely visible from here, jarring the line of the horizon.

"Shall we fly there?" I nod in the direction of the peaks.

"We can if you want to take a break, but that is not our destination now. We need to get to Uras. I think Baza and Mik'hael will be here any moment now after your little rattle and jingle."

His lopsided straining smile wakes the guilt again. Heat colours my cheeks.

"Okay. So how do we get there?" I sound more eager and upbeat than I feel. "Which direction do I fly to?"

"You don't even need to fly", he starts with a soft chuckle but stops abruptly, wheezing in pain. "That's the beauty of your powers. Once you have your wings, your powers are able to bring you anywhere you want to be, as long as you've been to that place before", he heaves, stopping now and again to gather some air. I'm not a doctor, but it looks like he's getting worse. I'm afraid he might pass out.

"And I will be able to get help with my wings there", he heaves, sweat rolling off his forehead. I reach out my arm and wipe his face with the back of my sleeve.

"But how am I supposed to take us to Uras if I have never been there? You just said it yourself that I should've been in the place at least once to be able to get there", I try to sound calm and level, like Rafe was before, but my voice spikes with alarm and I have to cough, to compose myself and to bring my voice down. He is probably already delirious, as there's no other plausible explanation for offering something that he already knows I can't do.

"I have been there", he grates through his teeth. "I can start getting us there, but you will need to push us through. Like jump starting a car. I will ignite it, but your powers will transport us there."

A coughing fit starts deep in his throat.

"Can't we just get back to my home? I've obviously been there and you can help transport us there. Maybe we can get you some medical help—"

He glares at me and I break mid-sentence.

"And you'll risk bringing Baza... and his malakhims to your home... to your sister just because you're feeling homesick? While you can't protect them?" Rafe is incredulous. His reprimanding tone annoys me but I know that he's right. A wet cough rumbles his chest and once his coughing fit is over, I answer.

"No", I grumble with a sigh. "Of course not."

"Good", he exhales. His eyes stay closed and I wonder if he's about to pass out. "I was worried that you were too childish for your new responsibilities."

He opens his eyes. The whites of his eyes have turned bloody red. His usually hazel-brown irises are barely visible on the backdrop of red. Blood, like tears, pools in the corners of his eyes.

I pull my head away from him, petrified, afraid of him and afraid to fall, wanting to let go and needing to hold on.

"Rafe", I stammer. "Your eyes..."

I don't know how to finish this sentence because I don't even understand what is happening to him. I don't know what I am expecting him to do, but I'm desperate for him to speak, I need to know that he is alright.

"Yes, I know. Now we're really running out of time. You need to open your wings as wide as they'll go and try to reach my two remaining wings. Keep our wings connected. Don't move."

A heaving cough stops him and a thin ribbon of blood snakes out of the corner of his mouth.

"Keep them connected", he stammers with the gurgling sound of the blood in his mouth, gazing at me with bloody unseeing eyes. He closes his eyes and this time bloody tears spill over, travelling down his cheeks.

I want to scream. I want to pull away. Shock rakes me and my mind picks up the pace.

I can't pull away. I'm not sure if I'll be able to hold on to him, but I have to try to do what he said. Worse comes to worst, I will have no choice but to get us where I know and so far with my limited life travels it is either my mum's house, the children's home or Baza's place. But then again, I don't know the technicalities of that sort of travel. My mind is like a ball in a pinball machine, bouncing from one thought to another.

I push the sickening thoughts and prospects of being stranded here to the back of my mind, forcing myself to concentrate on the task at hand.

Okay. Open my wings, then touch his wings. I can do that.

Rafe's body is suddenly heavy in my arms. His head lolls to the side as blood snakes down his chin and drips onto his chest.

"Rafe. Rafe." My trembling voice calls to him in the silence of the hell, but Rafe doesn't answer.

Breathe, breathe. I try to stamp out the panic in me. *Easy. Open wings, touch the wings.*

I take two flimsy shallow breaths.

I will my wings to open but nothing happens. They continue to move behind my back, rhythmic, unrushed, relaxed, belying the panic in my head. I don't know how to control them, how to make them listen to me. I strain, curving and bending my back, shrugging my shoulders, even doing a little jig with my hips but nothing happens. Frustration boils.

"Open. Open, damn you", I scream over the silent terrain. The left wing jolts, then opens, slams immobile, pressing flat against my back.

The moment my wing stops its movement, we fall, tumbling down, spiralling, spinning on our own axis, held up only by the movements of my right wings and a bit of a pull, provided by Rafe's still functioning wings.

My petrified scream fills the silence around us. I scream from the top of my lungs. Falling, head first, like a diver, I see the blanket of magma rushing towards us, but I can't stop the fall or straighten our descent.

The reflex to flap my arms like wings is so overwhelming that I have to grab hold of Rafe to make sure that I don't drop him. In a panicked frenzy, I move my shoulders up and down, up and down, screaming, falling.

But I managed to hold us up before.

I close my eyes, trying to block the rush of the wind in my face and its whoosh in my ears, counting. 1,2,3,4.... 13 and slowly I feel the change in our trajectory. It's not a harsh tug, but the soft curve of a controlled aircraft.

I open my eyes to see us doing half a loop, turning and climbing back up on my wings away from the deadly ocean of fire. My wings move again with a calm and even rhythm.

I throw my head back and roll my eyes skywards. Relief floods me and the desire to cry is so overwhelming that I start counting again. I can't come apart, not just yet. Besides my arms are busy holding Rafe so I wouldn't be able to wipe my running nose once I start.

Once calmer, I look around, racking my brain how to touch my wings to Rafe's. The only way I see is to slide around him, closer to his back, and to synchronise the rhythm of our wings so they stay connected while holding us in the air.

Rafe is still unconscious and heavy in my arms and, seeing him like that, limp and lifeless, I need to push to overpower the suffocating panic.

I'm scared. I feel so alone, lost, out of my depth in this bizarre and hostile place.

I take a practiced calming breath and ever so slowly, I slide sideways on Rafe. It's like sitting on top of a tree and moving around its trunk, one slip of a foot, a loose grip, and you will be falling. Only here I will drop Rafe.

Now I am almost at his back. His two left wings are still moving about. I sit there for a few minutes, watching their measured flexes, feeling the tempo of their beat, willing for my own to synchronise with his, and when I feel that I'm ready, I twist sideways, allowing my wing to touch his.

A sharp zap of energy shocks me.

I almost let go of Rafe again. I really begin to wonder about his chances of survival out here with me. If I knew how easily I could kill by accident, I would've taken Baza or Butcher with me on this trip.

I adjust my grip on Rafe, wriggle to hook my legs better, and go again.

I'm zapped again like I'm touching bare electric wires. I grit my teeth, holding on tight. The power is raking me, my body shakes and my teeth do a crazy chatter, but with the last of my strength, I hold on to Rafe's body. My legs are hooked around him, twisted at my ankles, my arms tight around his strong body.

Somewhere behind my back, I feel growing heat and a second later, I am blinded by the light of an explosion so strong that its wave throws us through the air. I slam my eyes shut.

It's like a nuclear bomb exploded behind us.

We tumble through the air, a tangled mess of limbs and bodies, and a second later we collide with a stone wall.

CHAPTER 19

The collision knocks the air out of my lungs, but my fall is padded by the softness of my feathers around me.

I lay disoriented on the hard stone floor. The air no longer has a stench of sulphur and urine, but smells of sea salt, sun and fruits. That's how I always imagined holidays would smell.

Balmy light warms up my skin and a soft breeze caresses and moves my hair. I'm comfortable and warm, and don't really want to get up, although my arm is bent at a weird angle under Rafe's heavy body and a corner of my wing is trapped under him.

I carefully lift his leg, freeing my wings and lean over to him.

"Rafe", I whisper above him. "Rafe, can you hear me?"

He is unconscious and unresponsive. Blood keeps trickling from the corner of his mouth, soaking into his shirt. His cheeks are stained with dried and crusted blood.

A sudden rush of approaching footsteps fills the hall, bouncing and echoing off the walls. They're running at us. A male's raspy voice is shouting commands in the language I heard at Baza's place.

I roll to the side, trying to push Rafe's body off my arm, so at least I can get up and meet the new problem head on. I'm on my knees, busy pushing at Rafe's limp body, when footsteps break off around us, and the next instance my wings shoot out wide open around us, creating a purple canopy over our bodies. My wings seem to be living a life of their own.

I raise my head.

We're surrounded, trapped in a tight dome by a crowd of angels. Most of them are on the ground, but a few hover on their wings above, obscuring the warm light.

I look up, waiting for their move, while calculating my options. An escape would be problematic, I would need to fight my way out of this tight circle first, and with this number of angels I don't have much chance. I don't even have a weapon.

Negotiations it is then.

The older looking male towers above me just a foot away, at the forefront of the group. The authoritative air around him and his military stance give away a warrior in charge.

His silver grey hair, cut short atop his head, is plaited into an intricate braid, which rests over his left shoulder. Dark, royal blue tunic and trousers peek from under his silvery white armour. The sleeves of his tunic are covered in intricate heavy silver embroidery, which looks like the tangled mess of some ancient hieroglyphs, symbols and images, some of which look strangely familiar. A short thick sword and double-faced axe hang heavily from the belt around his waist.

His arms are folded at me as his sharp iceberg blue eyes scrutinise me from under grey bushy eyebrows. Two stern deep wrinkles run from his nose to the corner of his mouth. The four icy blue wings behind him match his piercing blue eyes perfectly. An intelligent gaze bounces between me and Rafe, taking in every detail.

But I'm checking out the surrounding crowd as well.

There are mainly males in here but I spy a few female angels among the group. All the angels are breathtakingly beautiful. The female faces look fragile and innocent with full red lips, butterfly lashes and glowing skin, whilst the males look formidable with the handsome faces of marble statues of the Greek gods.

All of them are dressed in floating clothing of blue tones, ranging from the royal blue of the angel in charge to the subtle, almost white, of a few females. Intricate silver threaded embroidery spills over every angel's clothing, covering the edges of their tunics and dresses, shoulders, or their entire sleeves. All the angels have long hair, which is either plaited or flowing freely in the breeze.

A few males among the group wear silvery-white armour over their clothing, which so scarily reminds me of my armour in my dreams, and against my will my eyes keep coming back to the polished, reflecting surface of their breastplates. These angels have swords and axes attached to their belts.

The angels are quiet around us, studying me with guarded and surprised expressions, as if they didn't expect any guests, let alone me. Their eyes dart between me and Rafe's bloodied body, barely visible under my wings. Silence hangs heavily around us.

My worn out mind miserably spins, looking for a solution out of my newly acquired mess, when the old warrior extends his arm to me, bowing slightly in, offering me assistance to get up.

And as if on a cue, one by one, they raise their right arm and touch their four fingers to the middle of their forehead and then bow, deeply, to me. The moment freezes, suspended in time, as they all stand, unmoving around me with their heads down. Only the general is no longer bowing, but stands straight and tall in front of me.

"Welcome home, Uriel", he says with a little nod. "Or would you prefer me to use your human name?" he asks after a moment, drawing his brows.

"My name is Ariel. Not Uriel", I bristle.

"Of course. As you wish." He bows again, unfazed by my attack. "We are very happy to finally have you with us."

The angels raise their heads. Their bright eyes gaze openly at me from every direction and I even spy a few delighted, awed smiles. I shift uncomfortably, shocked by such a merry reception.

Suddenly, I sense a commotion behind my back and spin in time to see angels swoop in on Rafe.

"Oi", I yelp, rushing back to Rafe, but I'm blocked by a wall of bodies. "Let him go!"

As I try to push through the wall of angels, my wings shoot out wide open, and with that, the angels around me stumble and fall away, sneaking shocked glances at my wings as if they are poisonous.

Maybe they are?

"That's all right", a commanding baritone calls behind me. "They are going to take him to the revivification sanctorum. He needs help."

I spin back to him, about to argue, when a strong gust from dozens of large wings pushes at my back and as I turn again, I see Rafe's broken body being taken up to the sky by six angels.

My gaze follows them, as they take to the sky and, for the first time, I notice that this hall has no ceiling. Grey polished stone floor, white painted stone walls and no ceiling. The high and imperiously cloudless light blue sky is open high above us and I stare at the endless sky, speechless.

"I'm glad that Rafe has managed to bring you to us. We were all concerned whether you would choose to join us", the commander says behind me.

"I want to go with Rafe", I demand. "I need to be with him."

As he is gone, I feel weirdly unsettled. Of course I feel scared of the unknown, but it's more than that. I'm absolutely petrified for him and feel the growing distance between us, like a physical pain which increases with every minute. That new feeling disturbs me and it takes a lot out of me to pretend, to close off my expressions, pushing that feeling to the back of my ever so growing queue of shitty issues I have been dealing with lately.

"I understand and you will, but I can assure you that he is being taken care of, whereas we have more pressing issues to discuss", he bows again. "If you would like to follow me."

He takes a side step, gesturing with an open arm to the corridor behind him.

"As soon as you explain where I am", I snap, folding my arms over my chest.

He bats his eyelids at me in confusion, as two deep wrinkles fold between his brows, matching the ones around his nose. But as I remain silent, he speaks.

"It's Castle Uras in Sarukh. Your castle, Beyelai", he bows again. For god's sake, I wish he would stop bowing and just explain everything properly.

"Okay. And who are you?" I sigh, continuing my interrogation.

"I'm Chamuel, my Beyelai", he bows again, deeper this time, placing his four right fingers to the middle of his forehead.

"And that is supposed to mean something to me?" I shrug my shoulders.

Confused and frustrated wrinkles cover his forehead for a moment longer, before his face relaxes, as if a thought has caught him.

"Of course", he mumbles to himself, "Ophanims warned me that there will be relapses during the transfer and a lot of knowledge might be lost..."

"I'm Chamuel, my Beyelai", he starts again. "I am in command of your Meh'ita, your apocalypse army of twelve thousand angels. I am here to protect Uras, you and to follow your orders", he bows again, his fingers again touching his forehead, "and I would like to explain more to you, but right now we do have a more pressing issue that requires your attention."

"What is it?"

"I had better show you, my Beyelai", he says. "If you would please follow me."

He sets off down the bright sunny corridor, which strangely tugs at my memory.

I don't know why he doesn't offer for us to fly, maybe he isn't sure if I can use my wings, maybe some other reason, but we walk down the corridor and then up three flights of a wide spiral staircase, carved out of solid stone with wide stone banisters following it, before coming to an open ledge, suspended high over the emerald rolling hills.

Or what I know should be there. Somehow I remember that beautiful shade of green, stretching into the horizon like a plush carpet, and the joy I used to find in flying over it.

But right now, the greenery of the hills is swallowed by a living dark sea of moving bodies, covering the ground to the horizon.

The sinister sea breathes and ripples, and when I sweep my gaze over its beastly enormity, I childishly want to crawl under my blanket, tightly close my eyes and pretend that all of it isn't real.

The morbid army is paraded in front of me, spread under my feet. Its enormous volume is divided into sharp segments of different forms and colours.

At the forefront stands a small group of angels, no more than a hundred, sealed in uniformed granite grey military modern hi-tech gear. Only the different muted colours of their wings break the solid grey segment. The sun fails to reflect off their grey breastplates and the pauldrons, and it feels as if the light has been *absorbed* by them. They stay in the perfect military formation, immobile, their arms folded behind, their wings shot up above them.

And scarier still is the fact they look faceless. All of them wear a grey mask which fits like a second skin, completely hiding their faces, leaving only their eyes visible. The silent power and motionless of their bodies scare me more than the rowdy crowd of torturous wasteland lizards behind them.

There are twenty, maybe forty times more lizards from the wasteland in here than warrior angels. Their gold spiky collars and bracelets wink in the sun with their swaying, shifting movements. Blood encrusted whips hang lifeless from the dirty, ragged pieces of fabric that are wrapped around their waists, serving as belts and loin cloths.

As one, their eyeless, scaly heads are directed to the sky, as if these blind creatures are trying to see the glorious sky above or to smell the sweet air.

Blood stains some of the lizards' faces. Some blood has crusted over, while some is still wet, running thickly out of their razor teethed holes, down their chins, dripping to their slime-coated bare chests.

Now and again the lizards' thick tongues escape their blind holes, searching for freedom and then it's easy to spot the ones who recently fed, as their tongues are thickly covered in red sticky blood.

The lizards at the back are scruffier and not as nourished as the ones at the front. The scaly skin is strung tighter over their skeletons, the rags over their waists are dirtier, and they don't have whips. Their necklaces and bracelets are made of dull, blackened, rough iron. The iron's jagged edges cut into their skin and black blood trickles down their necks and wrists.

These lizards are not as organised as the ones with gold bands. They don't stand upright and seem agitated, moving erratically on all fours, bumping blindly into each other, hissing, their tongues flying out.

Sometimes a high pitched shrill would slice the silence when one would bite another with its tongue. But somehow the wild herd keeps to its boundaries, propped tightly from each side by a few rows of organised lizards with golden accessories.

The largest division of this army is spread wide to the horizon and at first glance it looks like a slimy, moving brown mass. Only looking closer, am I able to see the tangled mess of millions and millions of brown worms, sliding, crawling over each other.

Dozens of stacked rings of secreted brown skin cover their bodies, flexing with each move. The worms' tubular naked bodies are gigantic, not your average sized earthworm. These are five to six feet long and as large as small dolphins.

And just as I think they are just over inflated earthworms, a worm lifts its head up and a pair of aware and intelligent human eyes shines at me.

I clamp my hand over my mouth before I scream or throw up.

All these worms have human eyes.

My wings shoot open.

The legion below is paraded in front of me to demonstrate its strength and magnitude. And at the forefront of this circus of horrors is a familiar, round body with a neat crop of silver hair above the grey suit.

"What is this?" I whisper, stammering through the nausea, waving my hand at the army below, at the 'worms', and turn to Chamuel, but before he can answer, a familiar voice rises above the landscape.

"It's nice to see you again, Ariel. You look truly glorious with your new wings, the archangel you were always meant to be", Baza calls up to me and the wind carries his voice with ease. "And they suit you rather well, I couldn't be prouder. But I have to confess, I'm a bit disappointed in you, to leave without saying goodbye after everything we've done for you..." He shakes his head at me, tutting softly, like a displeased grandpa.

"But it's still not too late for you to return to us. Your battle is coming and with that small army behind you, you will never withstand the force of Mik'hael, but my army will. Look how vast and glorious my soldiers are!" He calls to me, spreading his arms wide. "And there will be many more!"

I am so bone tired.

I stand here and listen to more of his lies, but all that I want to do is to curl up in my bed, throw a blanket over my head, and pretend that the last few days were just a bad dream, a nightmare, from which I can wake up at any moment.

And I desperately want a shower and a change of clothes. My black sweatshirt and black jeans are no longer black, covered in a thick layer of caked-in dust from the wasteland and they reek of the ammonia of the magma ocean. I want to shower, to wash my hair and to brush my teeth, but instead I stand here, listening to more of Baza's bullshit. I don't have the energy for that little scheming tango that he wants me to dance with him.

I cut to the chase.

"I saw plenty, Baza, thanks", I shout into the wind. "You used me! You lied to me at every turn and you forgot to mention so many important details. Like the wasteland for example, and who you are." *And Sam.* My hands ball into fists. I wish I had a stone in my hand right now, to hurl it at Baza's smug, lying face.

"And I can see my mistake", Baza calls back, raising his arms towards me, like an over acting fat woman in opera. "I underestimated you. I thought you were weak but now I see that you're strong and able. That's why I am here and showing you my entire army. I'm sure that with this knowledge, you'll be able to make the right decision."

"And what decision is that?"

He takes a step forward, flashes his wings open and takes to the sky on his powerful big wings. He flies towards me and, instinctively, I take a step back on the ledge, while Chamuel takes a step forward, blocking me with his body.

In a silent gesture of warning, Chamuel draws his liquid-fire sword, but Baza ignores it, as he stops mid-air, floating leisurely, level to the ledge, his face close to mine. His beard is neatly trimmed, his hair is combed and soft wrinkles fold in the corners of his eyes, as if he is about to smile, but I know better, I have seen the calculated evil behind this gingerbread house.

"Your choice is very simple", he says, floating in the air across from me. "Mik'hael is coming for you. Your army is weak and will never win against his. I probably would not be wrong in assuming that you are not in full control of your powers, so you either stand against Mik'hael and die for something that has nothing to do with you, for a battle you hadn't begun, or you can join me, finally and fully. You now know everything. You know what I want and what I'm prepared to do for it. I'm offering you a partnership in changing the worlds."

"At the cost of all humans", I cut, taking a sidestep around Chamuel.

"What are these humans to you? When did any of them do anything good for you? I truly fail to see your compelling attachment to these creatures." He shakes his head at me.

"For starters, I am one, my sister is one", I start, but he raises his hand to interrupt me.

"You are no human, my dear child. Your glorious wings are the glaring proof of this. With regards to your sister, I would be honoured to have her living with us and, you have seen my place first hand, so you can be assured that we will have more than enough space for all of us and eventually..." He leans in closer dropping his voice as if sharing a secret, "we'll have worlds and worlds to choose from. Mine, yours, this one, Mik'hael's..." He laughs in the low musical baritone and his belly rumbles softly.

If I hadn't heard him issuing the orders for Sam to use my sister as leverage, and hadn't seen Hell with my own eyes, I would never have believed that this cosy grandpa is an evil mastermind.

"So, you promise me that nothing will happen to my sister and she'll be able to stay with me forever, and she will be safe?" I narrow my eyes at him. "Can you promise me that?" I demand louder.

"Beyelai", Chamuel's confused voice interjects behind me, "maybe you should–".

He is silenced the instant I turn to glare at him.

"Chamuel, this doesn't concern you and it is not your decision to make", I cut him off and turn back to Baza, who's clearly pleased with that little exchange, smiling wider.

"And what will I get out of this little partnership?" I ask, folding my arms across my chest, starting my hard negotiations. Baza's smile spreads wider, the Cheshire cat in front of a saucer of milk. He's got me. From the point of a firm 'no', we are now settling the details. I can practically see him rubbing his hands in anticipation.

"The same as I promised earlier", he says. "A place at my council's table as my right hand and an equal share of all dividends that will come out of our cooperation."

"And let me tell you, there will be plenty", he adds quieter.

"I want to be in charge of the Earth", I say, lifting my chin and straightening my back.

"After I've taken everything that my council needs for our progression, the Apkallu is yours", he offers easily, outstretching his hand to me for a handshake.

I pointedly look at him, then at his hand, and back to him, "I need to think."

"That would be very wise of you, Ariel. But please don't take too long, the news about your return has already spread, and I can guarantee that Mik'hael will be here soon."

With a last long look at Baza, taking him in with all his scheming and without a further word, I turn on the spot and head back to the stairs, taking the spiralling steps down.

The tips of my bottom wings brush over the smooth stone. I hear Chamuel's heavy boots boom on the stone behind me and an unsettling fear nags at me, as I can practically feel his emotions ripple off him, pushing at my back, and I wonder if he'll follow its call and push me down the stairs. But he is silent as he follows me downstairs, three flights of stairs to the hall where we started.

Once back in the hall, I turn to face him.

My stomach drops at the sight of Chamuel's fierce scowl, and I have to push at my feet to stop myself from taking a step back. His piercing blue eyes are throwing lightning bolts, his jaw muscles rippling under his skin as he grinds his teeth at me.

Although I manage to keep my feet in place, my heart is less obedient and doing little skips. The heat colours my cheeks as I clear my throat. I just isolated the person whose job it is to keep me safe. Nice going!

"Chamuel", I sound weak so I clear my throat again. "Can you please take me to Rafe?" I ask as evenly as my small voice lets me.

"Absolutely, Ariel." He jerks his head in a most resentful bow I've ever seen. "If you'll follow me", he grunts and turns, about to lead me down the hall.

"Chamuel", I grab his hand. Chamuel's big rigid frame spins to me. His surprised eyes shuttle between my face and my hand over his wrist. I drop my hand, releasing him. Probably I've overstepped some angelic boundaries as Chamuel's face relaxes the moment I release him.

"Sorry", I mumble as I raise my eyes to his. "Is it true what Baza said about Mik'hael's chances over us? Me?"

"He is right there", he huffs, glaring at me. "Without your full control over your powers, and you are still lacking there, as far as I can see –", he gives me a once over, "we don't have a chance against Mik'hael. But I don't see how that is of any importance to you now, if you have decided to join Baza. If you will excuse me, I need to go and prepare your kyriotes for a battle without their leader", he snaps, as his angry gaze rakes over me. Only his spittle at my feet is missing, to convey his repugnance in full.

"I need to find a way to avoid the battle altogether. *We* need more time."

"*We?*" he asks, hesitating, his gaze searching my face. "What for?"

"Let's face it, I'm never going to join Baza", I sigh. "I'm not that naïve. I know he's going to screw me over, and that it's only a matter of time. But if he and you are right, then we can't take on Mik'hael right now either. I still don't know what I'm doing with my powers most of the time, and to lead the army into an uneven battle is suicide, even I understand that. I need to buy us some time."

With every word I utter, his face relaxes. His forehead soothes and a small careful smile starts on his lips.

"Those are very wise words, my Beyelai", he gazes at me, and then bows, deep this time, holding his hand to his forehead longer than before.

"But what about Baza?" I ask, looking at Chamuel for guidance. At the end of the day, he said it is his job to keep me and the castle safe, and to lead my army, so he should be more knowledgeable in strategies and other warfare rubbish. "How long do you think I've got before he comes knocking on the door, demanding an answer?"

"Baza is not known for his patience, my Beyelai", Chamuel replies, "maybe a day. Two at the most."

"Okay. One day to find a solution. Great", I huff out a long sigh.

"May I propose a possible resolution, Ariel", Chamuel cautiously utters, taking another step closer to me. "If you were to disappear from here and leave the castle, there will be no need to engage with Mik'hael or give an answer to Baza. If you are gone, the earlier status quo will be restored by default. You could use this time to learn about your powers, learn how to control them, and come back on your conditions when you deem appropriate to do so."

"Where will I go?" I'm taken aback by his suggestion.

"I feel that Apkallu might be the best place for you to retreat to. You'll be able to hide among the humans, you know the way of life there, and with a bit of essence veiling, you'll be able to conceal the Qal of your essence from other realms."

Like a rag doll I have been dragged here, there and everywhere, without as much as asking my opinion on it, and now one of them suggests for me to go back where I started from? Go screwed logic!

I stand for a minute, chewing my lip, looking up at the endless sky, thinking on his proposal and on my options here, which are not that great.

I can join Baza and he will take care of Mik'hael for me, but I know for damn sure that he will stab me in the back. I can bet my last knickers that Baza is withholding something from me. I just know it!

And even without that knowledge, I'm not sure if I am comfortable to release a horde of lizards and human eyed worms on Earth. The thought of the horror army below roaming over my sleepy town sends a chill over me. *"Apocalypse tomorrow" – today!*

Or I can stay here, and when Mik'hael arrives, take my chances against him and fight. But to die for a squabble that I did not start and have not been party to, after everything I went through, is my least favourite option.

Of course, there is the option to have a heart to heart chat with Mik'hael, settle all of our differences, and let him do whatever he wants with the humans, but the main issue with that plan is my sister. Somehow, I doubt Mik'hael will let me keep her as she is disagreeable, strong minded and cheeky.

"Chamuel, can I please see Rafe?" I ask turning back to him.

"Oh. Sure", he stumbles, not expecting this sudden change of the direction in our conversation. "If you can follow me", he takes a step, but then as a thought hits him, he turns back to me, "unless you would prefer to fly there", he offers with a serene face, and I can't read behind his composed, military-trained face.

"That's okay", I mumble. "I'd rather walk". I feel embarrassed and uncomfortable. What sort of angel, especially the one who holds the key to the apocalypse, is unsure of flying? Oh well, at least it's not my first rodeo at failing expectations and providing high quality disappointments.

I follow Chamuel down the corridor, and then another one, and a forever winding set of stairs, and more corridors, and when I regret the decision to walk, he stops in front of an inconspicuous set of doors, opening one, letting me into a wide white room, which even smells sterile.

The ceiling high wide windows occupy the entire wall. Rafe's black tactical gear, weapons and ammunition are thrown in a black heap on the floor under a window. A wide but flat bed with wheels, which looks like an expensive type of gurney, is parked in the middle of the room, mostly obstructed from my view by a female angel with amber wings.

She turns to us the moment I step into the room and smiles kindly at me, taking a few steps away from the gurney, giving me a side view of Rafe's naked body, stretched out on the bed.

He lies on his front, his head turned to the side. His brown silky hair is pooling next to his head, his black long lashes casting shadows over his high cheeks, making his eye sockets look even more hollowed.

I can't take my eyes away from his face and body as I take a few cautious steps closer to the gurney. Behind me, Chamuel says something to the female angel in a hushed voice and she goes to him, giving me and Rafe some space and privacy.

Rafe's strong, muscular body lays relaxed on the bed. His silky skin is stretched over his taught muscles. His back rises and falls with his even breathing, but as I take another step closer, I clamp my hand over my mouth to stifle the horrified cry.

Rafe's beautiful, perfect body is broken.

The right side of his body is burned, from the buttocks all the way up to and over his shoulder. Charred black skin surrounds the huge wound on his back. His skin is seared right off and some muscles are missing as if slashed off by the flame. Or as if dissolved by acid. Raw bloodied meat is exposed over his back, with the white snowy peaks of the spinal bones extruding through it.

His two left wings hang lifelessly over the side of the gurney and there's nothing left of his right wings, even the earlier charred stubs are now gone.

Shock and guilt claw at me as I stumble around the gurney, unable to take my eyes away from his ravaged back, in stark contrast to his glorious body.

I'm next to his head. His face is relaxed, his eyes are closed. I want to stroke his soft hair, to tell him how sorry I am, but I don't want to wake him, so I stand there for another long minute, looking at his ruined back.

"Aren't you going to say hi?"

I jump up, startled. Rafe's croaky voice is barely audible.

"Hi", I whisper, taking a small step closer to the gurney. I raise my hand and before I can stop myself, I stroke the silk of his hair, moving it out of his face as I kneel next to him.

"How are you feeling?" I whisper, looking at Rafe's perfect face. The metal click of a shut door resonates in the empty room, and I lift my eyes to find that Chamuel and the female have left, leaving us alone.

"Hurts, but not as much as before", he answers, lifting his eyelids. His eyes are liquid warm amber as he gazes at me. "I'm glad you're here. You'll be safe in here, and Chamuel will take care of you", his content, small smile tugs at my heart. His warm gaze travels behind me. "Your wings shimmer. I like it."

I turn my head over my shoulder to see the sun from the window lightening my wings with a gold hue, breaking it into a million facets, dusting a golden haze over me.

"Thank you, Rafe", I reach and stroke his hair again, tucking it behind his ear. "Thank you for everything you have done for me. And I'm very sorry, more than I can express, for what happened to your wings. I am so, so sorry. I never meant for anything like that to happen", I rush in a guilty whisper.

"Ariel, please", Rafe's anxious voice rustles quietly. "Please. Don't cry."

I didn't realise I was crying. I lift my hand and quickly wipe at my eyes, pulling my lips into a forced smile.

"I came to say goodbye. I'll have to go away for a bit. I don't know for how long, but hopefully when I see you next time, you will wear more on your back."

Shit!

I flinch as the last word of my stupid joke leaves my mouth. Not very sensitive. Sometimes I wish I had a better filter between my brain and my mouth.

"Wait", he cuts in, raising his head and flinching in pain. "What do you mean, you are going away? Where? Does Chamuel know?" The words come out in a rush as his worried gaze searches my face.

"Chamuel knows. In fact, he suggested it. Baza's already here and Mik'hael is on his way. Every choice in front of me is as bad as the next. I just need to take some time to regroup and come back to handle my business when I'm ready." And before he can interrupt me I add, "And I'm okay with it. You know, it's the first decision I've made myself and haven't been forced into since this whole crap exploded", I say with faked upbeat, inwardly wincing at my pathetic attempt to sell the bubonic plague to the masses as a planned population control measure.

"Where are you going?" he demands. His voice is firm as he glares at me.

"Chamuel suggested back home, to my sister", I answer. "I wasn't sure about that, but after my little stunt that I am planning today, I think whoever is guarding her isn't going to be able to protect her. Everyone will be after her then, so I shall go back and try to keep her safe. Maybe we could both disappear, just as I've done before, and at least it will be more familiar than this", I sweep my gaze over the room.

"Rafe, I'm sorry to ask you for another favour, especially after everything that you have done for me, and I will understand if you say no..." I mumble, but can't seem to stop.

He doesn't want to know any of it. He probably hates you for what you've done to him already. Just ask your question, take the 'no' on the chin and go!

I suck in a deep breath.

"Do you think you can show me how to dampen my essence? I'll need a head start with Mik'hael and Baza", I say, gazing at him.

"Sure, I will show you when I come with you", he snaps.

"Wait, what? No". What's he talking about? Has he seen his back? Of course not, because he was *comatose* when we arrived. I take another deep breath, steadying myself.

"Rafe, you can't come with me", I say, trying to reason with him, like I was once with my little sister, when she was demanding to walk under November rain in her swimsuit.

"You're in pain, your back is a mess, and you need to heal, with the help of the gorgeous angel who was here before".

"I know what I need", he barks, cutting me off.

His jaw is set and sweat begins to bead on his forehead as he slowly, with long pauses, manoeuvres himself to his healthy side.

I practically feel his pain as mine and can hear his agonising cries in my head.

"Rafe, can you please stop it!"

I clap my hands over my ears, trying to stop the screams in my head.

But he ignores me as he finishes the slow turn to his side and now, laboriously, pushes himself up on his arms. As he rises, the sliced muscles of his wound twist. Blood beads over the wound and then, drip by drip begins to trickle like thawing spring brooks. Blood flows down his body, soaking his back and pooling on the gurney under him.

"Rafe, please!" I scream, but he is deaf to me.

"I'm going now, and by the time you are up, I will be gone!" I yell at him, pushing through the tears.

I storm out of the room, but my half opened wings hit the doorframe as I push through, sending sharp, blinding pain to my head. Tears are now freely flowing down my cheeks, brought on by the guilt from seeing Rafe's raw back and the pain of jamming my wings.

CHAPTER 20

"Hello, Ariel".

I freeze to the spot at the familiar melodic voice behind me. The fresh scent of lily of the valley knocks the air out of me, sending my heart into overdrive.

She's here! She's here!

On stiff legs, I turn around and stumble, taking two frightened steps back at the sight of a glorious warrior of God in front of me.

The pictures of angels like her were drawn by every generation since the dawn of time and on each one, these soldiers of God were as magnificent as the one before me.

Her pure white, large wings are spread wide behind her back. The sun, seeping through the limitless sky above, reflects and twinkles off her polished, silver armour. Her blonde hair shines like a halo around her head.

A calm and pleasant smile plays on her lips, failing to touch the glacial depths of her calculating eyes focused on me. She leisurely twirls two short thin swords by her sides as she takes two more deceivingly relaxed soft steps towards me. She is light on her feet and comfortable in her armour, silent and lethal with her weapons.

I was lucky to escape her once, and her eyes tell me that it was the last time. Killers like her do not make mistakes and certainly not twice.

That's it! "*Final destination, dear passengers, please remember your belongings*".

I look into the beautiful bright eyes of a beautiful angel and, with sharp clarity, realise that only one of us will walk out of here alive, and right now I would not bet that it will be me.

She takes another step towards me, matching mine backwards. She is not the school student I remember. The angel in front of me has nothing in common with my classmate apart from the voice and this disturbing spring flowers scent.

"I like your wings, darling. You look good", she dishes out pleasantries in her soft, melodic voice, as if she is not here to kill me.

I don't answer, hypnotised by the light catching off the twirling swords in her hands. These swords are made of the liquid fire, the one from the science class. The silver colour of the blades changes, shifting. These are the swords of the liquid fire from my dreams.

Her upper body and arms are sealed in sparkling armour. Her breastplate, pauldrons and gorget are covered in an intricate, intertwined design with a picture of the sun carved deeply at the centre of her breastplate. Exquisite, thin chain mail gloves hide her delicate hands. A poppy red tunic with heavy silvery embroidery pokes from under her armour like a mini skirt, matching the tight trousers over her legs. She looks stunning, magnificent, glorious!

"Listen, Ariel, it's just business", she says, "nothing personal, I promise, no hard feelings. I need to think about my reputation here and, unfortunately for you, I have to finish my job. I know that you are innocent in all of it, I understand, so how about I make it clean and fast? I'll make it as painless as possible. The way I will do it, you won't feel a thing. But only if you don't do anything stupid", she warns as she lowers her voice on the last sentence. I can hear the detached and steely notes of a cold blooded killer in it now.

"You run from me and I promise I shall make you pay. Then I will make it so long and painful for you that it will be hours before your body loses consciousness, allowing you to die slowly."

I take a careful step backwards and she takes one towards me. We keep progressing down the hall like that, under the accompaniment of her speech. My eyes dart around, bouncing off of the empty walls. I glance behind me, nothing! Nobody is around and there's no weapon I can see or think of.

My eyes shoot up to the wide open sky above us.
I can take off right now! Fly off, away from her!

"That's so sad", she snaps and I bring my eyes back to her, "when you try to give someone a chance and they still screw up."

Her eyes narrow to slits as she glares at me and any resemblance of a smile that she wore before disintegrated.

"I said no funny business. I warned you, but you didn't listen." Her body leans forward slightly, taking another wide step forward, ready to launch herself at me, and I still don't know what to do, spinning my head around, desperately seeking heavenly intervention.

"Sad", she purrs at me and it sounds final, like the signal to herself, and the next second she jumps up, airborne, and I can't help but follow her graceful movement with my eyes as she shoots her wings wide open mid-air, and the next second dives at me, completing the graceful and lethal trajectory.

I turn and try to run, but I'm too clumsy and too slow. She slams into me, sending me flying sideways. Again. Lately I've been feeling like a punching bag. Not that it's different from before this mess began.

That thought makes me angry.

My best friend Rage is wide awake, skipping impatiently inside her boxing ring and cracking her knuckles. Today she put on a Lucha Libre mask and black tutu. She is ready for a fight without rules, and ready to fight until our death.

I spin, as fast as I can, just a second before Mia lands her weight on top of me, knocking the air out of my lungs. Now I'm facing her, my wings pinned under me. With lightning speed, she raises her thin sword above me, ready to plunge it in, but before she has the chance to do so, my hand shoots out, seizing her wrist in my tight grip.

Surprise registers on her face when I stop the descent of her weapon.

But I'm surprised just as much as she is. And before she can shake off the grip or the shock, I throw a punch with my right hand.

My fist connects with her temple, rocking her above me, and her eyes open wider in surprise.

I'm equal to her in strength. I am no longer a weak and powerless human, and she is no longer stronger than me. And I can see that she had not factored that in, so I push an advantage making a second connection with her jaw.

"Nice", she gurgles through the blood in her mouth, which is now trickling out, droplets of it landing on my chest. My grubby sweatshirt is now totally ruined.

"I like a good match", Mia smiles, stretching her broken lips. Her bloodied smile looks creepy on the backdrop of her blonde curls and angelic face. "Where is the interest in slaughtering a sheep?"

And before she finishes the last word, she whips her left hand with the sword at me, slicing the air in its wake, as I throw my arm in to protect myself. The sword cuts deep at the back of my arm, and I swear I can hear the blade scraping at my ulna bone. I scream. I roar.

A distant rumble answers me. The vibration of the ground under me rises up the castle walls, increasing and soon the building starts to shake, swaying. I can hear voices scream in the distance.

Confusion freezes Mia for just a second but it's a second long enough for me to buck her off me, simultaneously twisting her wrist in my grip away from my chest, driving it up towards Mia's neck. The realisation of what I'm planning catches up with her and she twists, sliding off me sideways.

The blade willingly cuts deep into her shoulder and she screams, releasing her grip on the handle, leaving the sword embedded in her body and as she rolls off of me. I close my hand around its hilt, yanking it out of her and Mia screams again as the blade twists inside her on the way out.

Both bleeding and in pain, we roll in opposite directions. Now, both of us have a weapon.

Mia is up before me, as I groan in pain on the floor, pushing myself up with my left hand. My wings shoot out open. With the distance created between us, maybe I should try to fly away.

I thrust the hand with the knife in front of me, as I open my wings wide, bend my knees and launch myself up. My wings know what to do better than I. Their powerful pushes raise me up, into the sky, away from the ground and the hall where Mia still stands, watching me.

But my gloating smile dies as I watch Mia, raising her hand with the sword, and with a practiced move, flings it in the air. The tip of the blade lands into her open palm.

With a calculated look, she lifts her arm again and the next second her sword spins, cutting through the air, flying towards me with incredible speed.

My brain is sluggish, mesmerised by the acrobatic sword and when I eventually shake off the stupor and wake up to danger, my wings are far too slow.

Suddenly a solid body appears in front of me, obstructing my vision. The recognisable scent of undergrowth and moss pinches my nose. Surprise, pleasure, anger, hate are non-stop changing emotions inside me.

"Argh!" The pained bellow in Sam's voice rings in the air and then his body, carried by his glorious wings, dives away from me, towards Mia. I only see the black threaded soles of his boots and the folded white wings behind his back.

And then they collide.

A tangled mess of two bodies crash into the wall, vibrating the castle which only now has settled. Cracks burst from the point of the impact along the wall, snaking between the stones in the floor.

Sam's wide back obstructs my view of Mia. Her kicks and punches rock and shake Sam's body, as her elegant hand thrusts from under him, grabs hold of Sam's jacket and with a last punch, she flies in perfect salto from under him, using his body as leverage to push herself up, throwing Sam into the wall, head first.

Ouch! I almost feel sorry for him, but not enough to rescue that cheating bastard!

She is on her feet behind him. A whip is now in her hand, maybe even the one that she flexed in the science class. I wonder where she hid it before, maybe her armour has secret pockets?

He unsteadily rises, shaking off her earlier strike.

With a graceful and practiced move, she sends the whip toward Sam's unprotected back. The fiery tail of the whip cuts at Sam, slicing deep through his left wing, through his jacket and bites into his skin.

Sam's bellow bounces off the walls, echoing in my head. The strike sends him back on all fours, the blood flows freely out of his wing and back, rapidly turning his snow white feathers mottled red.

But he is stubborn and he pushes himself up. Mia's small sword is clutched in his hand.

I don't know who I should bet on in this match. Is my preference for my assassin to win and to kill that cheating lying bastard, or for him to win and to kill an assassin, but leaving me to kick his ass later?

Another strike of the whip flies towards Sam. This time it cleaves a corner of Sam's wing, leaving it to hang, swinging lifelessly by a thread of the skin and muscle. His wing is no longer white, covered in free-flowing blood.

Sam's agonising roar vibrates the walls, tearing at me, and this second my mind is made up and I'm sure I will regret it later, but now I can't stop myself. As I adjust my grip on the sword in my hand, I dive in, with all the speed I can get out my wings, towards Mia.

My shadow grows on the wall, expanding on and around Sam and just before I reach Mia, she turns to me, flicking her whip towards me.

But now I'm as fast as her whip. She showed me her tricks, now I'll try them myself.

Just as the whip is about to connect with me, I tuck my chin in and kick my right leg up, sending my body into a somersault towards her. Thank you mum, for three terms of gymnastics lessons when I was nine. My wings are folded tight around my body, giving me the perfect speed and trajectory.

The whip catches the side of my shoe, pulling it off, but doesn't hurt or stop me. With a thud I land in front of her, my wings burst open to ease the landing. Her dead whip strings on the floor.

"Enough!" I yell. "Mia, please. Don't make me choose which one of us will live today because I'll always choose myself. I don't have any problem with you. Just walk away and promise me never to come back", I shout as I hold the sword an arm's length away from her.

I never killed anyone and I don't think that I could do it. Right now I'm not protecting her, I'm protecting myself.

"I told you before, Uriel", she answers, stretching her lips in a creepy bloodied smile. "My reputation is at stake here and I always finish the job."

With that, she lunges herself at me.

On instinct, I thrust my arm with the sword towards her.

It surprises me when the sword is not stopped by anything hard. Its travel is only slowed, continuing now into something soft and warm. My hand, holding the hilt, brushes the wet warmth, and my surprise and realisation mirroring Mia's.

I let go of the hilt and Mia's body, no longer supported, collapses next to my feet, as aghast, I take two steps back.

The quiet settles in the hall, the rumbles and vibrations are long settled, and only my panting and Sam's pained wheezing break the silence.

I kneel next to him as he pushes himself to sit up against the wall. But his wing must be hurting him too much as he twists, leaning his side into it.

"What are you doing here?" I demand, looking into his gorgeous face. My hurt and anger are back with a vengeance.

His piercing blue eyes are on me and a smile tugs at the corner of his lips.

"I missed you. Thought that you might get yourself into trouble, and it seems I was right", he grunts, pushing through the pain.

"Quit the crap!" I snap. "I heard you! You practically saluted and clicked your heels at Baza when he told you to get my sister! You can't deny that. I saw you!" And now I yell, surprising myself. "Don't you dare lie to me! I hate you! You're full of crap! Just like everyone else", and before I can stop myself, I hit him.

My fist connects with his jaw. His head bangs against the wall and rolls back.

"Zu ku Izi", he hums through clutched teeth, glaring at me. "I guess I deserve it, but can we please stop with the physical violence?"

He spits blood, returning his gaze to me.

"I would've never brought your sister to Baza. You have to trust me on that, Ariel. If I had declined his order, he would have found someone else to carry it out and I would have lost my position in protecting you and your sister. I planned to find her and hide her among your kind with my little brother in tow. He hasn't pledged his alliance to Baza yet, so his essence will be obstructed from Baza's view. But then you disappeared..." He wipes the corner of his mouth with his finger.

"I would never have hurt you, Ariel. I love you", he whispers, gazing at me. My heart stops, then jumps up, starting to beat like a butterfly caught in a net. Liquid warmth and happiness spread through my veins.

He loves me! He loves me!

A stupid girly giggle threatens to burst out and I have to fight with myself to stop the smile, taking over my face, and with my arms, yearning to wrap around him.

Maybe he's telling the truth? It's possible, right? Oh, god, how much I wish it was the truth...

The heavy shuffle of footsteps echoes down the hall, growing closer. I dart to Sam, scooping Mia's sword out of his hand, ready to fight off more assassins.

Rafe's slim frame, sealed in his earlier black tactical gear, comes into a view, freezing at the sight of me and Sam.

I don't know what's going through his head, as he steadily sweeps his gaze over my hand, squeezing the hilt of Mia's sword, Sam, and his cut wing. His gaze then jumps behind me, taking in Mia's body. But it's not me, who he addresses first.

"What are you doing here, Samael?" he hisses at Sam. Now I notice the black, curved meat cleaver in his hand.

"Doing your job, by the looks of it", Sam spits at him as the pissing contest begins.

"How did you manage to get into Uras?" Rafe demands, swinging the cleaver slightly by his side, but I can see the pain he is in as sweat beads on his forehead.

"Why don't you ask your trustful Chamuel?" Sam barks at Rafe. "And that's how she got in here." He jerks his head towards Mia's body.

A fierce light starts behind Rafe's eyes, and his jaw sets as he mumbles profanities.

"Yeah, that's right. He has probably made a deal with Mik'hael, and Ariel is as good as dead staying in here", Sam confirms.

"It's a good thing she is not staying then", Rafe barks.

It's amazing how these two, both injured and in pain, still manage to find the energy to bite at each other.

"Okay", I call out, raising my hands up. "Will you two quit?" I glare at each one in turn.

The light catches in the sword's blade in my hand, blinding me for a second. I should take the sword with me. I would have loved to have had a shower, but that will have to wait now. I had probably better take Mia's other sword with me as well. I turn around to Mia's lifeless body behind me.

She lies on her back, spread like a starfish, staring with surprised unseeing eyes into the vast, bright sky above. Blood pools under her.

I try to force myself towards her, but my body refuses to obey me. Guilt, fear, sickness are wrapped around the absolute shock and the sharp realisation that I've just killed someone.

"I had to do it! I had to do it!" I mumble over and over, whispering to her, and the rocking begins.

"Ariel."

I jolt as someone's arms wrap around me. Rafe holds me tight, stopping my rocking.

"It's not your fault. None of it is your fault", he murmurs into my ear. "You had to do what you needed to survive. If you hadn't done it, you'd be dead now."

I clamp my hand over my mouth, shoving at his arms and when he finally lets go, I run down the hall. But I don't manage to go far before I fold in half, vomiting the remnants of my last meal I had in the cave. I heave, over and over.

After a while, not even bile comes up. I realise that it's been a while since I'd last eaten, but I'm not even hungry anymore, and surprising myself, I start to weep, the quiet and sad sound of a lost and hurt puppy.

I lean on the wall, wiping my mouth with my sleeve.

Why me? Why me?! All I ever wanted was a normal life. And now I'm an angel, hunted, on the run, expected to sacrifice myself. And now I'm a killer as well.

Can you still be yourself if you are no longer you?

"Ariel", Sam's scent wraps around me and a second later, I'm wrapped in his warm and strong arms. The warmth from his body pushes away the panic from my head and the chill from my body. He turns me around, carefully tucking my head under his chin, gently stroking my hair. I relax, feeling content next to him. Maybe even happy.

"Ariel, please don't cry. It hurts me seeing you like that", he hushes above me. "Remember when I called you

"Mermaid" for the first time?" He smiles against my hair. "You were so fierce, a small girl with big glasses in the school hall, and at that exact moment, I knew that I liked you. You landed in my arms when I needed you the most. You made me laugh, and you were so loyal to your sister, so strong and you are just as fierce and strong now. I know that you'll be fine. You will have to be fine, for me, for your sister. You have to come through it and I'll be here for you. Always. No matter how far I am, I'll be looking out for you. I will protect you by any means I have."

The rhythmic strokes calm my heart, soothing me.

"I'd offer you to sell my soul to the devil for you, but Baza already has it." His sad chuckle is like a knife in my heart. "Don't repeat my mistake, Ariel. The easy route or the revengeful one is never going to lead to happiness. I know it better than anyone else. You have to go with Rafe now and you have to survive, by any means you have. You hear me?" His soft hands lift my chin. His gaze is warm and intense, and I want to stay like that, next to him, forever.

"Can't you come with me?" I whisper.

"No", he says softly. "Baza owns my essence and with fibril attached to it, he will pull me back wherever I may go. But I'll keep you safe from a distance, however I can. Like your personal guardian angel", he smiles at his joke, but sadness hangs heavily in his eyes.

Rafe's heavy steps shuffle behind my back.

"You keep her safe", he barks to Rafe, over my head. "Anything I can do to help you, find a way to let me know.

And for An's sake, find an essence somewhere and heal yourself. What use are you to her like that?"

Sam leans his head back to me.

"I love you", he murmurs, and his warm and soft lips are on mine. His lips, his scent, his warmth encase me. My hands are in his hair, tugging him closer to me. I don't want to let him go. His hands and arms are tight around me and I feel that I belong and am happy for the first time in a very long while.

He gives a delicate stroke to my face with his warm hand, but he pulls it back too soon.

"Off you go! You need to go now, Ariel", he commands.

"Rafe, take her and go. And remember", he jabs his finger at Rafe's chest, "I hold you responsible for her safeguarding."

"I don't need a warning from an ibnatum", Rafe spits at Sam. "Some of us keep their loyalties no matter the cost."

"You", Sam hisses back at Rafe in a warning and I think he is about to jump at Rafe's throat, but instead he just stays there for a few more seconds as they glare at each other before Sam turns back to me.

He shoves Mia's little swords' hilts into my hands and I automatically close my fingers over them.

"I love you", he whispers into my lips one last time. His lips brush over mine, but he pulls away, then nudging me towards Rafe.

"Go!"

HALLOW

BOOK 2

CHAPTER 1

O chre yellow empty polystyrene cartons from a local fish and chips shop litter the pavement, dimly glowing in the dark like little islands amongst a dark night sea.

Small pieces of rubbish, sweets wrappers and old newspapers twirl and dance under our feet, but when picked up by a strong gust of wind, they would race past us as if alive, hurrying like a morning heard of commuters flooding a platform at Victoria station on their way to work.

The streets are pitch-black as the street lamps are already turned off for the night – it must be well past midnight. But the steady, soft, pearly glow comes off his body, dimly illuminating the pavement and the surrounding air as if we're followed by a personal street lamp.

The streets of the town are filled with the salty smell of the sea and a faint stench of rotting rubbish from nearby takeaways and restaurants that are now closed for the night. Rats rustle and squeak in the bins, fighting for the juiciest scraps.

The air has the faint, crisp smell of upcoming winter and it probably will be a week before rain puddles begin to freeze at night, giving young children the acute satisfaction of jumping into the thin crust of bright ice in the mornings and hearing it crunch under their feet. And a week after that, the snow will come.

The day of the fire in the science class, the day when my life irreversibly changed, and I learnt not only that angels exist but I'm one of them, was a breezy English summer. Somehow it is late autumn now. Somehow, somewhere I've lost half a year.

A chilling east wind throws fine drizzle in my face, whipping my damp hair around, seeping its numbing cold fingers through my muddy jeans and a sweatshirt. I didn't have a chance to change earlier and now I'm paying for it with smelly crusted over attire, which stands rigid like stinky armour.

My wings are behind me.

It's weird to have them there.

Most of the time I don't even think about them, don't feel them. But now and again they would flutter ever so slightly, move my hair or brush past my shoulders or arms, reminding me of their presence. They are there like long hair over the back of my neck, constant, familiar and inconspicuous. I only notice and think about them in the moments like now, when they gently rise and spread, covering me from the wind and rain.

But I'm still cold.

A few streets back my teeth began to chatter. At first it was short, sporadic clucks of a convulsing chicken, but now the chatter has upgraded to a steady rhythmic pulse. The shiver descends over my body, raking over me, twisting and shortening my muscles as if I touch exposed wires.

I need to get warm. I need to get to warmth, but I don't know what to do or where to go next.

I left Uras decisively.

I made the decision and now I need to follow through with it. The problem is I knew I needed to leave, and I knew I needed to come here, needed to see my sister, to make sure that she's alright, safe, but that was as far as I went in my preparations or in my planning.

I have no idea what to do next or even where to begin.

Rafe's heavy footsteps echo behind my back and I can hear his laboured breathing.

I can feel his presence. I sense him with the hair at my nape, and I can smell the scent of ripe fruits and sun around me. I can feel his pulsating life energy with my wings.

My wings know without a shadow of doubt that it is him behind me. My wings know that he is in pain and know that it's bad.

But he doesn't share it with me. He doesn't say a word.

He just walks behind me, keeping up with my intentionally shortened steps. He didn't want to share his pain with me then, and he's not sharing it now. He is just here for me, insistent and constant, even after everything I put him through.

Without a question, he followed me on the path that I chose for us, and the earlier guilt stirs again inside me.

The swords that Sam gave me are awkwardly stashed away, looped through the belt at the back of my jeans. I've never carried weapons before nor have I used them until today.

I sober in an instant thinking of Mia. I still can't believe that I've done it, done to another human, to another living being.

And then answering my call, the memories of our fight rush back, spreading the dark chill from within, matching the chill of the autumnal wet wind. The memories bring the crisp stabbing details of her beautiful porcelain pixie face: frozen in shock, with her eyes and red mouth wide open, her surprised gaze locked to mine.

I remember watching her body unnaturally folded on the floor. I remember that feeling, that knowledge: she's dead.

ACKNOWLEDGEMENTS

Foremost I would like to thank my family, and my girls in particular, for their constant support. Without them, there simply would be no book.

I owe a great debt to my daughter Lidia for all her support, 'hands-on' management and the advice I've received on the characters, plot, my writing and everything and anything in between. Thank you, my darling, for putting up with me while I was writing, for not letting me give up.

My gratitude goes to my personal cheerleader, my patient and calm husband for tolerating my craziness all these years and for believing in me. For all the encouragement and support you gave me with this book – I will be forever grateful.

I owe a huge thank you to my friend Gina – YA enthusiast and beta-reader extraordinaire, who provided me with the most detailed and helpful feedback on the book, everything from the structure and characters, to the corrections of my typos in the manuscript. Thank you for sharing your excitement about all things YA with me and thank you for your friendship.

And thank you to my second beta-reader Izzy for reading my story and providing such valuable feedback, as a representative of the target audience.

Thank you all.

ABOUT AUTHOR

Olga Gibbs lives in a leafy-green town, nestled amongst the green fields of West Sussex, England. She lives with her husband and their two daughters and a cat.

Please visit her author website for more information on upcoming books.